T0166757

RING AROUND THE SUN

RING AROUND THE SUN

CLIFFORD D. SIMAK

OPEN ROAD
INTEGRATED MEDIA
NEW YORK

FOR CARSON

All rights reserved, including without limitation the right to reproduce this
book or any portion thereof in any form or by any means, whether electronic
or mechanical, now known or hereinafter invented, without the express written
permission of the publisher.

This is a work of fiction. Names, characters, places, events, and incidents
either are the product of the author's imagination or are used fictitiously. Any
resemblance to actual persons, living or dead, businesses, companies, events,
or locales is entirely coincidental.

Copyright © 1952, 1953 by Clifford D. Simak

ISBN: 978-1-5040-7981-5

This edition published in 2023 by Open Road Integrated Media, Inc.
180 Maiden Lane
New York, NY 10038
www.openroadmedia.com

RING
AROUND
THE SUN

1

Vickers got up at an hour outrageous for its earliness, because Ann had phoned the night before to tell him about a man in New York she wanted him to meet.

He had tried to argue about it.

"I know it breaks into your schedule, Jay," she had said, "but I don't think this is something you can pass up."

"I can't do it, Ann," he'd told her. "I've got the writing going now and I can't get loose."

"But this is big," Ann had said, "the biggest thing that has ever broken. They picked you to talk to first, ahead of all the other writers. They think you're the man to do it."

"Publicity."

"This is not publicity. This is something else."

"Forget it—I won't meet the guy, whoever he is," he had said, and hung up. But here he was, making himself an early breakfast and getting ready to go into New York.

He was frying eggs and bacon and making toast and trying to keep one eye on the coffee maker, which was temperamental, when the doorbell rang.

He wrapped his robe around him and headed for the door.

It might be the newsboy. He had been out on the regular collection day and the boy probably had seen the light in the kitchen.

Or it might be his neighbor, the strange old man named Horton Flanders, who had moved in a year or so ago and who dropped over to spend an idle hour at the most unexpected and inconvenient times. He was an affable old man and distinguished looking, although slightly moth-eaten and shabby at the edges, pleasant to talk with and a good companion, even though Vickers might have wished that he were more orthodox in his visiting.

It might be the newsboy or it might be Flanders. It could scarcely be anyone else at this early hour.

He opened the door and a little girl stood there, wrapped in a cherry-colored bathrobe and with bunny rabbit slippers on her feet. Her hair was tousled from a night of sleep, but her blue eyes sparkled at him and she smiled a pretty smile.

"Good morning, Mr. Vickers," she said. "I woke up and couldn't go back to sleep and I saw the light burning in your kitchen and I thought maybe you was sick."

"I'm all right, Jane," Vickers told her. "I'm just getting breakfast. Maybe you would like to eat with me."

"Oh, yes," said Jane. "I was hoping maybe if you was eating breakfast you'd ask me to eat with you."

"Your mother doesn't know you're here, does she?"

"Mommy and Daddy are asleep," said Jane. "This is the day that Daddy doesn't work and they was out awful late last night. I heard them when they came in and Mommy was telling Daddy that he drank too much and she said she wouldn't go out with him, never again, if he drank that much, and Daddy . . ."

"Jane," said Vickers, firmly, "I don't think your mommy and daddy would like you to be telling this."

"Oh, they don't care. Mommy talks about it all the time. I heard her telling Mrs. Traynor she had half a mind to divorce my Daddy. Mr. Vickers, what is divorce?"

"Now, I don't know," said Vickers. "I can't recollect I ever heard the word before. Maybe we oughtn't to talk about what your mommy says. And look, you got your slippers all wet crossing the grass."

"It's kind of wet outside. The dew is awful heavy."

"You come in," said Vickers, "and I'll get a towel and dry your feet and then we'll have some breakfast and call your mommy so she knows where you are."

She came in and he closed the door.

"You sit on that chair," he said, "and I'll get a towel. I'm afraid you might catch cold."

"Mr. Vickers, you aren't married, are you?"

"Why, no. It happens that I'm not."

"Most everyone is married," said Jane. "Most everyone I know. Why aren't you married, Mr. Vickers?"

"Why, I don't rightly know. Never found a girl, I guess."

"There are lots of girls."

"There was a girl," said Vickers. "A long time ago, there was a girl."

It had been years since he had remembered sharply. He had forced the years to obscure the memory, to soften it and hide it away so that he did not think of it, and if he did think of it, to make it so far away and hazy that he could quit thinking of it.

But here it was again.

There had been a girl and an enchanted valley they had walked in, a springtime valley, he remembered, with the pink of wild crab apple blossoms flaming on the hills and the song of bluebird and of lark soaring in the sky, and there had been a wild spring breeze that ruffled the water and blew along the grass so that the meadow seemed to flow and become a lake with whitecaps rolling on it.

They had walked in the valley and there was no doubt that it was enchanted, for when he had gone back again the valley wasn't there—or at least not the same valley. It had been, he remembered, a very different valley.

He had walked there twenty years ago and through all of twenty years he had hidden it away, back in the attic of his mind, yet here it was again, as fresh and shining as if it had been only yesterday.

"Mr. Vickers," said Jane, "I think your toast is burning."

2

After Jane had gone and he had washed the dishes, he remembered that he had intended for a week or more to phone Joe about the mice.

"I got mice," Vickers told him.

"You got what?"

"Mice," said Vickers. "Little animals. They run around the place."

"Now that's funny," said Joe. "A well-built place like yours. It shouldn't have no mice. You want me to come over and get rid of them?"

"I guess you'll have to. I tried traps but these mice don't go for traps. Got a cat a while back and the cat left. Only stayed a day or two."

"Now, that's a funny thing. Cats like places where they can catch a mouse."

"This cat was crazy," said Vickers. "Acted like it was spooked. Walked around on tiptoe."

"Cats is funny animals," Joe confided.

"I'm going down to the city today. Figure you could do it while I'm gone?"

"Sure thing," said Joe. "The exterminating business is kind of slack right now. I'll come over ten o'clock or so."

"I'll leave the front door unlocked," said Vickers.

He hung up the phone and got the paper off the stoop. At his desk, he laid down the paper and picked up the sheaf of manuscript, holding it in his hand, feeling the thickness of it and the weight of it, as if by its thickness and its weight he might reassure himself that what it held was good, that it was not labor wasted, that it said the many things he wished to say and said them well enough that other men and women might read the words and know the naked thought that lay behind the coldness of the print.

He should not waste the day, he told himself. He should stay here and work. He should not go traipsing off to meet this man his agent wanted him to meet. But Ann had been insistent and had said that it was important and even when he had told her about the car being in the garage for repairs she still had insisted that he come. That story about the car had been untrue, of course, for he knew even as he told her that Eb would have it ready for him to make the trip.

He looked at his watch and saw he had no more than half an hour until Eb's garage would open and half an hour was not worth his while to spend in writing.

He picked up the paper and went out on the porch to read the morning's news.

He thought about little Jane and what a sweet child she was and how she'd praised his cooking and had chattered on and on.

You aren't married, Jane had said. Why aren't you married, Mr. Vickers?

And he had said: once there was a girl. I remember now. Once there was a girl.

Her name had been Kathleen Preston and she had lived in a big brick house that sat up on a hill, a many-columned house with a wide porch and fanlights above the doors—an old house that had been built in the first flush of pioneer optimism when the country had been new, and the house had stood when the land had failed and ran away in ditches and left the hillsides scarred with gullied yellow clay.

He had been young then, so young that it hurt him now to think of it; so young he could not understand that a girl who lived in an old ancestral home with fanlights above the doors and a pillared portico could not seriously consider a boy whose father farmed a worn-out farm where the corn grew slight and sickly. Or rather, perhaps, it had been her family that could not consider it, for she, too, must have been too young to fully understand. Perhaps she had quarreled with her family; perhaps there had been angry words and tears. That was something he had never known. For between that walk down the enchanted valley and the next time he had called they had bundled her off to a school somewhere in the east and that was the last he had seen or heard of her.

For remembrance sake he had walked the valley again, alert to catch something that would spell out for him the enchantment of that day he had walked with her. But the crab apples had dropped their blossoms and the lark did not sing so well and the enchantment had fled into some never-never land. She had taken the magic with her.

The paper fell out of his lap and he bent to pick it up. Opening it, he saw that the news was following the same drab pattern of all other days.

The latest peace rumor still was going strong and the cold war still was in full cry.

The cold war had been going on for years, of course, and gave promise of going on for many more. The last forty years had seen crisis after crisis, rumor after rumor, near-war always threatening and big war never breaking out, until a cold-war-weary world yawned in the face of the new peace rumors and the crises that were a dime a dozen.

Someone at an obscure college down in Georgia had set a new record at raw egg-gulping and a glamorous movie star was on the verge of changing husbands once again and the steelworkers were threatening to strike.

There was a lengthy feature article about missing persons and he read about half of it, all that he wanted to. It seemed that more and more people were dropping out of sight all the time, whole families at a time, and the police throughout the land were getting rather frantic. There always had been people who had disappeared, the article said, but they had been individuals. Now two or three families would disappear from the same community and two or three from another community and there was no trace of them at all. Usually they were from the poorer brackets. In the past, when individuals had dropped from sight there had usually been some reason for it, but in these cases of mass disappearances there seemed to be no reason beyond poverty and why one would or could disappear because of poverty was something the article writer and the people he had interviewed could not figure out.

There was a headline that read: More Worlds Than One, Says Savant.

He read part of the story:

> BOSTON, MASS. (AP)—There may be another earth just a second ahead of us and another world a second behind us and another world a second behind that one and another world a second behind . . . well, you get the idea.
>
> A sort of continuous chain of worlds, one behind the other.
>
> That is the theory of Dr. Vincent Aldridge. . . .

Vickers let the paper drop to the floor and sat looking out across the garden, rich with flowers and ripe with sunshine. There was peace here, in this garden corner of the world, if there were nowhere else, he thought. A peace compounded of many things, of golden sunshine and the talk of summer leaves quivering in the wind, of bird and flower and sundial, of picket fence that needed painting and an old pine tree dying quietly and tranquilly, taking its time to die, being friends with the grass and flowers and other trees all the while it died.

Here there was no rumor and no threat; here was calm acceptance of the fact that time ran on, that winter came and summer, that sun would follow moon and that the life one held was a gift to be cherished rather than a right that one must wrest from other living things.

Vickers glanced at his watch and saw that it was time to go.

3

Eb, the garage man, hitched up his greasy britches and squinted his eyes against the smoke from the cigarette that hung from one corner of a grease-smeared mouth.

"You see, it's this way, Jay," he explained. "I didn't fix your car."

"I was going to the city," said Vickers, "but if my car's not fixed . . ."

"You won't be needing that car anymore. Guess that's really why I didn't fix it. Told myself it would be just a waste of money."

"It's not that bad," protested Vickers. "It may look ramshackle, but it still has lots of miles."

"Sure, it's got some miles in it. But you're going to be buying this new Forever car."

"Forever car?" Vickers repeated. "That's a queer name for a car."

"No, it isn't," Eb told him, stubbornly. "It'll really last forever. That's why they call it the Forever car, because it lasts forever. Fellow was in here yesterday and told me about it and asked if I wanted to take it on and I said sure I would and this fellow, he said I was smart to take it on, because, he said, there isn't going to be any other car selling except this Forever car."

"Now, wait a minute," said Vickers. "They may call it a Forever car, but it won't last forever. No car would last forever. Twenty years, maybe, or a lifetime, maybe, but not forever."

"Jay," declared Eb, "that's what this fellow told me. 'Buy one of them,' he says, 'and use it all your life. When you die, will it to your son and when he dies he can will it to his son and so on down the line.' It's guaranteed to last forever. Anything goes wrong with it and they'll fix it up or give you a new one. All except the tires. You got to buy the tires. They wear out, just like on any other car. And paint, too. But the paint is guaranteed ten years. If it goes bad sooner than ten years you get a new job free."

"It *might* be possible," said Vickers, "but I hardly think so. I don't doubt a car could be made to last a lot longer than the ones do now. But if they were built too well, there'd be no replacement. It stands to reason a manufacturer in his right mind wouldn't build a car that would last forever. He'd put himself out of business. In the first place, it would cost too much . . ."

"That's where you're wrong," Eb told him. "Fifteen hundred smackers, that's all you pay. No accessories to buy. No buildups. You get it complete for fifteen hundred."

"Not much to look at, I suppose."

"It's the classiest job you ever laid your eyes on. Fellow that was here was driving one of them and I looked it over good. Any color that you want. Lots of chrome and stainless steel. All the latest gadgets. And drive . . . man, that thing drives like a million dollars. But it might take some getting used to it. I went to open the hood to take a look at the motor and, you know, that hood doesn't open. 'What you doing there?' this fellow asked me and I told him I wanted to look at the motor. 'There isn't any need to,' this fellow says. 'Nothing ever goes wrong with it. You never need to get at it.' 'But,' I asked him, 'where do you put in the oil?' And you know what he said? Well, sir, he said you don't put in no oil. 'All you put in is gasoline,' he tells me.

"I'll have a dozen or so of them in within a day or so," said Eb. "You better let me save you one."

Vickers shook his head. "I'm short on money."

"That's another thing about it. This company gives you good trade-in value. I figure I could give you a thousand for that wreck of yours."

"It's not worth a thousand, Eb."

"I know it's not. Fellow says, 'Give them more than they're worth. Don't worry about what you give them. We'll make it right with you.' It doesn't exactly seem the smart way to do business, come to think about it, but if that's the way they want to operate I won't say a word against it."

"I'd have to think about it."

"That would leave five hundred for you to pay. And I can make it easy on you. Fellow said I should make it easy. Says they aren't so much interested in the money right now as getting a few of them Forever cars out, running on the road."

"I don't like the sound of it," protested Vickers. "Here this company springs up over night with no announcement at all with a brand new car. You'd think there would have been something in the papers about it. If I were putting out a new car, I'd plaster the country with advertising . . . big ads in the newspapers, announcements on television, billboards every mile or so."

"Well, you know," said Eb, "I thought of that one, too. I said, look, you fellows want me to sell this car and how am I going to sell it when you aren't advertising it? How am I going to sell it when no one knows about it? And he said that they figured the car was so good everyone would up and tell everybody else. Said there isn't any advertising that can beat word of mouth. Said they'd rather save the money they put in advertising and cut down the cost of the car. Said there was no reason to make the consumer pay for the cost of an advertising campaign."

"I can't understand it."

"It does sort of hit you that way," Eb admitted. "This gang that's putting out the Forever car isn't losing any money on it, you can bet your boots on that. Be crazy if they did. And if they aren't losing any money at it, can you imagine what the rest of them companies have been making all these years, two or three thousand for a pile of junk that falls apart second time you take it out? Makes you shiver to think of the money they been making, don't it?"

"When you get the cars in," said Vickers, "I'll be down to take a look at them. We might make a deal, at that."

"Sure," said Eb. "Be sure to do that. You say you was going to the city?"

Vickers nodded.

"Be a bus along any minute now," said Eb. "Catch it down at the drugstore corner. Get you there in a couple of hours. Those fellows really wheel it."

"I guess I could take a bus. I never thought of it."

"I'm sorry about the car," said Eb. "If I'd known you was going to use it, I'd have fixed her up. Not much wrong with it. But I wanted to see what you thought about this other deal before I run you up a bill."

The drugstore corner looked somehow unfamiliar and Vickers puzzled about it as he walked down the street toward it. Then, when he got closer, he saw what it was that was unfamiliar.

Several weeks ago old Hans, the shoe repairman, had taken to his bed and died and the shoe repair shop, which had stood next to the drugstore for almost uncounted years, finally had been closed.

Now it was open again—or, at least, the display window had been washed, something which old Hans had never bothered to do in all his years, and there was a display of some sort. And there was a sign. Vickers had been so intent on figuring out what was wrong with the window that he did not see the sign until he was almost even with the store. The sign was new and neatly lettered and it said GADGET SHOP.

Vickers stopped before the window and looked at what was inside. A layer of black velvet had been laid along the display strip and arranged upon it were three items—a cigarette lighter, a razor blade and a single light bulb. Nothing else.

Just those three items. There were no signs, no advertising, no prices. There was no need of any. Anyone who saw that window, Vickers knew, would recognize the items, although the store would not sell only those. There would be a couple of dozen others, each of them in its own way as distinguished and efficient as the three lying on the strip of velvet.

There was a tapping sound along the walk and Vickers turned when it came close to him. It was his neighbor, Horton Flanders, out for his morning walk, with his slightly shabby, carefully brushed clothes and his smart malacca cane. No one else, Vickers told himself, would have the temerity to carry a cane along the streets of Cliffwood.

Mr. Flanders saluted him with the cane and moved in to stand beside him and stare at the window.

"So they're branching out," he said.

"Apparently," Vickers agreed.

"Most peculiar outfit," said Mr. Flanders. "You may know, although I presume you don't, that I have been most interested in this company. Just a matter of curiosity, you understand. I am curious, I might add, about many different things."

"I hadn't noticed." Vickers said.

"Oh, my, yes," said Mr. Flanders. "About so many things. About the carbohydrates, for instance. Most intriguing setup, don't you think so, Mr. Vickers?"

"I hadn't given it much thought. I have been so busy that I'm afraid . . ."

"There's something going on," said Mr. Flanders. "I tell you that there is."

The bus came down the street, passed them and braked to a stop at the drugstore corner.

"I'm afraid I shall have to leave you, Mr. Flanders," Vickers said. "I'm going to the city. If I'm back tonight, why don't you drop over."

"Oh, I will," Mr. Flanders told him. "I nearly always do."

4

It had been the blade at first, the razor blade that would not wear out. And after that the lighter that never failed to light, that required no flints and never needed filling. Then the light bulb that would burn forever if it met no accident. Now it was the Forever car.

Somewhere in there, too, would be the synthetic carbohydrates.

There is something going on, Mr. Flanders had said to him, standing there in front of old Hans' shop.

Vickers sat in his seat next to the window, well back in the bus, and tried to sort it out in his mind.

There was a tie-up somewhere—razor blades, lighters, light bulbs, synthetic carbohydrates and now the Forever car. Somewhere there must be a common denominator to explain why it should be these five items and not five other things, say roller curtains and pogo sticks and yo-yos and airplanes and toothpaste. Razor blades shaved a man and light bulbs lit his way and a cigarette lighter would light a cigarette and the synthetic carbohydrates had ironed put at least one international crisis and had saved some millions of people from starvation or war.

There is something going on, Flanders had said, standing there in neat, but shabby clothes and with that ridiculous stick clutched in his fist, although, come to think of it, it was not ridiculous when Mr. Flanders held it.

The Forever car would run forever and it used no oil and when you died you willed it to your son and when he died he willed it to his son and if your great-great-grandfather bought one of the cars and you were the eldest son of the eldest son of the eldest son you would have it, too. One car would outlast many generations.

But it would do more than that. It would close every automotive plant in a year or so; it would shut down most of the garages and repair shops; it would be a blow to the steel industry and the glass industry and the fabric makers and perhaps a dozen other industries as well.

The razor blade hadn't seemed important, nor the light bulb, nor the lighter, but now they suddenly all were. Thousands of men would lose their jobs and they would come home and face the family and say: "Well, this is it. After all these years I haven't got a job."

The family would go about their everyday affairs in tight and terrible silence, with a queer air of dread hanging over them, and the man would buy all the newspapers and study the want ad columns, then go out and walk the streets and men in little cages or at desks in the outer offices would shake their heads at him.

Finally the man would go to one of those little places that had the sign "Carbohydrates, Inc." over its door and he would shuffle in with the embarrassment of a good workman who cannot find a job, and he would say, "I'm a little down on my luck and the cash is running low. I wonder . . ."

The man behind the desk would say, "Why, sure, how many in your family?" The man would tell him and the one who was at the desk would write on a slip of paper and hand it to him. "That window over there," he'd say. "I figure there's enough there to last you for a week, but if there isn't be sure to come back anytime you want to."

The man would take the slip of paper and try to say his thanks, but the carbohydrates man would brush them easily aside and say,

"Look, now, that's what we're here for. This is our business, helping guys like you."

The man would go to the window and the man behind the window would look at the slip of paper and hand him packages and one package would be synthetic stuff that tasted like potatoes and another one would taste like bread and there would be others that would make you think you were eating corn or peas.

That was what had happened before, that was what was happening all the time.

It wasn't like relief—anyhow, you could say it wasn't like relief. These carbohydrates people didn't ever insult you when you came to ask for help. They treated you like a paying customer and they always said that you should come back and sometimes when you didn't they came around to see what had happened—if maybe you had got a job or were bashful about coming in again. If it turned out that you were bashful, they'd sit down and talk to you and before they left they had you thinking you were doing them a favor by taking the carbohydrates off their hands.

Because of the carbohydrates millions who would have died were still alive in India and in China. Now the thousands who would lose their jobs when the automotive plants shut down and the steel mills curtailed their operations and the repair shops shut their doors, would travel the same trail to the doors with the carbohydrates sign.

The automotive industry would have to shut down. No one would buy any other car when you could walk down the street and buy one that would last forever. Just as the razor blade industry was already closing its doors, now that it was possible to get an everlasting blade at the gadget shops. The same thing was happening with light bulbs and with cigarette lighters and the chances were, Vickers told himself, that the Forever car wasn't the last that would be heard from these manufacturers, whoever they might be.

For it must be, he told himself, that those who made the razor blades also made the lighters and the light bulbs, and that those who made the gadget items must have designed the Forever car. Not the same companies, perhaps, although he couldn't know, for it had never occurred to him to try to find out who had made any of them.

The bus was filling up, but Vickers still sat by himself, staring out the window and, sorting out his thoughts.

Just behind him a couple of women were talking and, without consciously trying to eavesdrop, he picked up their words.

One of them giggled and said, "We have the *most* interesting group. So *many* interesting people in it."

And the other woman said, "I been thinking about joining one of those groups, but Charlie, he says it's all baloney. Says we're living in America in the year 1987 and there's no reason in the world why we should pretend we aren't. Says this is the best country and the best time the world has ever known. Says we got all the modern conveniences and everything. Says we're happier than people ever been before. Says this pretending business is just a lot of communist propaganda and he'd like to get hold of the ones that got it started. Says . . ."

"Oh, I don't know," interrupted the first woman. "It *is* kind of fun. It takes a *lot* of work, of course, reading about them old times and all of that, but you get something out of it, I guess. One fellow was saying at a meeting the other night you get out of it what you put into it and I guess he's right. But I don't seem to be able to put much into it. I guess I must be the flighty type. I'm not too good a reader and I don't understand too well and I got to have a lot explained to me, but there are them as get a lot of it, seems like. There's a man in our group living back in London, back in the times of a man named Samuel Peeps. I don't know who this Peeps was, but I guess he was an important man or something. You don't know who Peeps was, do you, Gladys?"

"Not me," said Gladys.

"Well, anyhow," continued the other, "this fellow, he talks all the time about this Peeps. He wrote a book, this Peeps, and it must be an awful long book because he tells about so many things. This man I was telling you about writes the *most* wonderful diary. We always like to have him read it to us. You know, it sounds almost as if he was *really* living there."

The bus stopped for a railroad crossing and Vickers glanced at his watch. They'd be in the city in another half an hour.

It was a waste of time, he told himself. No matter what sort of scheme Ann had up her sleeve, it would be a waste of time, for he was not going to allow anything to interrupt his writing. He shouldn't have allowed himself to be talked into wasting even this one day.

Back of him, Gladys was saying, "Did you hear about these new houses they're putting out. I was talking to Charlie about them the other night and I was saying maybe we ought to look into them. Our place is getting kind of shabby, you know, and we'll have to paint it and sort of fix it up, but Charlie he said that it was a sucker game of some sort. He said no one would put out them kind of houses on the sort of deal they offer without there was a catch somewhere. Charlie, he said he was too old a hand to be taken in by something like them houses. Mabel, have you seen any of them houses or read anything about them . . ."

"I was telling you," Mabel persisted, "about this group I belong to. One of the fellows is pretending that he's living in the future. Now, I ask you, ain't that a laugh. Imagine anyone pretending he's living in the future . . ."

5

Outside the door, Ann Carter stopped and said, "Now, please remember, Jay, his name is Crawford. You're not to call him Cranford or Crawford or any other name but Crawford."

Vickers said humbly, "I'll do my very best."

She came close to him and tightened his tie and straightened it and flicked some imaginary dust off his lapel.

"We're going out as soon as this is over and buy you a suit," she said.

"I have a suit," said Vickers.

The letters on the door read: North American Research.

"What I can't understand," protested Vickers, "is why North American Research and I should have anything in common."

"Money," said Ann. "They have it and you need it."

She opened the door and he followed her in obediently, thinking what a pretty woman she was and how efficient. Too efficient. She knew too much. She knew books and publishers and what the public wanted and she was onto all the angles. She drove herself and everyone around her. She was never so happy as when three telephones were ringing and there were five dozen letters to be answered and a dozen calls to make. She had bullied him into coming here this day and it was not beyond reason, he told himself, that she had bullied Crawford and North American Research into wanting him to come.

"Miss Carter," said the girl at the desk, "you can go right in. Mr. Crawford is waiting for you."

She's even got the Indian sign on the receptionist, Vickers thought.

6

George Crawford was a big man who overflowed the chair in which he sat. He held his hands folded over his paunch and talked with no change of tone, with no inflection whatsoever, and was the stillest man Vickers had ever seen. There was no movement in him nor any sense of movement. He sat huge and stolid and his lips scarcely moved and his voice was not much louder than a whisper.

"I have read some of your work, Mr. Vickers," he said. "I am impressed by it."

"I am glad to hear you say so," Vickers said.

"Three years ago, I never would have thought that I would ever read a piece of fiction or be talking to its author. Now, however, I find that we need a man like you. I have talked it over with my directors and we are all agreed that you are the man who could do the job for us."

He paused and stared at Vickers with bright blue eyes that peered out like bullet points from the folds of flesh.

"Miss Carter," he said, "tells me that, at the moment, you are very busy."

"That is right."

"Some important piece of work, I presume," said Crawford.

"I hope it is."

"This thing I have in mind would be more important."

"That," Vickers told him crisply, "is a matter of opinion."

"You don't like me, Mr. Vickers," Crawford said. It was a statement of fact, not a question, and Vickers found that it irritated him.

"I have no opinion of you," he replied. "I am totally disinterested in everything except what you have to say."

"Before we go any further," said Crawford, "I would like to have it understood that what I have to say is of a confidential nature."

"Mr. Crawford," Vickers told him, "I have little stomach for cloak and dagger business."

"This is not cloak and dagger business," said Crawford and for the first time there was an edge of emotion in his voice. "It is the business of a world with its back against the wall."

Vickers stared at him, startled. My God, he thought, the man really means exactly what he is saying. He really believes that the world does have its back against the wall.

"Perhaps," said Crawford, "you have heard of the Forever car."

Vickers nodded. "The garage owner in my home town tried to sell me one this morning."

"And about the everlasting razor blades and the lighter and the light bulbs."

"I have one of the blades," said Vickers, "and it is the best blade I ever owned. I doubt that it is everlasting, but it is a good blade and I've never had to sharpen it. When it wears out, I intend to buy another one."

"Unless you lose it, you will never have to. Because, Mr. Vickers, it *is* an everlasting blade. And the car is an everlasting car. Maybe you've heard about the houses, too."

"Not enough to matter."

"The houses are prefabricated units," said Crawford, "and they sell at the flat rate of five hundred dollars a room—set up. You can trade in your old home on them at a fantastic trade-in value and the credit terms are liberal—much more liberal, I might add, than any sane financing institution would ever countenance. They are heated and air conditioned by a solar plant that tops anything—you hear me, *anything*—that we have today. There are many other features, but that gives you a rough idea."

"They sound like a good idea. We've been talking about low-cost housing for a long time now. Maybe this is it."

"They are a good idea," said Crawford. "I would be the last to deny they are. Except that they will ruin the power people. That solar plant supplies it all—heat, light, power. When you buy one of them, you don't need to tie up to an electric outlet. And they will put thousands of carpenters and masons and painters out of work and in the carbohydrates lines, too. They eventually will wreck the lumber industry."

"I can understand about the power angle," Vickers said, "but that business about the carpenters and the lumber industry doesn't quite make sense. Surely these houses use lumber and it must take carpenters to build them."

"They use lumber, all right, and someone builds them, but we don't know who it is."

"You could check," suggested Vickers. "It seems rather elementary. There must be a corporate setup. There must be mills and factories somewhere."

"There's a company," admitted Crawford. "A sales company. We started with that and we found the warehouse from which the units are shipped for delivery after they are sold. But that's the end of it. There is, so far as we can find, no factory that builds them. They are consigned from a certain company and we have its name and address. But no one has ever sold a stick of timber to that company. They have never bought a hinge. They hire no men. They list factory sites and the sites are there, but there aren't any factories. And, to the best of our knowledge, no single person has gone into or come out of the home office address since we've been watching it."

"That's fantastic," Vickers objected.

"Of course it is," agreed Crawford. "Lumber and other materials go into those houses and somewhere there are men who build them."

"Mr. Crawford, just one question. Why are you interested?"

"Well, now," said Crawford, "I wasn't quite ready to tell you that."

"I know you weren't, but tell me anyway."

"I had hoped to sketch in a bit more of the background, so that you would understand what I am driving at. Our interest—I might say our organization—sounds just a little silly until you know the background."

"Someone has you scared," said Vickers. "You wouldn't admit it, of course, but you're scared livid."

"Queerly enough, I will admit it. But it's not me, Mr. Vickers— it's industry, the industry of the entire world."

"You think the people who are making and selling these houses," said Vickers, "are the same ones who are making the Forever car and the lighters and the bulbs."

Crawford nodded. "And the carbohydrates, too," he added. "It's terrifying, when you think about it. Here we have someone who wrecks industries and throws millions out of work, then turns around and offers those same millions the food to live on—offers it without the red tape and the investigations and all the quibbling that always heretofore has characterized relief."

"A political plot?"

"It's more than that. We are convinced that it is a deliberate, well-planned attack on world economy—a deliberate effort to undermine the social and economic system of our way of life, and after that, of course, the political system. Our way of life is based on capital, be it private capital or state control of resources and on the wage that the worker earns at his daily job. Take away those two things, capital and jobs, and you have undercut the whole basis of an orderly society."

"We?" asked Vickers. "Who are we?"

"North American Research."

"And North American Research?"

"You're getting interested," said Crawford.

"I want to know who I'm talking to and what you want of me and what it's all about."

Crawford sat for a long time without speaking, and then he finally said, "That is what I meant when I told you what I had to say was highly confidential."

"I will swear no oath," said Vickers, "if that is what you mean."

"Let's go back," said Crawford, "and review some history. Who we are and what we are will become apparent then.

"You remember the razor blade. It was the first to come out. An everlasting razor blade. The news spread quickly and everyone went out and bought one of the razor blades.

"Now, the ordinary man will get anywhere from one to half a dozen shaves out of a blade. Then he throws that blade away and puts in another one. That means he is a continuous buyer of new razor blades. And as a result the razor blade industry was a going concern. It employed thousands of workers, over the course of a year it represented a certain profit for thousands of dealers, it was a factor in a certain type of steel production. In other words, it was an economic factor which, linked in with thousands of other similar economic factors, make up the picture of world industry. So what happens?"

"I'm no economist, but I can tell you that," said Vickers. "No one bought any more razor blades. So the razor blade industry was out the window."

"Not quite as quickly as that, of course," said Crawford. "A huge industry is a complex thing, and it dies somewhat slowly, even after the handwriting is on the wall, even after sales stop almost completely—and then quite completely. But you're correct; that's what's happening right now: out the window.

"And then, there was the lighter. A small thing in itself, of course, but fairly large when you look at it from the world point of view. The same thing happened there. And the everlasting light bulbs. And the same thing once again. Three industries doomed, Mr. Vickers. Three industries wiped out. You said a while ago that

I was scared and I told you that I was. It was after the bulbs that we got scared. Because if someone could wipe out three industries, why not half a dozen, or a dozen or a hundred—why not all of them?

"We organized, and by we I mean the industry of the world— not American industry alone, but the industry of America and the British Commonwealth and the continent of Europe and Russia and all of the rest of them. There were a few, of course, who were skeptical. There still are a few who never have come in, but by and large I can tell you that our organization represents and is backed by every major industry of the entire world. As I have said, I would prefer you not to mention this."

"At the moment," Vickers told him, "I have no intention of saying anything about it."

"We organized," said Crawford, "and we swung a lot of power, as you can well imagine. We made certain representations and we brought certain pressures and we got a few things done. For one thing, no newspaper, no periodical, no radio station, now will accept advertising for any of the gadgets nor give them any mention in the news. For another, no reputable drug store or any other place of business will sell a razor blade or a bulb or lighter."

"That was when they set up the gadget shops?"

"Exactly," said Crawford.

"They're branching out," said Vickers. "One opened in Cliffwood just the other day."

"They set up the gadget shops," said Crawford, "and they developed a new form of advertising. They hired thousands of men and women who went around from place to place and said to people they would meet: 'Did you hear about those wonderful new gadgets they are getting out? You haven't? Well, just let me tell you . . .' You get the idea. Something like that, involving personal contact, is the best kind of advertising that there is. But it's more expensive than you can possibly imagine.

"So we knew that we were up against not merely inventive and productive genius, but almost unlimited money as well.

"And we investigated. We tried to run these folks to earth, to find out who they were and how they operated and what they meant to do. As I've told you, we ran into stone walls."

"There might be legal angles," said Vickers.

"We have run down the legal angles, and these people, whoever they may be, are covered hell to breakfast. Taxes? They pay taxes. They're eager to pay taxes. So there won't be any investigation, they actually pay more taxes than they need to pay. Rules of corporation? They are more than meticulous in meeting all the rules. Social security? They pay social security on huge payrolls that we are convinced are utterly fictitious, but you can't go to the social security people and say, 'Look, there aren't any such people as these they're paying taxes on.' There are other points, but those serve as illustration. We've run down so many legal blind alleys that our legal force is dizzy."

"Mr. Crawford," said Vickers, "you make out a most interesting case, but I can't see the point of what you said earlier. You said this was a conspiracy to break world industry, to destroy a way of life. If you study our economic history, you will find example on example of cut-throat competition. Surely that's all this is."

"You forget," Crawford replied, "about the carbohydrates."

And that was true, thought Vickers. The carbohydrates were something apart from cut-throat competition.

There had been, he remembered, a famine in China, as usual, and another threatening, as usual, in India, and the American Congress had been debating, along strictly personal and political lines, as to whom they should help and how, and should they help anyone at all.

The story had broken for the morning papers. Synthesis of carbohydrates had been accomplished by an obscure laboratory. The story didn't say it was an obscure laboratory; that had come out later. And much later it came out that the laboratory was one that had never been heard of before, one which literally had sprung out of the ground overnight. There had been certain captains of industry, Vickers recalled, who had from the very first attacked these manufacturers of synthetic carbohydrates with the smear of "fly-by-night."

They were not fly-by-night. The company might have been unorthodox in its business dealings, but it was here to stay. A few days after the initial announcement the laboratory had made it known that it did not intend to sell its product, but would give it away to persons who might need it—persons, you understand, not populations or countries, but persons who were in need and who could not earn the money necessary to buy sufficient food. Not only the starving, but the simply undernourished, the whole wide segment of the world's population who would never actually starve from insufficient food, but who would suffer disease and handicaps, both physical and mental, from never getting quite enough to eat.

Offices appeared, as if by magic, in India and China, in France and England and Italy, in America and Iceland and Ireland and New Zealand, and the poor came in droves and were not turned away. There were those, no doubt, who took advantage of the situation, those who lied and took food they had no right to have, but the offices, it appeared after a time, did not seem to mind.

Carbohydrates by themselves were not sufficient food. But they were better than no food at all, and for many the saving represented by free carbohydrates provided the extra pennies to buy the bit of meat which had been a stranger to their table for many long months.

"We checked into the carbohydrates," Crawford was saying, "and we found nothing more to go on than with any of the others. So far as we're concerned, the carbohydrates aren't being manufactured— they simply exist. They are shipped to the distribution offices from several warehouses and none of the warehouses are big enough to carry more than a day or two's supply. We can find no factories and we can't trace transportation—oh, sure, from the warehouses to the distribution points, but not from anywhere to the warehouses. It's like the old story that Hawthorne told—about the pitcher of milk that never ran dry."

"Maybe you should go into the carbohydrates business yourself."

"Good idea," said Crawford, "but we don't know how. We'd like to make a Forever car, or everlasting razor blades, too, but we don't know how to do that, either. We've had technicians and scientists working on the problems, and they are no nearer to solution than the day they started."

"What happens when the men who are out of work need more than just a gift of food?" asked Vickers. "When their families are in tatters and they need clothes? What happens when they're thrown into the street?"

"I think I can answer that. Some other philanthropic society will spring up over night and will furnish clothes and shelter. They're selling houses now for five hundred a room and that's no more than token payment. Why not give them away? Why not clothing that will cost no more than a tenth, or a twentieth of what you pay today? A suit for five dollars, say. Or a dress for fifty cents."

"You have no idea of what is coming next?"

"We've tried to dope it out," said Crawford. "We figured the car would come quickly, and it did. We figured houses, too, and they have put them out. Clothing should be one of the next items to go on the market."

"Food, shelter, transportation, clothing," said Vickers. "Those are four basics."

"They also have fuel and power," Crawford added. "Let enough of the world's population shift to these new houses, with their solar power, and you can mark the power industry completely off the books."

"But who is it?" asked Vickers. "You've told me you don't know. But you must have some idea, some educated guess."

"Not an inkling. We have tables of organization for their corporation setups. We can't find the men themselves; they are names we've never heard of."

"Russia?"

Crawford shook his head. "The Kremlin is worried, too. Russia is co-operating. That should prove how scared they are."

For the first time, Crawford moved. He unfolded his hands from across his paunch, grasped the arms of his massive chair and pulled himself straight, sitting upright now.

"I suppose," he said, "that you are wondering where you fit in on this."

"Naturally."

"We can't come out and say, 'Here we are, a combine of the world's industrial might, fighting to protect your way of life.' We can't explain to them what the situation is. They'd laugh at us. After all, you can't tell people that a car that will last forever or a house that cost only five hundred a room is a bad thing for them. We can't tell them anything and yet this needs telling. We want you to write a book about it."

"I don't see . . ." Vickers began, but Crawford stopped him in mid-sentence.

"You would write it as if you had doped it out yourself. You would hint at informed sources that were too high to name. We'd furnish all the data, but the material would appear as yours."

Vickers came slowly to his feet. He reached out a hand and picked up his hat.

"Thanks for the chance," he said. "I'm not having any."

7

Ann Carter said to Vickers: "Some day, Jay, I'm going to get sore enough at you to take you apart. And when I do maybe I'll have a chance to find what makes you tick."

"I got a book to write," said Vickers. "I'm writing it. What more do you want?"

"That book could keep. You could write it anytime. This one won't."

"Go ahead, tell me I threw away a million bucks. That's what you're thinking."

"You could have charged them a fancy fee for writing and gotten a contract with the publisher like there never was before and . . ."

"And pushed aside the greatest piece of work I've ever done," said Vickers, "and come back to it cold and find I'd lost the touch."

"Every book you write is your greatest one. Jay Vickers, you're nothing but a literary ham. Sure, you do good work and your darn books sell, although sometimes I wonder why. If there were no money in it you'd never write another word. Tell me, honest, why do you write?"

"You've answered it for me. You say for money. All right, so it's for money."

"All right, so I have a sordid soul."

"My God," said Vickers, "we're fighting as if we were married."

"That's another thing. You've never married, Jay. It's an index of your selfishness. I bet you never even thought of it."

"Once I did," said Vickers. "Once long ago."

"Here, put your head down here and have a good long cry. I bet it was pitiful. I bet that's how you got some of those excruciating love scenes you put into your books."

"Ann, you're getting maudlin drunk."

"If I'm getting drunk, you're the man who drove me to it. You're the one who said, 'Thanks for the chance, but I'm not having any.'"

"I had a hunch there was something phony there," insisted Vickers.

"That was you," said Ann.

She finished off her drink.

"Don't use a hunch," she said, "to duck the responsibility for turning down the best thing you ever had. Any time someone dangles money like that in front of me, I'm not letting any hunch stand in my way."

"I'm sure you wouldn't," Vickers agreed.

"That was a nasty thing to say," Ann told him. "Pay for the drinks and let's get out of here. I'm putting you on that bus and don't you come back again."

8

The huge sign was draped diagonally across the front of the huge show window. It read:

HOUSES
TAILORED TO ORDER
$500 a-room
LIBERAL TRADE-IN ON YOUR OLD HOME

In the window was a five or six room house, set in the middle of a small, beautifully planned lawn and garden. There was a sundial in the garden and a cupola with a flying duck weather vane on the attached garage. Two white lawn chairs and a white round table stood on the clipped grass and there was a new and shiny car standing in the driveway.

Ann squeezed Vickers' arm. "Let's go in."

"This must be what Crawford was talking about," said Vickers.

"You got lots of time to catch the bus," Ann said.

"We might as well. If you get interested in looking at a house you won't be chewing me."

"If I thought it were possible, I'd trap and marry you."

"And make my life a hell."

"Why, certainly," Ann told him sweetly. "Why else would I do it?"

They went in the door and it swung to behind them and the noise of the street was shut away and they walked on the deep green carpeting that doubled as a lawn.

A salesman saw them and came over.

"We were just passing by," said Ann, "and we thought we would drop in. It looks like a fine house and . . ."

"It is a fine house," the salesman assured them, "and it has many special features."

"Is that true what the sign said?" asked Vickers. "Five hundred dollars a room?"

"Everyone asks me that. They read the sign, but they don't believe it, so the first thing they ask me when they come in is whether it is really true we sell these houses for five hundred a room."

"Well, is it?" insisted Vickers.

"Oh, most certainly," said the salesman. "A five room house is twenty-five hundred dollars and a ten room house would be five thousand dollars. Most people of course aren't interested in a ten room house at first."

"What do you mean, at first?"

"Well, you see, it's this way, sir," the salesman said. "This is what you might call a house that grows. You buy a five room house, say, and in a little while you figure that you want another room so we come out and redesign the house and make it a six room house."

"Isn't that expensive?" Ann asked.

"Oh, not at all," the salesman said. "It only costs you five hundred dollars for the extra room. That is a flat and standard charge."

"This is a prefabricated house, isn't it?" asked Ann.

"I suppose you would call it that, although it does the house injustice. When you say 'prefabricated' you are thinking of a house that is pre-cut and sort of stuck together. Takes a week or ten days to put it together and then you just have a shell—no heating plant, no fireplace, no nothing."

"I'm interested in this extra room angle," said Vickers. "You say that when they want an extra room they just call you up and you come out and stick one on."

The salesman stiffened slightly. "Not *exactly*, sir. We stick nothing on. We *redesign* your house. At all times, your house is well planned and practical, designed in accordance with the highest scientific and esthetic concepts of what a home should be. In some cases, adding another room means that we have to change the whole house around, rearrange the rooms and such.

"Of course," he added, "if you wanted to change the place completely the best thing might be to trade the house in on a new one. For doing that we make a service charge of one percent per year of the original cost, plus, of course, the charge for the extra rooms."

He looked at the two of them, hopefully. "You have a house, perhaps?"

"A little cottage up the valley," said Vickers. "It's not much of a place."

"Worth how much, would you say?"

"Fifteen or twenty thousand, but I doubt if I could get that much."

"We'd give you twenty thousand," said the salesman, "subject to appraisal. Our appraisals are most liberal."

"Look," said Vickers, "I'd only want a five or six room house. That would only come to twenty-five hundred or three thousand."

"Oh, that's all right," the salesman told him. "We'd pay the difference in cash."

"That doesn't make sense!"

"Why, of course it does. We're quite willing to pay the going market value on existing structures in order to introduce our own. In your case, we'd pay you the difference, then we'd take your old place and move it away and set up the new one. It's as simple as that."

Ann spoke to Vickers. "Go ahead and tell the man that you aren't having any. This sounds like a good sound business proposition to me, so of course you'll turn it down."

"Madam," said the salesman, "I don't quite understand."

"It's just a private joke," Vickers interpreted.

"Ah . . . well, I was telling you that this house has some special features."

"Go ahead, please," said Ann. "Tell us about them."

"Very happy to. For instance there is the solar plant. You know what a solar plant is."

Vickers nodded. "A power plant operated by the sun."

"Exactly," said the salesman. "This plant, however, is somewhat more efficient than the usual solar plant. It not only heats the house in winter, but supplies electrical power for all the year around. It eliminates the necessity of relying upon a public utility for your power. I might add there is plenty of power, much more than you will ever need."

"A nice feature," said Ann.

"And it comes fully equipped. You get a refrigerator and a home freezer, an automatic washer and dryer, a dish washer, a garbage disposal unit, a toaster, a waffle-iron, radio, television, and other odds and ends."

"Paying extra for them, of course," said Vickers.

"Oh, indeed not. *All* you pay is five hundred a room."

"And beds?" asked Ann. "Chairs and stuff like that?"

"I'm sorry," said the salesman. "You have to furnish those yourself."

"There is an extra charge," Vickers persisted, "for carting away the old house and putting up the new one."

The salesman drew himself erect and spoke with quiet dignity. "I want you to understand that this is an honest offer. There are *no* hidden costs. You buy the house and pay—or arrange to pay—at the rate of five hundred a room. We have trained crews of workmen who move away your old house and erect the new one. All of that is included in the original cost. There is nothing added on. Of course, some buyers want to change location. In that case we are usually able to work out an acceptable exchange plan between their old real estate and the new location they select. You, I presume, would want to stay where you are. You said you were up the valley. A most attractive place."

"Well, I don't know," said Vickers.

"I forgot to mention one thing," the salesman went on. "You never have to paint this house. It is built of material that is of the same color all the way through. The color never wears off or fades. We have a wide range of very attractive color combinations."

"We don't want to take up too much of your time," said Vickers. "You see, we're not really customers. We just dropped in."

"But you have a house?"

"Yes, I have a house."

"And we stand ready to replace the house with a new one and pay you a comfortable sum besides."

"I know all that," said Vickers, "but . . ."

"It seems to me," the salesman said, "that you should be the one trying to sell me instead of me trying to sell you."

"I have a house, and I like it. How would I know I'd like one of these new houses?"

"Why, sir," said the salesman, "I just been telling you—"

"I'm used to my house. I'm acquainted with it and it's got used to me. I've become attached to it."

"Jay Vickers!" said Ann. "You can't become that attached to a house in three years. To hear you talk about it, you'd think it was your old ancestral home."

Vickers was obstinate. "I have the feel of it. I know the place. There's a creaky board in the dining room and I step on it on purpose at times just to hear it creak. And there's a pair of robins that have a nest in the vine on the porch and there's a cricket in the basement. I've hunted for that cricket, but I never could find him; he was too smart for me. And now I wouldn't touch him if I could, because he's a part of the house and—"

"You'd never be bothered with crickets in one of our houses. They have bug repellent built right into them. You never are bothered with mosquitoes or ants or crickets or anything of the sort."

"But I'm not bothered with this cricket," said Vickers. "That is what I was trying to tell you. I like it. I'm not sure I'd like a house where a cricket couldn't live. Now, mice, that's a little different."

"I dare say," declared the salesman, "that you would not have mice in one of our houses."

"I won't have any in mine, either. I called in an exterminator to get rid of them, and they'll be gone by the time I get home."

"One thing is bothering me," said Ann to the salesman. "You remember all that equipment you mentioned, the washer and refrigerator and . . ."

"Yes, certainly."

"But you didn't mention anything about a stove."

"Didn't I?" asked the salesman. "Now, how could I have let it slip my mind? Of course you get a stove."

9

When the bus reached Cliffwood, darkness was beginning to fall. Vickers bought a paper at the corner drugstore and made his way across the street to the town's one clean cafe.

He had ordered the meal and was just starting on the paper when a piping voice hailed him.

"Hi, there, Mr. Vickers."

Vickers put down the paper and looked up. It was Jane, the little girl who had come for breakfast.

"Why, hello, Jane," he said. "What are you doing here?"

"Me and Mommy came down to buy some ice cream for supper," Jane explained. She perched herself on the edge of the chair across the table from him. "Where you been today, Mr. Vickers? I came across to see you, but there was a man there and he wouldn't let me in. He said he was killing mice. What was he killing mice for, Mr. Vickers?"

"Jane," a voice said.

Vickers looked up and a woman stood there, sleek and maturely beautiful, and she smiled at him.

"You must not mind her, Mr. Vickers," she said.

"Oh, indeed, I don't, I think she's wonderful."

"I am Mrs. Leslie," said the woman. "Jane's mother. We've been neighbors for a long time now, but we've never met."

She sat down at the table.

"I have read some of your books," she said, "and they are wonderful. I haven't read them all. One has so little time."

"Thank you, Mrs. Leslie," said Vickers and wondered if she would think that he was thanking her for not reading all his books.

"I had meant to come over and see you," Mrs. Leslie said. "Some of us are organizing a Pretentionist Club and I have you on my list."

Vickers shook his head. "I am pressed for time," he said. "I make it a rule to belong to nothing."

"But this," said Mrs. Leslie, "would be—well, you might say, this would be down your alley."

"I am glad you thought of me."

She laughed at him. "You think us foolish, Mr. Vickers."

"No," he said, "not foolish."

"Infantile, then."

"Since you supplied the word," said Vickers, "I'll agree to it. Yes, I must admit, it does seem just faintly infantile."

Now, he thought, I've done it. Now she will twist it around so that it will appear it was I, not she, who said it. She'll tell all the neighbors how I told her to her face the club was infantile.

But she didn't seem insulted. "It must seem infantile to someone like you who has every minute filled. But I've been told that it's a wonderful way to work up an interest—an outside interest, that is."

"I have no doubt it is," said Vickers.

"It's a lot of work, I understand. Once you decide on the period you'd like to pretend you are living in, you must read up on the period and do a lot of research on it and then you have to write your diary and it must be day to day and it must be a full account of each day's activities and not just a sentence or two and you must make it interesting and, if you can, exciting."

"There are many periods of history," said Vickers, "that could be made exciting."

"Now, I'm glad to hear you say that," Mrs. Leslie told him, eagerly. "Would you tell me one? If you were going to choose a period for excitement, Mr. Vickers, which one would you choose?"

"I'm sorry. I'd have to think about it."

"But you say there were many . . ."

"I know. And yet, when I think of it, it seems to me that the present day might prove as exciting as any of the others."

"But there's nothing going on."

"There's too much going on," said Vickers.

The whole idea was pitiful, of course—grown people pretending they lived in some other age, publicly confessing that they could not live at peace with their own age, but most go burrowing back through other times and happenings to find the musty thrill of vicarious existence. It marked some rankling failure in the lives of these people, some terrible emptiness that would not let them be, some screaming vacuum that somehow had to be filled.

He remembered the two women who had talked in the bus seat behind him and he wondered momentarily what vicarious satisfaction the Pretentionist living back in Pepys' time might get out of it. There was, of course, Pepys' well filled life, the scurrying about, the meetings with many people, the little taverns where there were cheese and wine, the theaters, the good companionship and the midnight talks, the many interests that had kept Pepys as full of life, as naturally full of life, as these Pretentionists were empty.

The movement itself was escapism, of course, but escapism from what? From insecurity, perhaps. From tension, from a daily, ever-present uneasiness that never quite bubbled into fear, yet never quieted into peace. The state, perhaps, of never being sure—a state of mind that all the refinements of a highly advanced technology could not compensate.

"They must have our ice cream packed by now," said Mrs. Leslie, gathering up her gloves and purse. "You must come over, Mr. Vickers, and spend an evening with us."

Vickers rose with her. "Certainly. Some evening very soon," he promised.

He knew he wouldn't and he knew she didn't want him to, but they both paid lip service to the old fable of hospitality.

"Come on, Jane," said Mrs. Leslie. "It was nice to meet you, Mr. Vickers, after all these years."

Without waiting for his answer, she moved away.

"Everything is fine at our house now," said Jane. "Mommy and Daddy have made up again."

"I'm glad of that," said Vickers.

"Daddy says he won't run around with women any more," said Jane.

"I'm glad to hear that, too," said Vickers.

Her mother called to her across the store.

"I got to go now," said Jane. She slipped off the chair and ran across the store to her mother's side. She turned and waved at him as they went out the door.

Poor kid, he thought, what a life she has ahead of her. If I had a little girl like that—he shut the thought away. There was no little girl for him. There was a shelf of books; and there was the manuscript that lay waiting for him, in all its promise and its glory. And suddenly he realized how faint the promise was, how false and shallow the glory might be. Books and manuscript; he thought. Not much to build a life on.

And that was it, of course. That was the trouble with not himself alone, but with everyone—no one seemed now to have much on which to build his life. For so many years the world had lived with war or the threat of war. First it had been a frantic feeling, a running to escape, and then it was just a moral and mental numbness that one didn't even notice, a condition that one accepted as the normal way of life.

No wonder there were Pretentionists, he told himself. With his books and his manuscript, he was one himself.

10

___

He looked under the flower pot on the corner of the stoop to find the key, but it wasn't there and then he remembered that he had left the door unlocked so that Joe could come in and get rid of the mice.

He turned the knob and went in and made his way across the room to turn on the desk lamp. A white square of paper with awkward pencil scrawls upon it lay beneath the lamp.

Jay: I did the job, then came back and opened up the windows to clean out the smell. I'll give you a hundred bucks a throw for every mouse you find. Joe.

A noise brought him around from the desk and he saw that there was someone on the porch, sitting in his favorite chair, rocking back and forth, a cigarette making a little wavy line dancing in the dark.

"It's I," said Horton Flanders. "Have you had anything to eat?"

"I had something in the village."

"That's a pity. I brought over a tray of sandwiches and some beer. I thought you might be hungry and I know how you hate to cook . . ."

"Thanks," said Vickers. "I'm not hungry now. We can have them later."

He threw his hat onto a chair and went out onto the porch.

"I have your chair," said Mr. Flanders.

"Keep it," Vickers said. "This one is just as comfortable."

"Did you notice if there was any news today? I have a most deplorable habit, at times, of not looking at the papers."

"The same old thing. Another peace rumor that no one quite believes."

"The cold war still goes on," said Mr. Flanders. "It's been going on for almost forty years. It warms up now and then, but it never does explode. Has it ever occurred to you, Mr. Vickers, that there have been a dozen times at least when there should have been real war, but somehow or other it has never come to be?"

"I hadn't thought of it."

"But it's the truth. First there was the Berlin airlift trouble and the fighting in Greece. Either one of them could have set off a full scale war, but each of them was settled. Then there was Korea and that was settled, too. Then Iran threatened to blow up the world, but we got safely past it. Then there were the Manila incidents and the flareup in Alaska and the Indian crisis and half a dozen others. But all of them were settled, one way or another."

"No one really wants to fight," said Vickers.

"Perhaps not," agreed Mr. Flanders, "but it takes more than just the will for peace to prevent a war. Time and again a major nation has climbed out on a limb to a point where they had to fight or back up. They always have backed up. That isn't human nature, Mr. Vickers, or at least it wasn't human nature until forty years ago. Does it seem to you that something might have happened, some unknown factor, some new equation, that may account for it?"

"I don't quite see how there could be any new factor. The human race is still the human race. They've always fought before. Forty years ago they had just finished the greatest war that ever had been fought."

"Since then, there has been provocation after provocation and there have been regional wars, but the world has not gone to war. Can you tell me why?"

"No, I can't."

"I have thought about it," said Mr. Flanders, "in an idle way, of course. And it seems to me that there must be some new factor."

"Fear, perhaps," suggested Vickers. "Fear of our frightful weapons."

"That might be it," admitted Mr. Flanders, "but fear is a funny thing. Fear is just as apt to start a war as it is to hold one off. It is quite possible that fear alone might make a people go out and fight to be rid of fear—willing to go against the fear itself to be rid of it. I don't think, Mr. Vickers, that fear alone can account for peace."

"You're thinking of some psychological factor?"

"Perhaps that might be it," said Mr. Flanders. "Or it might be intervention."

"Intervention! Who would intervene?"

"I really couldn't say. But the thought is not a new one to me and not in this respect alone. Starting about ninety years or so ago something happened to the world. Up until that time man had stumbled along pretty much in the same old ruts. There had been some progress here and there, some changes, but not very many of them. Not many changes in thinking especially and that is the thing that counts.

"Then mankind, which had been shambling along, broke into a gallop. The automobile was invented and the telephone and motion pictures and flying machine. There was the radio and all the other gadgetry that characterized the first quarter of the century.

"But that was largely mechanics, pure and simple, putting two and two together and having four come out. In the second quarter of the century classical physics was largely displaced by a new kind of thinking, a thinking which admitted that it didn't know when it came face to face with the atoms and electrons. And out of that came theories and the physics of the atom and all the probabilities that today still are probabilities.

"And that, I think, was the greatest stride of all—that the physicists who had fashioned neat cubicles of knowledge and had classified and assigned all the classical knowledge to fit into them snugly should have had the courage to say they didn't know what made electrons behave the way they do."

"You're trying to say," Vickers put in, "that something happened to whip man out of his rut. But it wasn't the first time a thing like that had happened. Before it there had been the Renaissance and the Industrial Revolution."

"I did not say it was the only time it had ever happened," Mr. Flanders told him. "I merely said it happened. The fact that it had happened before, in a slightly different manner, should prove that it is not an accident, but some sort of cycle, some sort of influence which is operative within the human race. What is it that kicks a plodding culture out of a shuffle into a full-fledged gallop and, in this case at least, keeps it galloping for almost a hundred years without a sign of slackening?"

"You said intervention," said Vickers. "You're off on some wild fantasy. Men from Mars, maybe?"

Mr. Flanders shook his head. "Not men from Mars. I don't think it's men from Mars. Let's be a little more general."

He waved his cigarette at the sky above the hedge and trees, with its many stars twinkling in the night. "Out there must be great reservoirs of knowledge. At many points in all that space out beyond our earth there must be thinking beings and they would create knowledge that we had never dreamed of. Some of it might be applicable to humans and to earth and much of it would not."

"You're suggesting that some one from out there—"

"No," said Mr. Flanders. "I'm suggesting that the knowledge is there and waiting, waiting for us to go out there and get it."

"We haven't even reached the moon yet."

"We may not need to wait for rockets. We may not have to go physically to get it. We might reach out with our minds. . . ."

"Telepathy?"

"Perhaps. Maybe that is what you could call it. A mind probing out and searching—a mind reaching out for a mind. If there is such a thing as telepathy, distance should make no difference—a half a mile or a light year, what would be the difference? For the mind is not a physical property, it is not bound, or should not be bound, by the laws that say that nothing can exceed the speed of light."

Vickers laughed uneasily, feeling the slow crawl of invisible, many-footed creatures moving on his neck.

"You can't be serious," he said.

"Perhaps I'm not," admitted Mr. Flanders. "Perhaps I'm an old eccentric who has found a man who will listen to him and will not laugh too much."

"But this knowledge that you talk of. There is no evidence that such knowledge can be applied, that it ever could be used. It would be alien, it would involve alien logic and apply to alien problems and it would be based on alien concepts that we could not understand."

"Much of it would," said Mr. Flanders. "You would have to sift and winnow. There would be much chaff, but you would find some kernels. You might find, for instance, a way in which friction could be eliminated and if you found that you would have machines that would last forever and you would have—"

"Wait a minute," snapped Vickers, tensely, "what are you getting at? What about this business of machines that would run forever? We have that already. I was talking to Eb just this morning and he was telling me—"

"About a car. That, Mr. Vickers, is exactly what I mean."

11

For a long time after Mr. Flanders left, Vickers sat on the porch, smoked his cigarettes and stared at the patch of sky he could see between the top of the hedge and the porch's roof . . . at the sky and its crystal wash of stars, thinking that one could not sense the distance and the time that lay between the stars.

Flanders was an old man with a shabby coat and a polished stick and his queer, stilted way of talking that made you think of another time and another culture. What could he know, what possibly could he know of knowledge in the stars?

Anyone could dream up talk like that. What was it he had said? He had thought of it, in an idle way. And that, Vickers decided, was the way it must be—an idle old eccentric with nothing on his mind except the idle thoughts that took his mind off another life, an old and faded life that he wanted to forget.

And there, thought Vickers, I am speculating, too, for there's no way that I can know the kind of a life the old man may have led.

He got up and went into the living room. He pulled the chair out from his desk and sat down and stared at the typewriter sitting there, accusing him of wasted time, of an entire wasted day, pointing with accusing finger at the pile of manuscript that should have been a little thicker if he had stayed at home.

He picked up a few pages of the manuscript and tried to read, but he had no interest and he was gripped by the terrifying thought that he had gone cold, had lost the spark which drove him day after day to the task of setting down the words that must be written—that literally *must* be written, as if the writing of them were a means of purging himself of a confusion that lurked inside his mind, as if the writing of them were a task, or penance, that must be done as a condition of his living.

He had said no, that he wasn't interested in writing Crawford's book and he had said it because he *wasn't* interested, because he had wanted to come back here and add to the pile of manuscript that lay there on the desk.

And yet that had not been the only factor—there had been something else. Hunch, he had told Ann, and she had scoffed at him. But there had been a hunch—that and a feeling of danger and of fear, as if a second self had been standing at his side, warning him away.

It was illogical, of course, for there was no reason why he should have a sense of fear. There had been no reason why he could not have taken on the job. He could have used the money. Ann could have used the fee. There was no logic, no sense, in refusing. And yet, without an instant's hesitation, he had refused the offer.

He put the sheets of manuscript back on top of the pile, rose from the chair and pushed it flush against the desk.

As if the whisper of the chair sliding on the carpeting might have been a signal, a scurrying sound came out of one darkened corner and traveled to the next and then was still, so still that Vickers could hear the faint swish of a vine, swung slowly by the wind, scraping against the screen of the porch outside the open door. Then even the vine stopped swaying and the house was still with a deathly stillness that was unnatural, as if the whole house might be waiting for whatever happened next.

Slowly Vickers turned around to face the room, moving his feet cautiously, pivoting his body with an exaggerated, almost ridiculous, effort to be quiet, to get turned around so he could face the corner from which the sound had come without anything knowing he had turned.

There were no mice. Joe had come up, while he was in the city, and had killed the mice. There were no mice and there should be no scurrying from one corner to the next. Joe had left a note which even now still lay beneath the desk lamp saying that he would pay one hundred bucks a throw for every mouse that Vickers could produce.

The silence hung, not so much a silence as a quietness, as if everything were waiting without breathing.

Moving only his eyeballs, for it seemed that if he moved his head his neck would creak and betray him to whatever danger there might be, Vickers examined the room, with particular emphasis upon the darkened areas in the corners and underneath the furniture and in the shadowed places that were farthest from the light. Cautiously he put his hands behind him, to grasp the desk edge, to get hold of something that was solid so that he did not stand so agonizingly alone, transfixed in the room.

The fingers of his right hand touched something that was metallic and he knew that it was the metal paper weight that he had lifted off the pile of manuscript when he had sat down at the desk. His fingers reached out and grasped it and dragged it forward into the hollow of his hand and he closed his fingers on it and he had a weapon.

There was something in the corner by the yellow chair and although it seemed to have no eyes, he knew it was watching him. It didn't know that he had spotted it, or it didn't seem to know, although in the next instant it more than likely would.

"Now!" said Vickers and the word exploded from him like a cannon blast. His right arm swung up and over and followed through and the paperweight, turning end over end, crashed into the corner.

There was a crunching sound and the noise of metallic parts rolling on the floor.

12

There were many little tubes, smashed, and an intricate mass of wiring that was bent and broken and funny crystal discs that were chipped and splintered, and the metallic outer shell that had held the tubes and wiring and the discs and the many other pieces of mechanical mystery that he did not recognize.

Vickers pulled the desk lamp closer to him, so that the light might shine down upon the handful of parts he had gathered from the floor and he put out a finger and stirred it among them, gingerly, listening to the tinkling sounds they made as they clinked together.

No mouse, but something else—something that scuttled in the night, knowing that he would think it was a mouse; a thing that had scared the cat which knew it was no mouse, and a thing that would not be attracted to traps.

An electronic contraption, maybe, from the looks of the tubes and wiring. Vickers stirred the pieces again with a probing finger and listened to the tinkling as they clinked together.

An electronic spy, he speculated, a scuttling, scurrying, listening thing that watched his every moment, a thing that stored what it heard and saw for future reference or transmitted directly the knowledge that it gained. But direct to whom? And why? And maybe it wasn't a spying thing, at all. Maybe it was something else, something for which there might be a simpler—or a more weird—explanation. If it were a listening or a seeing device, planted here to spy on him, he would not have caught it. He had never seen one of them before, and for months now he'd heard the scurrying and the scampering that he had thought were mice.

If it were a spying device it would be made so well, so cleverly that it would be able not only to observe him, but to keep out of sight itself. To have any value it must keep its presence undetected. There would have been no careless moment. It would not have been seen unless it wanted itself to be seen.

Unless it wanted itself to be seen!

He had been sitting at the desk and had gotten up and pushed the chair flush with the desk and it had been then that he had heard the scampering. If it had not run, he never would have seen it. And it need not have run, for the room was in shadow, with only the desk lamp burning, and his back had been toward the room.

The cold certainty came to him that it had wanted to be seen, that it had wanted to be trapped in a corner and crushed with a paperweight—that it had run deliberately to call his attention to it and that once he'd seen it, it had not tried to get away.

He sat at the desk and cold beads of perspiration came out of his forehead and he felt them there but did not lift a hand to brush them off.

It had wanted to be seen. It had wanted him to know.

Not it, of course, but the thing behind it—whoever or what-ever it was that had caused the contraption to be placed inside his house. For months it had scampered and scurried, had listened and watched, and now the time for the scampering and the watching had come to an end and it was time for something else; time to serve notice on him that he was being watched.

But why, and who?

He fought down the cold, screaming panic that rose inside of him, forced himself to stay sitting in the chair.

There was a clue somewhere in this very day, he thought. Somewhere there was a clue, if he could recognize it. Something happened today that made the agency behind the watcher decide it was time to let him know.

He ticked off the day's events, marshalling them in his mind as they might be written in a notebook:

> *The little girl who had come to breakfast.*
> *The remembrance of a walk that he had taken twenty years before.*
> *The story in the paper about more worlds than one.*
> *The women who had talked in the seat behind him on the bus, and Mrs. Leslie and the club she was organizing.*
> *Crawford and his story of a world with its back against the wall.*
> *The houses at five hundred dollars a room.*
> *Mr. Flanders sitting on the porch and saying that there was a new-found factor which kept the world from war.*
> *The mouse that was not a mouse.*

But that wasn't all, of course; somewhere there was something else that he had forgotten. Without knowing how he knew it, he knew that he had forgotten something, some other tabulated fact that should be inserted somewhere in the list of things that had happened in the day.

There was Flanders saying that he was interested in the setup of the gadget shops and that he was intrigued by the riddle of the carbohydrates and that he was convinced there was something going on.

And later in the day he had sat on the porch and talked of reservoirs of knowledge in the stars and of a factor which kept the world from war and of another factor which had whipped Man out of his rut almost a hundred years ago and had kept him at the gallop ever since. He had speculated about these matters in an idle way, he had said.

But was his speculation idle?

Or did Flanders know more than he was telling?

And if he knew, what then?

Vickers shoved back the chair and got to his feet.

He looked at the time. It was almost two o'clock.

No matter, he thought. It's time that find out. Even if I have to break into his house and jerk him out of bed, screaming in his nightshirt (for he was sure that Flanders would not wear pajamas), it's time that I find out.

13

Long before he reached Flanders' house, Vickers saw that there was something wrong. The house was lighted up, from basement to garret. Men with lanterns were walking about the yards and there were other knots of men who stood around and talked, while all along the street women and children stood on the porches in hastily snatched-up robes. As if, Vickers thought, they were waiting for a strange three o'clock parade that might at any moment come winding down the street.

A group of men was standing by the gate and as he turned in, he saw there were some he knew. There was Eb, the garage man, and Joe, the exterminator, and Vic, who ran the drugstore.

"Hello, Jay," said Eb, "we're glad that you are here."

"Hello, Jay," said Joe.

"What's going on?" asked Vickers.

"Old Man Flanders," said Vic, "has up and disappeared."

"His housekeeper got up in the night to give him some medicine," said Eb, "and found he wasn't there. She looked around for him for a while and then she went to get some help."

"You've searched for him?" asked Vickers.

"Around the place," said Eb. "But we're going to start branching out now. We'll have-to organize and get some system in it."

The drugstore owner said: "We thought at first maybe he'd been up during the night wandering around the house or out into the yard and might have had a seizure, of one sort or another. So we looked near at hand at first."

"We've gone over the house," said Joe, "from top to bottom and we've combed the yard and there ain't hide nor hair of him."

"Maybe he went for a walk," Vickers offered.

"No man in his right mind," declared Joe, "goes walking after midnight."

"He wasn't in his right mind, if you ask me," said Eb. "Not that I didn't like him, 'cause I did. Never saw a more mannerly old codger in all my born days, but he had funny ways about him."

Someone with a lantern came down the brick paved walk.

"You men ready to get organized?" asked the man with the lantern.

"Sure, sheriff," said Eb. "Sure, we're ready, any time you are. We just been waiting for you to get it figured out."

"Well," said the sheriff, "there ain't much that we can do until it gets light, although that's only a couple hours away. But I thought maybe until it got light enough to see we might take some quick scouts out around. Some of the other boys are going to fan out and cover the town, go up and down all the streets and alleys and I thought maybe some of you might like to have a look along the river."

"That's all right with us," said Eb. "You tell us what you want us to do and we sure will do it."

The sheriff lifted his lantern to shoulder height and looked at them. "Jay Vickers, ain't it? Glad you joined us, Jay. We need all the men there are."

Vickers lied, without knowing why he lied: "I heard some commotion going on."

"Guess you knew the old gent pretty well. Better than the most of us."

"He used to come over and talk to me almost every day," said Vickers.

"I know. We remarked about it. He never talked to no one else."

"We had some common interests," Vickers said, "and I think that he was lonely."

"The housekeeper said he went over to see you last night."

"Yes, he did," said Vickers. "He left shortly after midnight."

"Notice anything unusual about him? Any difference in the way he talked?"

"Now, look here, sheriff," said Eb. "You don't think that Jay had anything to do with this?"

"No," the sheriff said. "No, I guess I don't." He lowered the lantern and said, "If you fellows would go down to the river. Split up when you get there. Some of you go upstream and some of you go down. I don't expect you to find anything, but we might as well look. Be back by daylight and we'll really start combing for him."

The sheriff turned away, walking back up the brick pavement, with his lantern swinging.

"I guess," said Eb, "we might as well get started. I'll take one bunch down the river and Joe will take the others up. That all right with the rest of you?"

"It's all right with me," said Joe.

They walked out the gate and down the street until they hit the cross street, then went down to the bridge. They halted there.

"We split up here," said Eb. "Who wants to go with Joe?"

Several men said they would.

"All right," said Eb. "The rest of you come with me."

They separated and plunged down from the street to the river bank. Cold river mist lay close along the bank and in the darkness they could hear the swift, smooth tonguing of the river. A night bird cried across the water and looking out to the other bank, one could see the splintered starlight that had shattered itself against the running current.

Eb asked, "You think we'll find him, Jay?"

Vickers spoke slowly. "No, I don't. I can't tell you why, but somehow I am pretty sure we won't."

14

It was early evening before Vickers returned home.

The phone was ringing when he stepped inside the door and he strode across the room and picked it up.

It was Ann Carter. "I've been trying to get you all day. I'm terribly upset. Where have you been?"

"Out looking for a man," said Vickers.

"Jay, don't be funny," she said. "Please don't be funny."

"I'm not being funny. An old man, a neighbor of mine, disappeared. I've been out helping look for him."

"Did you find him?"

"No, we didn't."

"That's too bad," she said. "Was he a nice old man?"

"The best."

"Maybe you'll find him later."

"Maybe we will," said Vickers. "Why are you upset?"

"You remember what Crawford said?"

"He said a lot of things."

"But what he said about what would come next. You remember that?"

"I can't say that I do."

"Well, he said clothing would be next. A dress for fifty cents."

"Now that you mention it," said Vickers, "it all comes back to me."

"Well, it happened."

"What happened?"

"A dress. Only it wasn't fifty cents. It was *fifteen*!"

"You bought one?"

"No, I didn't, Jay. I was too scared to buy one. I was walking down Fifth Avenue and there was a sign in the window, a little discreet sign that said the dress on the model could be had for fifteen cents. Can you imagine that, Jay! A dress for fifteen cents on Fifth Avenue!"

"No, I can't," Vickers confessed.

"It was such a pretty dress," she said. "It shone. Not with stones or tinsel. The material shone. Like it was alive. And the color . . . Jay, it was the prettiest dress I have ever seen. And I could have bought it for fifteen cents, but I didn't have the nerve. I remembered what Crawford had told us and I stood there looking at the dress and I got cold all over."

"Well, that's too bad," said Vickers. "Buck up your nerve and go back in the morning. Maybe they'll still have it."

"But that isn't the point at all, Jay. Don't you see? It proves what Crawford told us. It proves that he knew what he was talking about, that there really is a conspiracy, that the world really does have its back against the wall."

"And what do you want me to do about it?"

"Why, I—I don't know, Jay. I thought you would be interested."

"I am," said Vickers. "Very interested."

"Jay, there's something going on."

"Keep your shirt on, Ann," said Vickers. "Sure, there's something going on."

"What is it, Jay? I know it's more than Crawford said. I don't know how—"

"I don't know, either. But it's big—it's bigger than you and I can handle. I have to think it out."

"Jay," she said, and the sharp tenseness was gone from her voice. "Jay, I feel better now. It was nice to talk to you."

"You go out in the morning," he told her, "and buy up an armful of those fifteen-cent dresses. Get there early ahead of the crowd."

"Crowd? I don't understand."

"Look, Ann," Vickers said, "when the news gets around, Fifth Avenue is going to have a crush of bargain hunters like nothing you've ever seen before."

"I guess you're right at that," she said. "Phone me tomorrow, Jay?"

"I'll phone."

They said good night and he hung up, stood for a moment, trying to remember the next thing that he should do. There was supper to get and the papers to get in and he'd better see if there was any mail.

He went out the door and walked down the path to the mailbox on the gatepost. He took out a slim handful of letters and leafed through them swiftly, but there was so little light he could not make out what they were. Advertising mostly, he suspected. And a few bills, although it was a bit early in the month for the bills to start.

Back in the house he turned on the desk lamp and laid the pile of letters on the desk. Beneath the lamp lay the litter of tubes and discs that he had picked up from the floor the night before. He stood there staring at them, trying to bring them into correct time perspective. It had only been the night before, but now it seemed as if it were many weeks ago that he had thrown the paperweight and there had been a crunching sound that had erupted with a shower of tiny parts rolling on the floor.

He stood there then, as he stood now, and knew there was an answer somewhere, a clue, if only he knew where to find it.

The phone rang again and he went to answer it.

It was Eb, asking: "What do you think of it?"

"I don't know what to think," said Vickers.

"He's in the river," Eb maintained. "That is where he is. That's what I told the sheriff. They'll start dragging tomorrow morning as soon as the sun is up."

"I don't know," said Vickers. "Maybe you are right, but I don't think that he is dead."

"Why don't you think so, Jay?"

"No reason in the world," said Vickers. "No actual, solid reason. Just a hunch."

"The reason I called," Eb told him, "is that I got some of those Forever cars. Came in this afternoon. Thought maybe you might want one of them."

"I hadn't thought much about it, Eb, to tell you the truth. But I might be interested."

"I'll bring one up in the morning," said Eb. "Give you a chance to try it out. See what you think of it."

"That'll be fine," said Vickers.

"All right, then," said Eb. "See you in the morning."

Vickers went back to the desk and picked up the letters. There were no bills. Of the seven letters, six were advertising matter, the seventh was in a plain white envelope addressed in a craggy hand.

He tore it open. There was one sheet of white note paper, neatly folded.

He unfolded it and read:

My dear friend Vickers:

I hope that you are not unduly worn out by the strenuous efforts which you undoubtedly will have thrown into the search for me today.

I feel very keenly that my actions will impose upon the kind people of this excellent village a most unseemly amount of running around to the neglect of their business, although I do not doubt that they will enjoy it most thoroughly.

I feel that I can trust your understanding not to reveal the fact of this letter nor to engage any further than is necessary to convince our neighbors of your kindly intentions in what must necessarily be a futile hunt for me. I can assure you that I am most happy and that only the necessity of the moment made me do what I have done.

I am writing this note for two reasons. Firstly, to quiet any fear you may feel for me. Secondly, to presume upon our friendship to the point of giving some unsolicited advice.

It has seemed to me for some time now that you have been confining yourself too closely to your work and that a holiday might be an excellent idea for someone in your situation. It might be that a visit to your childhood scene, to walk down the paths you walked when you were a boy, might clear away the dust and make you see with clearer eyes.

Your friend,
Horton Flanders.

15

I will not go, thought Vickers. I cannot go. The place means nothing to me now and I do not want it to mean anything after all these years of trying to forget it.

He could have shut his eyes and seen it—the yellow clay of the rain-washed cornfields, the roads all white with dust winding through the valleys and along the ridgetops, the lonely mailboxes sitting on forlornly leaning fence posts stuck into the ground, the sagging gates, the weather-beaten houses, the scraggy cattle coming down the lane, following the rutted path that their hoofs had made, the mangy dogs that ran out and barked at you when you drove past their farms.

If I go back they'll ask me why I came and how I'm getting on. "Too bad about your Pa, he was a damn good man." They'd sit on the upturned boxes in front of the general store and chew slowly on their cuds of tobacco and spit out on the sidewalk and look at him out of slanted eyes and say: "So you write books. By God, some day I'll have to read one of your books. I never heard of them."

He'd go to the cemetery and stand before a stone with his hat held in his hand and listen to the wind moan in the mighty pines that grew all around the cemetery fence and he'd think, if only I could have amounted to something in time that you could have known, so that the two of you could have been proud of me and bragged about me a little when the neighbors dropped in for a visit—but of course, I never did.

He'd drive the roads he'd known when he was a boy and stop the car beside the creek and get out and climb the barbed wire fence and walk down to the hole where he always caught the chubs and the stream would be a trickle and the hole would be a muddy widening of the trickle and the tree where he had sat would be gone in some springtime flood. He'd look at the hills and they would be familiar and at the same time strange, and he would try to puzzle out what was wrong with them and he could not tell for the life of him what was wrong with them and he'd go on, thinking about the creek and the unfamiliar hills, feeling lonelier by the minute. And finally in the end, he'd flee. He would press the accelerator to the boards and cling to the wheel and try not to think.

And he would—finally, he admitted it—he would drive past the great brick house with the portico and the fanlights above the door. He would drive very slowly and he would look at it and he'd see how the shutters had come loose and were sagging and how the paint was flaking and how the roses that had bloomed beside the gate had died out in some cold and blustery winter.

I won't go, he said. I will not go.

And yet, perhaps, he should.

It might clear away the dust, Flanders had written, might make you see with clearer eyes.

Might make him see *what* with clearer eyes?

Was there something back there in his boyhood lanes that might explain this situation that had burst upon him, some hidden fact, some abstract symbol, that he had missed before? Some thing, perhaps, that he had seen before, even many times, and had not recognized?

Or was he imagining things, reading significance into words that had no significance? How could he be sure that Horton Flanders with his shabby suit and ridiculous cane had anything to do with the story that Crawford had spelled out about humanity standing with its back against the wall?

There was no evidence at all.

Yet Flanders had disappeared and had written him a letter.

Clear away the dust, Flanders had written, so that you may see the better. And all that he might have meant was that he should clear away the dust so that he could write the better, so that the manuscript which lay upon the desk might be the better piece of work because its creator had looked on life and fellow man with eyes that were clear of dust. The dust of prejudice, perhaps, or the dust of vanity, or simply the dust of not seeing as sharply as one should.

Vickers put down a hand on the manuscript and ruffled its pages with his thumb, an absent, almost loving gesture. So little done, he thought, so much still to do.

Now, for two whole days, he'd done nothing on it. Two full days wasted.

To do the writing that should be done, he must be able to sit down calmly and concentrate, shut out the world and then let the world come in to him, a little at a time, a highly selected world that could be analyzed and set up with a clarity and sharpness that could not be mistaken.

Calmly, he thought. My God, how can a man be calm when he has a thousand questions and a thousand doubts probing at his mind?

Fifteen cent dresses, Ann had said on the telephone. Fifteen cent dresses in a shop on Fifth Avenue.

There was some factor he was overlooking, some factor in plain sight waiting to be seen.

First there was the girl who had come to breakfast and after that the paper he had read. Then he'd gone down to get his car and Eb had told him about the Forever car and because his car had not been ready he'd gone to the drugstore corner to catch a bus and Mr. Flanders had come and joined him as he stared at the display in the gadget shop and Mr. Flanders had said—

Wait a second. He had gone to the drugstore corner to get a bus.

There was something about a bus, something that tugged at his mind.

He had gotten on the bus and sat down in a seat next to the window. He'd sat down in a seat and looked out the window and no one else had come and sat down with him. He'd ridden to the city in a seat all by himself.

That is it, he thought, and even as he thought it he felt a wild elation and then a sense of horror at an incident forgotten and he stood for a moment unmoving, trying desperately to blot out the incident from so many years ago. He stood and waited and it would not blot out and there was no getting away from it and he knew what he must do.

He turned to the desk and pulled out the top drawer on the left hand side and slowly, methodically took out the contents, one by one. He did this with all the drawers and did not find what he was looking for.

Somewhere, he thought, I'll find it. It was a thing I would not throw away.

The attic, perhaps. One of the boxes in the attic.

He climbed the stairs and, reaching the top, blinked at the glow of the unshielded light bulb hanging from the ceiling. There was a chill in the air, and the starkness of the rafters, coming down on either side like a mighty jaw about to close on him, went with the alien chill.

Vickers moved from the stairs across the floor to the storage boxes pushed against the eaves. In which one of the three would it be most likely to be found? There was no telling.

So he started with the first and he found it half way down, under the old pair of bird shooters that he had hunted for last fall and had finally given up for lost.

He opened the notebook and thumbed through it until he came to the pages that he was seeking.

16

It must have been going on for years before he noticed it.

At first, having noticed it, he speculated on it somewhat idly. Then he began a detailed observation, and when the observation bore out the idle speculation he tried to laugh it off, but it wasn't a thing that you could laugh off. He went through the observation again, for a period of a month, keeping a written record of the facts he noted.

When the written record bore out the evidence of his earlier observation, he had tried to tell himself it was imagination, but by now he had it down in black and white and he knew there must be something to it.

The record said that it was worse than he had first imagined, that it concerned not only one phase of his existence, but many different phases. As the evidence accumulated, he stood aghast that he had not noticed it before, because it was something which should have been obvious from the very first.

The whole thing started with the reluctance of his fellow passengers to ride with him on the bus. He lived, at the time, at an old ramshackle boarding house at the edge of town near the end of the line. He'd get on in the morning and, being one of the few who boarded at that point, would take his favorite seat.

The bus would fill up gradually as the stops were made, but it would be almost the end of the run before he'd have a seat companion. It didn't bother him, of course; in fact, he rather liked it to be that way, for then he could pull his hat down over his eyes and slump down in the seat and think and probably even doze a little without ever considering the need of civility. Not that he would have been especially civil in any case, he now admitted. The hour that he went to work was altogether too early for that.

People would get on the bus and they'd sit with other people, not necessarily people whom they knew, for sometimes, Vickers noticed, they didn't exchange a single word for the entire ride with their seat mate. They'd sit with other people, but they'd never sit with him until the very last, not until all the other seats were filled and they had to sit with him or stand.

Perhaps, he told himself, it was body odor; perhaps it was bad breath. He made a ritual of bathing after that, using a new soap that was guaranteed to make him smell fresh. He brushed his teeth more attentively, used mouth wash until he gagged at the sight of it.

It did no good. He still rode alone.

He looked at himself in the mirror and he knew it was not his clothes, for in those days he was a smart dresser.

So, he figured, it must be his attitude. Instead of slumping down in the seat and pulling his hat over his eyes, he'd sit up and be bright and cheerful and he'd smile at everyone. He'd smile, by God, if it cracked his face to do it.

For an entire week he sat there looking pleasant, smiling at people when they glanced at him, for all the world as if he were a rising young business man who had read Dale Carnegie and belonged to the Junior Chamber.

No one rode with him—not until there was no other seat. He got some comfort in knowing they'd rather sit with him than stand.

Then he noticed other things.

At the office the fellows were always visiting around, gathering in little groups of three or four at one of the desks, talking about their golf score or telling the latest dirty story or wondering why the hell a guy stayed on at a place like this when there were other jobs you could just walk out and take.

No one, he noticed, ever came to his desk. So he tried going to some of the other desks, joining one of the groups. Within a short time, the fellows would all drift back to their desks. He tried just dropping by to pass the time of the day with individual workers. They were always affable enough, but always terribly busy. Vickers never stayed.

He checked up on his conversational budget. It seemed fairly satisfactory. He didn't play golf, but he knew a few dirty stories and he read most of the latest books and saw the best of the recent movies. He knew something about office politics and could damn the boss with the best of them. He read the newspapers and went through a couple of news weeklies and knew what was going on and could argue politics and had armchair opinions on military matters. With those qualifications, he felt, he should be able to carry on a fair conversation. But still no one seemed to want to talk to him.

It was the same at lunch. It was the same, now that he had come to notice it, everywhere he went.

He had written it down, with dates and an account of each day, and now, fifteen years later, he sat on a box in a raw and empty attic and read the words he'd written. Staring straight ahead of him, he remembered how it had been, how he'd felt and what he'd said and done, including the original fact that no one would ride with him, until all the seats were taken. And that, he remembered, was the way it had been when he'd gone to New York just the other day.

Fifteen years ago he had sat and wondered why and there had been no answer.

And here it was again.

Was he somehow, in some strange way, *different?* Or was it merely some lack in him, some quirk in his personality that denied him the vital spark, the ready glow of comradeship?

It had not only been the matter of no one riding with him, no groups gathering at his desk. There had been more than that—

certain more elusive things that could not be put on paper. The feeling of loneliness which he had always had—not the occasional twinges that everyone must feel, but a continual sense of "different-ness" that had forced him to stand apart from his fellow humans, and they from him. His inability to initiate friendships, his outsize sense of dignity, his reluctance to conform to certain social stan-dards.

It had been these characteristics, he was certain—although until now he had never thought of it in exactly that way—that had led him to take up residence in this isolated village, that had confined him to a small circle of acquaintances, that had turned him to the solitary trade of writing, pouring out on paper the pent-up emo-tions and the lonely thoughts that must find some release.

Out of his differentness he had built his life; perhaps out of that very differentness had sprung what small measure of success he had achieved.

He had settled into a rut of his own devising, a polished and well-loved rut, and then something had come along to jolt him out of it. It had started with the little girl coming to the door, and after that Eb talking about the Forever car—and there had been Crawford, and Flanders' strange words on the porch and, finally, the notebook remembered after many years and found in an attic box.

Forever cars and synthetic carbohydrates, Crawford talking about a world with its back against the wall—some how he knew that all these things were connected, and that he was tied up in some way with all of it.

It was maddening, to be convinced of this without a scrap of evidence, without a shred of reason, without a single clue as to what his part might be.

It had always been like that, he realized, even in little things—the frightening feeling that he had but to stretch out his hand to touch a certain truth, but never being able to reach quite far enough to grasp it.

It was absurd to know that a thing was right without knowing why: to know that it had been right to refuse Crawford's offer, when every factor urged its acceptance; to have known from the very start that Horton Flanders could not be found, when there was no reason to suspect he might not be.

Fifteen years ago he had faced a certain problem and after a time, in his own way, had solved it, without realizing he had solved it, by retreat from the human race. He had retreated until his back was against the wall and there, for a while, he had found peace. Now, in some strange way, his sense of "hunch," this undefined feeling that was almost prescience, seemed to be telling him that the world and the affairs of men had sought him out again. But now he could retreat no further, even if he wanted to. Curiously, he did not seem to want to, and that was just as well, for there was no place to go. He had shrunk back from humanity and he could shrink no farther.

He sat alone in the attic, listening to the wind that whispered in the eaves.

17

Someone was hammering on the door downstairs and shouting his name, but it was a moment or two before he realized what was happening.

He rose from the box and the notebook fell from his fingers and fell rumpled on the floor, face downward, with its open pages caught and crumpled.

"Who is it?" he asked. "What's the matter down there?"

But his voice was no more than a croaking whisper.

"Jay," the voice shouted. "Jay, are you here?"

He stumbled down the stairs and into the living room. Eb stood just inside the door.

"What's the matter, Eb?"

"Listen, Jay," Eb told him, "you got to get out of here."

"What for?"

"They think you did away with Flanders."

Vickers reached out a hand and caught the back of a chair and hung on to it.

"I won't even ask you if you did," said Eb. "I'm pretty sure you didn't. That's why I'm giving you a chance."

"A chance?" asked Vickers. "What are you talking about?"

"They're down at the tavern now," said Eb, "talking themselves into a lynching party."

"They?"

"All your friends," Eb said, bitterly. "Someone got them all stirred up. I don't know who it was. I didn't wait to find out who. I came straight up here."

"But I liked Flanders. I was the only one who liked him. I was the only friend he had."

"You haven't any time," Eb told him. "You've got to get away."

"I can't go anywhere. I haven't got my car."

"I brought up one of the Forever cars," said Eb. "No one knows I brought it. No one will know you have it."

"I can't run away. They've got to listen to me. They've got to."

"You damn fool. This isn't the sheriff with a warrant. This is a mob and they won't listen to you."

Eb strode across the room and grabbed Vickers roughly by the arm. "Get going, damn you," he said. "I risked my neck to come up here and warn you. After I've done that, you can't throw the chance away."

Vickers shook his arm free.

"All right," he said, "I'll go."

"Money?" asked Eb.

"I have some."

"Here's some more." Eb reached into his pocket and held out a thin sheaf of bills.

Vickers took it and stuck it in his pocket.

"The car is full of gas," said Eb. "The shift is automatic. It drives like any other car. I left the motor running."

"I hate to do this, Eb."

"I know just how you hate to," said Eb, "but if you want to save this town a killing there's nothing else to do."

He gave Vickers a shove.

"Come on," he said. "Get going."

Vickers trotted down the path and heard Eb pounding along

behind him. The car stood at the gate. Eb had left the door wide open.

"In you go. Cut straight over to the main highway."

"Thanks, Eb."

"Get out of here," said Eb.

Vickers pulled the shift to the drive position and stepped on the gas. The car floated away and swiftly gathered speed. He reached the main highway and swung in toward the west.

He drove for miles, fleeing down the cone of brightness thrown by the headlights. He drove with a benumbed bewilderment that he should be doing this—that he, Jay Vickers, should be fleeing from a lynching party made up of his neighbors.

Someone, Eb had said, had got them all stirred up. And who would it have been who would have stirred them up?

Someone, perhaps, who hated him.

Even as he thought that, he knew who it was. He felt again the threat and the fear that he had felt when he had sat face to face with Crawford—the then-unrealized threat and fear that had made him refuse the offer to write Crawford's book.

There's something going on, Horton Flanders had said, standing with him in front of the gadget shop.

And there was something going on.

There were everlasting gadgets being made by non-existent firms. There was an organization of world businessmen, backed into a corner by a foe at whom they could not strike back. There was Horton Flanders talking of some new, strange factors which kept the world from war. There were Pretentionists, hiding from the actuality of today, playing dollhouse with the past.

And, finally, here was Jay Vickers fleeing to the west.

By midnight, he knew what he was doing and where he was going.

He was going where Horton Flanders had said that he should go, doing what he had said he would never do.

He was going back to his own childhood.

18

They were exactly the way he had expected them to be.

They sat out in front of the general store, on the bench and the upturned boxes, and turned sly eyes up toward him and they said: "Too bad about your Pa, Jay. He was a damn good man."

They said: "So you write books, do you. Have to read one of your books someday. Never heard of them."

They said: "You going out to the old place?"

"This afternoon," said Vickers.

"It's changed," they warned. "It's changed a whole lot. There ain't no one living there."

"Farming's gone to hell," they told him. "Can't make no money at it. This carbohydrates business. Lots of folks can't keep their places. Banks take them away from them, or they have to sell out cheap. Lots of farms around here being bought up for grazing purposes—just fix the fences and turn some cattle in. Don't even try to farm. Buy feeder stuff out in the west and turn it loose the summer, then fatten it for fall."

"That's what happened to the old place?"

They nodded solemnly at him. "That's what happened, son. Feller that bought it after your Pa, he couldn't make the riffle. Your

Pa's place ain't the only one. There's been lots of others, too. You remember the old Preston place, don't you?"

Vickers nodded.

"Well, it happened to it, too. And that was a good place. One of the best there was."

"No one living there?"

"No one. Somebody boarded up the doors and windows. Now, why do you figure anyone would go to all the work of boarding up the place?"

"I wouldn't know," said Vickers.

The storekeeper came out and sat down on the steps.

"Where you hanging out now, Jay?" he asked.

"In the East," said Vickers.

"Doing right well, I expect."

"I'm eating every day."

"Well," the storekeeper said, "you ain't so bad off, then. Anyone that can eat regular is doing downright well."

"What kind of car is that you got?" another of them asked.

"It's a new kind of car," said Vickers. "Just got it the other day. Called the Forever car."

They said: "Now ain't that a hell of a name to call a car."

They said: "I imagine it cost you a pile of jack."

They said: "How many miles to a gallon do you get on it?"

He got into the car and drove away, out through the dusty, straggling village, with its tired old cars parked along the streets, with the Methodist church standing dowdy on the hill, with old people walking along the street with canes and dogs asleep in dust wallows under lilac bushes.

19

The gate to the farm was chained and the chain locked with a heavy padlock, so he parked the car beside the highway and walked the quarter mile down to the buildings.

The farm road was overgrown with grass in places and knee-high with weeds in others and only here and there could you find the sign of wheel-ruts. The fields lay unplowed, with brush springing up along the fences and weed patches flourishing in the poorer spots, where years of cultivation had sapped the ground of strength.

From the highway, the buildings had looked about the same as he remembered them, cozily grouped together and strong with the feel of home, but as he drew nearer the signs of neglect became apparent, striking him like a hand across the face. The yard around the house was thick with grass and weeds and the flower beds were all gone and the rosebush at the corner of the porch was dying, a scraggly thing with only one or two roses where in other years it had been heavy with its bloom. The plum thicket in the corner of the fence had run riot, and the fence itself was rickety and in places had disappeared entirely. Some windows in the house were broken, probably by kids heaving idle stones, and the door to the back porch had become unlocked and was swinging in the wind.

He waded through the sea of grass, walking around the house, astonished at how tenaciously the marks of living still clung about the place. There, on the chimney, running up the outside wall, were the prints of his ten-year-old hands, impressed into wet mortar, and the splintered piece of siding still remained above the basement window, broken by poorly aimed chunks of wood chucked through the open window into the basement to feed the old, wood-eating furnace. At the corner of the house he found the old washtub where his mother each spring had planted the nasturtiums, but the tub itself was almost gone, its metal turned to rust, and all that remained was a mound of earth. The mountain ash still stood in the front yard and he walked into its shade and looked up into its canopy of leaves and put out his hand and stroked the smoothness of its trunk, remembering how he had planted it as a boy, proud that they should have a tree like no one else in the neighborhood.

He did not try the door, for the outside of the house was all he wished to see. There would be too much to see inside the house— the nail holes on the wall where the pictures had been hung and the marks upon the floor where the stove had stood and the stairway with the treads worn smooth by beloved footsteps. If he went in, the house would cry out to him from the silences of its closets and the emptiness of its rooms.

He walked down to the other buildings and they, he found, for all their silence and their emptiness, were not so memory-haunted as the house. The henhouse was falling in upon itself and the hoghouse was a place for the winter winds to whistle through and he found an old, worn-out binder stored in the back of the cavernous machine shed.

The barn was cool and shadowed, and of all the buildings it seemed the most like home. The stalls were empty, but the hay still hung in cobwebby wisps from the cracks in the floor of the mow and the place still smelled the way he had remembered it, the half-musty, half-acid smell of living, friendly beasts.

He climbed the incline to the granary and sliding back the wooden latch, went in. Mice ran squeaking across the floor and up the walls and beams. A pile of grain sacks were draped across the partition that held the grain back from the alley way and a broken harness hung from a peg upon the wall and there, at the end of the alley, lay something that stopped him in his tracks.

It was a child's top, battered now and with all its color gone, but once it had been bright and colorful and when you pumped it on the floor it had spun and whistled. He had gotten it for Christmas, he remembered, and it had been a favorite toy.

He picked it up and held its battered metal with a sudden tenderness and wondered how it had gotten there. It was a part of his past catching up with him—a dead and useless thing to everyone in all the world except the boy to whom it had once belonged.

It had been a striped top and the colors had run in spiraling streaks when you spun it and there had been a point, he remembered, where each streak ran and disappeared, and another streak came up and it disappeared, and then another.

You could sit for hours watching the streaks come up and disappear, trying to make out where they went. For they must go somewhere, a boyish mind would figure. They couldn't be there one second and be gone the next. There must be somewhere for them to go.

And there had been somewhere for them to go!

He remembered now.

It all came back to him, with the top clutched in his hands and the years peeling off and falling away to take him back to one day in his childhood.

You could go with the streaks, go where they went, into the land they fled to, if you were very young and could wonder hard enough.

It was a sort of fairyland, although it seemed more real than a fairyland should be. There was a walk that looked as if it were made of glass and there were birds and flowers and trees and some butterflies and he picked one of the flowers and carried it in his hand as he walked along the path. He had seen a little house hidden in a grove and when he saw it, he became a little frightened and walked back along the path and suddenly he was home, with the top dead on the floor in front of him and the flower clutched in his hand.

He had gone and told his mother and she had snatched away the flower, as if she might be afraid of it. And well she might have been, for it was winter.

That evening Pa had questioned him and found out about the top and the next day, he remembered, when he'd looked for the top he couldn't find it anywhere. He had cried off and on for days, secretly of course.

And here it was again, an old and battered top, with no hint of the original color, but the same one, he was sure.

He left the granary, carrying the battered top along with him, away from the unloved insecurity in which it had rested for so long.

Forgetfulness, he told himself, but it was more than that—a mental block of some sort that had made him forget about the top and the trip to fairyland. Through all the years he had not remembered it, had not even suspected that there was an incident such as this hidden in his mind. But now the top was with him once again and the day was with him, too—the day he'd followed the swirling streaks and walked into fairyland.

20

He told himself he would not stop at the Preston house. He would drive by, not too fast, of course, and would have a look at it, but he would not stop. For he was fleeing now, as he had known that he would flee. He had looked upon the empty shell of childhood and had found an artifact of childhood and he would not look once again upon the bare bones of his youth.

He wouldn't stop at the Preston house. He'd just slow up and look, then speed up the car and put the miles behind him.

He wouldn't stop, he said.

But, of course, he did.

He sat in the car and looked at the house and remembered how it once had been a proud house and had sheltered a family that had been proud as well—too proud to let a member of its family marry a country lad from a farm of sickly corn and yellow clay.

But the house was proud no longer. The shutters were closed and someone had nailed long planks across them, taping shut the eyes of the once-proud house, and the paint was scaling and peeling from the stately columns that ran across its front and someone had thrown a rock to break one of the fanlights above the carved front door. The fence sagged and the yard had grown to weeds and the brick walk that ran from gate to porch had disappeared beneath the running grass.

He got out of the car and walked through the drooping front gate up to the porch. Climbing the stairs, he walked along the porch and saw how the floor boards had rotted.

He stood where they had stood, the two of them, and first had known their love would last forever and he tried to catch that moment of the past and it was not there. There had been too much time, too much sun and wind, and it was there no longer, although the ache of it was there. He tried to remember how the meadows and the fields and yard had looked from the porch, with the white moonlight shattering on the whiteness of the columns, and how the roses had filled the air with the distilled sunshine of their scent. He knew these things, but he could not feel or see them.

On the slope behind the house were the barns, still painted white, although not so white as they once had been. Beyond the barns the ground sloped down and there stretched out before him the valley they had walked that last time he had seen her.

It had been an enchanted valley, he remembered, with apple blossoms and the song of lark.

It had been enchanted once. It had not been the second time. But what about the third?

He told himself that he was crazy, that he was chasing rainbow ends, but even as he told himself, he was walking down the slope, down past the barns and on into the valley.

At the head of it he stopped and looked at it and it was not enchanted, but he remembered it, as he had remembered the moonlight on the columns—the columns had still been there, and the valley still was there and the trees were where he had known they'd be and the creek still trickled down the meadows that flanked it on each side.

He tried to go back, and could not, but went on walking down the valley. He saw the crab apple thickets, with the blossoms fallen now, and once a lark soared out of the grass and flew into the sky.

Finally he turned back: it was the same as it had been that second time. The third visit, after all, had been the same as the second. It had been she who had turned this prosaic valley into an enchanted place. It had been, after all, an enchantment of the spirit.

Twice he had walked in enchanted places, twice in his life he had stepped out of old familiar earth.

Twice. Once by the virtue of a girl and the love between them. Once again because of a spinning top.

No, the top had been the first.

Yes, the top—

Now, wait a minute! Now, not so fast!

You're wrong, Vickers. It wouldn't be that way.

You crazy fool, what are you running for?

21

The manager of the dime store, when Vickers sought him out, seemed to understand.

"You know," he said, "I understand just how you feel. I had a top like that myself when I was a kid, but they don't make them any more. I don't know why—they just don't, I guess. Got too many other high powered, new fangled kinds of toys. But there's nothing like a top."

"Especially those big ones," said Vickers. "The ones with the handle on them and you pumped them on the floor and they whistled."

"I remember them," the manager said. "Had one myself when I was a kid. Sat and played with it for hours, just watching it."

"Watching where the stripes went?"

"I don't recall I worried much about where the stripes might go. I just sat and watched it spin and listened to it whistle."

"I used to worry about where they went. You know how it is. They travel round and then they disappear, somewhere near the top."

"Tell me," asked the manager. "Where do they go?"

"I don't know," Vickers admitted.

"There's another dime store down the street a block or two," the manager said. "Carries a lot of junky stuff, but they might have a top like that left over."

"Thanks," said Vickers.

"You might ask at the hardware store across the street, too. They carry quite a stock of toys, but I suppose they got them put away down in the basement. They only get them out at Christmas time."

The man at the hardware store said he knew what Vickers wanted, but he hadn't seen one for years. The other dime store didn't have one, either. No, said the girl, chewing gum and nervously thrusting a pencil back and forth into the wad of hair above her ear, no, she didn't know where he might get one. She'd never heard of one. There were a lot of other things here if he wanted to get something for a little boy. Like those toy rockets or these—

He went out on the sidewalk, watching the late afternoon crowd of shoppers in the little Midwestern town. There were women in print dresses and other women in sleek business suits and there were high school kids just out of class and businessmen out for a cup of coffee before they settled down to clean up the odds and ends of the day before they left for home. Up the street he saw a crowd of loafers gathered around his own car, parked in front of the first dime store. It was time, he thought, to feed that parking meter.

He reached into his pocket, looking for another dime, and he had one—a dime, a quarter and a nickel. The sight of the coins in his hand made him wonder about the money in his billfold, so he took it out and flipped it open and saw that all that he had left were two dollar bills.

Since he couldn't go back to Cliffwood, not right away at least, he had no place to call his home. He'd need money for lodging for the night and for meals and for gasoline to put into the car—but more than that, more than anything, he was in need of a singing top that had colored stripes painted on its belly.

He stood in the middle of the sidewalk, thinking about the top, arguing with himself, with all of his logical being telling him that he must be wrong about it. It is *not* wrong, said the illogic within him. It *will* work. It had worked once before, when he was a child, before Pa had taken the top away from him.

What would have happened to him if the top had not been taken and hidden away from him? He wondered if he would have gone again and again, once he had found the way, back into that fairyland and what might have happened there, who and what he might have met and what he would have found in the house hidden in the grove. For he would have gone to the house, he knew, after a time. Having watched it long enough and grown accustomed to it, he would have followed the path across the grove and gone up to the door and knocked.

He wondered if anyone else had ever watched a spinning top and walked into fairyland. And he wondered, if they had, what had happened to them.

The dime store manager had not done it, he was sure, for the dime store manager had said that he had never wondered where the stripes might go. He had just sat and watched and listened to the whistle.

He wondered why he, of all men, should find the way. And he wondered if the enchanted valley might not have been a part of fairyland as well and if somehow the girl and he might not have walked through another unseen gate. For surely the valley that he remembered was not the valley he had walked that morning.

There was only one way to find out, and that was to get a top.

But, of course, he had a top! Even while he frantically sought for one, he already had one. The handle would have to be straightened and it might need a bit of oil to clear away the rust and it would have to be painted.

More than likely it would be better than any other he could get, for it would be the original top that had sent him through before—and it pleased him to think that it might have certain special qualities, a certain mystic function no other top might have.

He was glad that he had thought of it, lying there, forgotten for the second time, in the glove compartment where he had tossed it after finding it again.

He walked up the street to the hardware store.

"I want some paint," said Vickers. "The brightest, glossiest paint you have. Red and green and yellow. And some little brushes to put it on with."

He figured, from the way the man looked at him, that, he thought he was insane.

22

He called Ann from his hotel room, collect, since, after eating dinner, he had only ninety cents.

She sounded harried. "Jay, where are you? Where in the name of heaven did you go?"

He told her where he was.

"But why are you *there?*" she asked him. "What is the matter with you?"

"There's nothing wrong with me," said Vickers. "That is, nothing yet. I am just a fugitive. I got run out of Cliffwood."

"You *what?*"

"They were fixing up a necktie party. Somehow or other they got it into their heads that I had killed a man."

"Now I know you're crazy. You wouldn't kill a fly."

"Of course I wouldn't. But I couldn't explain that to them. I didn't have a chance."

"Why," said Ann, "I talked to Eb . . ."

"You talked to who?"

"You know, the man in the garage. I'd heard you talk about him. I was hunting high and low for you. For two whole days I beat the bushes for you. I called your home and there was no one there, so I remembered you talking about Eb, the garageman, and I asked the operator to let me talk to him, and—"

"What did Eb say?"

"He didn't say a thing," said Ann. "He said he hadn't noticed you around, but he didn't know where you were. He told me not to worry."

"Eb was the one who tipped me off," said Vickers. "He told me they were getting set to lynch me and he gave me a car and some money and saw me out of town."

"Of all the silly things. Who was it they thought you killed?"

"Horton Flanders. He's the old man that got lost."

"But you wouldn't kill him. You said he was a nice old man. You told me so yourself."

"Look, Ann," said Vickers, "I didn't kill anyone. Someone just got the boys stirred up."

"But you can't go back to Cliffwood."

"No," said Vickers. "I can't go back to Cliffwood."

"What are you going to do, Jay?"

"I don't know. Just stay hid out, I guess."

"Why didn't you call me right away?" demanded Ann. "What are you way out West for? You should have come straight to New York. New York is the swellest place there is for someone to hide out. You might at least have called me."

"Now, wait a minute," Vickers said. "I called you, didn't I?"

"Sure. You called me because you're broke and want me to wire some money and you—"

"I haven't asked for any money yet."

"You will."

"Yes," he said, "I'm afraid I will."

"Aren't you interested in why I was trying to get hold of you?"

"Mildly," said Vickers. "Because you don't want me to get out from under your thumb. No agent wants their best author to get from under—"

"Jay Vickers," said Ann, "some day I'm going to crucify you and hang you up along the roadside as a warning."

"I would make a most pathetic Christ. You couldn't choose a better man."

"I'm calling you," said Ann, "because Crawford's practically frantic. The sky's the limit. I mentioned a fantastic figure and he didn't even shiver."

"I thought we disposed of Mr. Crawford," Vickers said.

"You don't dispose of Crawford," said Ann. Then she paused and silence hummed along the wires.

"Ann," said Vickers. "Ann, what's the trouble?"

Her voice was calm, but strained. "Crawford is a badly frightened man. I've never seen a man so thoroughly frightened. He came to me. Imagine that! I didn't go to him. He came into my office, puffing and panting and I was afraid I didn't have a chair in the place strong enough to hold him. But you remember that old oak one over in the corner, that old hunk over in the corner? It was one of the first sticks of furniture I ever bought for my office and I kept it as a sentimental piece. Well, it did the trick."

"What trick?"

"It held him," said Ann, triumphantly. "He'd have simply crushed anything else in the place. You remember what a big man he is."

"Gross," said Vickers. "That's the word you want."

"He said, 'Where's Vickers?' And I said, 'Why ask me, I don't keep a leash on Vickers.' And he says, 'You're his agent, aren't you?' And I said, 'Yes, the last time I heard, but Vickers is a very changeable sort of man, there's no telling about him.' He says, 'I've got to have Vickers.' And so I told him, 'Well, go get him, you'll find him around somewhere.' He said, 'The sky's the limit, name any price you want to, make any terms you want.'"

"The man's a crackpot," Vickers said.

"There's nothing crackpot about the kind of money he's offering."

"How do you know he's got the money?"

"Well, I don't know. Not for sure, that is. But he must have."

"Speaking of money," Vickers said. "Have you got a loose hundred lying around? Or fifty, even?"

"I can get it."

"Wire it here, right away. I'll pay you back."

"All right, I'll do it right away," she said. "It isn't the first time I've bailed you out and I don't imagine it will be the last. But will you tell me one thing?"

"What's that?"

"What are you going to do?"

"I'm going to conduct an experiment," said Vickers.

"An experiment?"

"An exercise in the occult."

"What are you talking about? You don't know anything about the occult. You're about as mystic as a block of wood."

"I know," said Vickers.

"Please tell me," she said. "What are you going to do?"

"As soon as I get through talking to you," said Vickers, "I'm going to do some painting."

"A house?"

"No, a top."

"The top of what?"

"Not the top of anything. A top. A toy kids play with. You spin it on the floor."

"Now listen to me," she said. "You cut out this playing around and come home to Ann."

"After the experiment," said Vickers.

"Tell me about it, Jay."

"I'm going to try to get into fairyland."

"Quit talking foolish."

"I did it once before. Twice before."

"Listen, Jay, this business is serious. Crawford is scared and so am I. And there's this lynching business, too."

"Send me the money," Vickers said.

"Right away."

"I'll see you in a day or two."

"Call me," she said. "Call me tomorrow."

"I'll call you."

"And, Jay . . . take care of yourself. I don't know what you're up to, but take care of yourself."

"I'll do that, too," said Vickers.

23

He straightened the handle which spun the top and he polished the metal before marking off the spirals with a pencil and he borrowed a can of sewing machine oil and oiled up the spinning spiral on the handle so that it worked smoothly. Then he went about the painting.

He wasn't much good at it, but he went about it doggedly. He carefully painted in the colors, red, then green, then yellow, and he hoped the colors were right, for he couldn't remember exactly what the colors had been. Although, probably it didn't make much difference what the colors were, just so they were bright and ran in a spiral.

He got paint on his hands and on his clothes and on the chair he laid the top on and he spilled the can of red paint on the floor, but he picked it up real quick so that scarcely any of it ran out onto the carpeting.

Finally the job was finished and it looked fairly good.

He worried about whether it would be dry by morning, but he read the labels on the cans and labels said the paint was quick drying, so he was somewhat relieved.

He was ready now, ready to see what he would find when he spun the top. It might be fairyland, and it might be nothing. Most likely it would be nothing. For more would go into it than the spinning of the top—the mind and the confidence and the pure simplicity of a child. And he didn't have that any longer.

He went out and closed and locked the door behind him, then went down the stairs. The town and the hotel were too small to have elevators. Although not so small a town as the little village that had been "town" to him in his childhood days, that little village where they still sat out on the bench in front of the store and looked up at you with sidewise glances and asked you impudent, prying questions out of which to weave the fabric of long gossiping.

He chuckled, thinking of what they'd say when the word got back to the little town, slowly, as news always gets back to a little town, of how he had fled from Cliffwood on the threat of being lynched.

He could hear them talking now.

"A sly one," they would say. "He always was a sly one and not up to any good. His Ma and Pa were real good people, though. Beats hell how a son sometimes turns out even when his Ma and Pa were honest people."

He went through the lobby and out the door and into the street.

He stopped at a diner and ordered a cup of coffee and the waitress said to him, "Nice night, isn't it."

"Yes, it is," he said.

"You want anything to go with that coffee, mister?"

"No," said Vickers. "Just the coffee." He had money now—Ann had sent it quickly enough—but he found, not surprisingly, that he had no appetite, no desire at all for food.

She moved on up the counter and wiped off imaginary spots with a cloth she carried in her hand.

A top, he thought. Where did it tie in? He'd take the top to the house and spin it and would know once and for all if there was a fairyland—well, no, not exactly that. He'd know if he could get back into fairyland.

And the house. Where did the house tie in?

Or did either the house or the top tie in?

And if they didn't tie in, why had Horton Flanders written: "Go back and travel the paths you walked in childhood. Maybe there you will find a thing you'll need—or something that is missing." He wished he could remember the exact words Flanders had used, but he could not.

So he had come back and he had found a top and, more than that, he had remembered fairyland. And why, he asked himself, in all the years since he had been eight years old, had he never before recalled that walk in fairyland?

It had made a deep impression on him at the time, of that there was no doubt, for once he had remembered it had been as clear and sharp as if it had just happened.

But something had made him forget it, some mental block, perhaps. Something had made him forget it. And something had made him know that the metal mouse had wanted to be trapped. And something had made him instinctively refuse Crawford's proposition. *Something.*

The waitress came back down the counter and leaned on her elbow.

"They're starting a new picture at the Grand tonight," said the girl. "I'd love to see it, but I can't get off."

Vickers didn't answer.

"You like pictures, mister?" asked the girl.

"I don't know," said Vickers. "I seldom go to them."

Her face said she sympathized with anyone who didn't. "I just live for them," she said. "They're so natural."

He looked up at her and saw that she wore the face of Everyone. It was the face of the two women who talked in the seat behind him on the bus; it was the face of Mrs. Leslie, saying to him, "Some of us are going to organize a Pretentionist Club . . ." It was the face of those who did not dare sit down and talk with themselves, the people who could not be alone a minute, the people who were tired without knowing they were tired and afraid without knowing that they were afraid.

And, yes, it was the face of Mrs. Leslie's husband, crowding drink and women into a barren life. It was the grinding anxiety that had become commonplace, that sent people fleeing for psychological shelters against the bombs of uncertainty.

Gayety no longer was sufficient, cynicism had run out, and flippancy had never been more than a temporary shield. So now the people fled to the drug of pretense, identifying themselves with another life and another time and place—at the movie theater or on the television screen or in the Pretentionist movement. For so long as you were someone else you need not be yourself.

He finished his coffee and went out into the quiet street.

Overhead a jet flashed past, streaking low, the mutter of its tubes bouncing back against the walls. He watched its lights draw twin lines of fire over the night horizon, and then went for a walk.

24

When Vickers opened the door of the room, he saw that the top was gone. He had left it on the chair, gaudy in its new paint, and it wasn't on the chair or on the floor. He got down on his belly and looked underneath the bed and it wasn't there. It wasn't in the closet and it wasn't in the hall outside.

He came back into the room again and sat down on the edge of the bed.

After all the worry and the planning the top had disappeared. Who would have stolen it? What would anyone want with a battered top?

What had he himself wanted with it?

It seemed faintly ridiculous now, sitting on the edge of the bed in a strange hotel room, to ask himself these questions.

He had thought the top would buy his way into fairyland and now, in the white glare of the ceiling light, he wondered at himself for the madness of his antics.

Behind him, the door came open and he heard it and wheeled around.

In the door stood Crawford.

The man was even more massive than Vickers had remembered

him. He filled the doorway and he stood motionless, without a single flicker, except for slowly winking eyelids.

Crawford said: "Good evening, Mr. Vickers. Won't you ask me to come in?"

"Certainly," said Vickers. "I was waiting for, a call from you. I never thought that you would take the trouble to travel here in person."

And that was a lie, of course, because he'd not been waiting for a call.

Crawford moved ponderously across the room. "This chair looks strong enough to hold me. You don't mind, I hope."

"It's not my chair," said Vickers. "Go ahead and bust it."

It didn't break. It creaked and groaned, but it held.

Crawford relaxed and sighed. "I always feel so much better when I get a good strong chair beneath me."

"You tapped Ann's phone," said Vickers.

"Why, certainly. How else would I have found you? I knew that, sooner or later, you would call her."

"I saw the plane come in." said Vickers. "If I had thought that it was you, I'd driven out to meet you. I have a bone to pick With you."

"I don't doubt it," Crawford said.

"Why did you almost get me lynched?"

"I wouldn't have you lynched for all the world," said Crawford. "I'm too much in need of you."

"What do you need me for?"

"I don't know," said Crawford. "I thought maybe you would know."

"I don't know a thing," said Vickers. "Tell me, Crawford, what is this all about? You didn't tell the truth that day I came in to see you."

"I told you the truth, or at least part of it. I didn't tell you everything we knew."

"Why not?"

"I didn't know who you were."

"But you know now?"

"Yes, I know now," said Crawford. "You are one of them."

"One of whom?"

"One of the gadgeteers."

"What in hell makes you think so?"

"Analyzers. That's what the psych boys call them. Analyzers. The damn things are uncanny. I don't pretend to understand them."

"And the analyzers said there was something strange about me?"

"Yes," said Crawford. "That's about the way it is."

"If I am one of them, why come to me?" asked Vickers. "If I am one of them, you are fighting me. Remember? A world with its back against the wall. Surely, you remember."

"Don't say 'if,'" said Crawford. "You *are* one of them all right, but quit acting as if I were an enemy."

"Aren't you?" asked Vickers. "If I am what you say I am, you are an enemy."

"You don't understand," said Crawford. "Let's try analogy. Let's go back to the day when the Cro-Magnon drifted into Neanderthaler territory . . ."

"Don't give me analogy," Vickers told him. "Tell me what's on your mind."

"I don't like the situation," Crawford said. "I don't like the way things are shaping up."

"You forget that I don't know what the situation is."

"That's what I was trying to tell you with my analogy. You are the Cro-Magnon. You have the bow and arrow and the spear. I am the Neanderthaler. I only have a club. You have the knife of polished stone; I have a piece of jagged flint picked out of a stream bed. You have clothing fashioned out of hides and furs and I have nothing but the hair I stand in."

"I wouldn't know," said Vickers.

"I'm not so sure myself," said Crawford. "I'm not up on that sort of stuff. Maybe I gave the Cro-Magnon a bit too much and the Neantherthaler less than what he had. But that's not the point at all."

"I appreciate the point," said Vickers. "Where do we go from there?"

"The Neanderthaler fought back," said Crawford, "and what happened to him?"

"He became extinct."

"They may have died for many reasons other than the spear and arrow. Perhaps they couldn't compete for food against a better race. Perhaps they were squeezed out of their hunting grounds. Perhaps they crawled off and starved. Perhaps they died of an overpowering shame—the knowledge that they were outdated, that they were no good, that they were, by comparison, little more than beasts."

"I doubt," said Vickers drily, "that a Neanderthaler could work up a very powerful inferiority complex."

"The suggestion may not apply to the Neanderthaler. It does apply to us."

"You're trying to make me see how deep the cleavage goes."

"That is what I'm doing," Crawford told him. "You can't realize the depth of hate, the margin of intelligence and ability. Nor can you realize how desperate we really are.

"Who are these desperate men? I'll tell you who they are. They're the successful ones, the industrialists, the bankers, the business-men, the professional men who have security and hold positions of importance, who move in social circles which mark the high tide of our culture.

"They'd no longer hold their positions if your kind of men took over. They'd be Neanderthaler to your Cro-Magnon. They'd be like Homeric Greeks pitchforked into the complex technology of this century of ours. They'd survive, of course, physically. But they'd be aborigines. Their values would be swept away and those values, built up painfully, are all they have to live by."

Vickers shook his head. "Let's not play games, Crawford. Let's try to be honest for a while. I imagine you think I know a whole lot more than I really do. I suppose I should pretend I know as much as you think I do—act smart and make you think I know all there is to know. Fence with you. Get you to tip your hand. But somehow I haven't got the heart to do it."

"I know you don't know too much. That's why I wanted to reach you as soon as possible. As I see it, you aren't entirely mutant yet, you haven't yet shed the chrysalis of an ordinary man. There's a lot of you that still is normal man. The tendency is to shift toward mutation—more today than yesterday, more tomorrow than today. But tonight, in this room, you and I still can talk man to man."

"We could always talk."

"No, we couldn't," said Crawford. "If you were entirely mutant, I'd feel the difference in us. Without equality there'd be no basis for discussion. I'd doubt the soundness of my logic. You'd look on me with a shade of contempt."

"Just before you came in," said Vickers, "I'd almost convinced myself it was all imagination . . ."

"It's not imagination, Vickers. You had a top, remember?"

"The top is gone."

"Not gone," said Crawford.

"You have it?"

"No," said Crawford. "No, I haven't got it. I don't know where it is, but it still is somewhere in this room. You see, I got here before you did and I picked the lock. Incidentally, a most inefficient lock."

"Incidentally," said Vickers, "a very sneaky trick."

"Granted. And before this is over, I'll commit other sneaky tricks. But to go back, I picked the lock and walked into the room and I saw the top and wondered and I—well, I—"

"Go on," said Vickers.

"Look, Vickers, I had a top like that when I was a kid. Long, long ago. I hadn't seen one in years, so I picked it up and spun it, see. For no reason. Well, yes, there may have been a reason. Maybe an attempt to regain a lost moment of my childhood. And the top . . ."

He stopped speaking and stared hard at Vickers, as if he might be trying to detect some sign of laughter. When he spoke again his voice was almost casual.

"The top disappeared."

Vickers said nothing.

"What was it?" Crawford asked. "What kind of top was that?"

"I don't know. Were you watching it when it disappeared?"

"No. I thought I heard someone in the hall. I looked away a moment. It was gone when I looked back."

"It shouldn't have disappeared," said Vickers. "Not without you watching it."

"There was some reason for the top," said Crawford. "You had painted it. The paint was still a little wet and the cans of paint are sitting on that table. You wouldn't go to all that trouble without some purpose. What was the top for, Vickers?"

Vickers told him. "It was for going into fairyland."

"You're talking riddles."

Vickers shook his head. "I went once—physically—when I was a kid."

"Ten days ago, I would have said the both of us were crazy, you for saying it and I for believing it. I can't say it now."

"We still may be crazy, or at best just a pair of fools."

"We're neither fools nor crazy," Crawford said. "We are men, the two of us, not quite the same and more different by the hour, but we still are men and that's enough of a common basis for our understanding."

"Why did you come here, Crawford? Don't tell me just to talk. You're too anxious. You had a tap on Ann's phone to find out where I'd gone. You broke into my room and you spun the top. And you had a reason. What was it?"

"I came here to warn you," Crawford said. "To warn you that the men I represent are desperate, that they will stop at nothing. They won't be taken over."

"And if they have no choice?"

"They have a choice. They fight with what they have."

"The Neanderthalers fought with clubs."

"So will Homo sapiens. Clubs against your arrows. That's why I want to talk to you. Why can't you and I sit down and try to find an answer? There must be some area for agreement."

"Ten days ago," said Vickers, "I sat in your office and talked with you. You described the situation and you said you were completely mystified, stumped. To hear you tell it then, you didn't have the ghost of an idea what was going on. Why did you lie to me?"

Crawford sat stolidly, unmoving, no change of expression on his face. "We had the machine on you, remember? The analyzers. We wanted to find out how much you knew."

"How much did I know?"

"Not a thing," said Crawford. "All we found out was that you were a latent mutant."

"Then why pick me out?" demanded Vickers. "Except for what you tell me of the strangeness that is in me, I have no reason to believe that I am a mutant. I know no mutants. I can't speak for mutants. If you want to make a deal, go catch yourself a real honest-to-God mutant."

"We picked you out," said Crawford, "for a simple reason. You are the only mutant we could lay a finger on. You and one other—and the other one is even less aware than you."

"But there must be others."

"Certainly there are. But we can't catch them."

"You sound like a trapper, Crawford."

"Perhaps that's what I am. These others—you can pin them down only when they want to see you. Otherwise they are always out."

"Out?"

"They disappear," explained Crawford harshly, "We track them down and wait. We send in word and wait. We ring doorbells and wait. We never find them in. They go in a door, but they aren't in the room. We wait for hours to see them and then find out they weren't in the place where we'd seen them go at all, but somewhere else, maybe miles away."

"But me—me you can track down. I don't disappear."

"Not yet, you don't."

"Maybe I'm a moronic mutant."

"An undeveloped one."

"You picked me out," said Vickers. "In the first place, I mean. You had some reason to suspect before I knew, myself."

Crawford chuckled. "Your writings. Some strange quality in them. Our psych department spotted it. We found some others that way. A couple of artists, an architect, a sculptor, one or two writers. Don't ask me how the psych boys do it. Smell it out, maybe. Don't look so startled, Vickers. When you organize world industry you have, in terms of cash and manpower, a crack outfit that can perform tremendous jobs of research—or anything else that you put it to. You'd be surprised how much work we've done, the areas we have covered. But it's not enough. I don't mind telling you that we've been licked at every turn."

"So now you want to bargain."

"I do. Not the others. They'll never want to bargain. They're fighting, don't you understand, for the world they've built through many bloody years."

And that was it, thought Vickers. *Through many bloody years.*

Horton Flanders had sat on the porch and rocked and the firefly of the lighted cigarette had gone back and forth and he had talked of war and why War III somehow hadn't happened and he had said that maybe someone or something had stepped in, time and again, to prevent it happening. Intervention, he had said, rocking back and forth.

"This world they built," Vickers pointed out, "hasn't been too good a world. It was built with too much blood and misery, it mixed too many bones into the mortar. During all its history there's hardly been a year when there wasn't violence—organized, official violence—somewhere on the earth."

"I know what you mean," said Crawford. "You think there should be a reorganization."

"Something like that."

"Let's do some figuring, then," Crawford invited. "Let's try to thrash it out."

"I can't. I have no knowledge and I have no authority. I haven't even contacted or been contacted by these mutants of yours—if they are really mutants."

"The machines say they are mutants. The analyzer said that you are mutant."

"How can you be sure?" asked Vickers.

"You don't trust me," said Crawford. "You think I'm a renegade. You think I see sure defeat ahead and have come running, waving the white flag, anxious to prove my nonbelligerence to the coming order. Trying to make my individual peace and to hell with all the rest of them. Maybe the mutants will keep me as a mascot or a pet."

"If what you say is true, you and the rest of them are licked, no matter what you do."

"Not entirely licked," said Crawford. "We can hit back. We can raise a lot of hell."

"With what? Remember, Crawford, you only have a club."

"We have desperation."

"And that is all? A club and desperation?"

"We have a secret weapon."

"And the others want to use it."

Crawford nodded. "But it isn't good enough, which is why I'm here."

"I'll get in touch with you," said Vickers. "That's a promise. That's the best that I can do. When and if I find you're right, I'll get in touch with you."

Crawford heaved himself out of the chair. "Make it quick as possible," he said. "There isn't much time. I can't hold them off forever."

"You're scared," said Vickers. "You're the most frightened man I ever saw. You were scared the first day I saw you and you still are."

"I've been scared ever since it started. It gets worse every day."

"Two frightened men," said Vickers. "Two ten-year-olds running in the dark."

"You, too?"

"Of course. Can't you see me shaking?"

"No, I can't. In some ways, Vickers, you're the most cold-blooded man I have ever met."

"One thing," said Vickers. "You said there was one other mutant you could catch."

"Yes, I told you that."

"Any chance of telling who?"

"Not a chance," said Crawford.

"I didn't think there was."

The rug seemed to blur a little, then it was there, spinning slowly, flopping in wild wobbles, its hum choked off, its colors blotched with its erratic spinning. The top had come back.

They stood and watched it until it stopped and lay upon the floor.

"It went away," said Crawford.

"And now it's back," Vickers whispered.

Crawford shut the door behind him and Vickers stood in the cold, bright room with the motionless top on the floor, listening to Crawford's footsteps going down the hall.

25

When he could hear the footfalls no longer, Vickers went to the telephone and lifted it and gave a number, then waited for the connection to be made. He could hear the operators along the line setting up the call, faint, tenuous voices that spoke with a reedy nonchalance.

He'd have to tell her fast. He couldn't waste much time, for they would be listening. He'd have to tell her fast and make sure she did the thing he wanted her to do. She must be out and gone before they could reach her door.

He'd say: "Will you do something for me, Ann? Will you do it without question, without asking why?"

"He'd say: "You remember that place where you asked about the stove? I'll meet you there."

Then he'd say: "Get out of your apartment. Get out and hide. Stay out of sight. Right this minute. Not an hour from now. Not five minutes. Not a minute. Hang up this phone and go."

It would have to be fast. It would have to be sure. It would have to be blind.

He couldn't say: "Ann, you're a mutant," then have her want to know what a mutant was and how he came to know and what it meant, while all the time the listeners would be moving toward her door.

She had to go on blind faith. But would she?

He was perspiring. Thinking of how she might want to argue, how she might not want to go without knowing the reason, he felt the moisture trickle down across his ribs.

The phone was ringing now. He tried to recall how her apartment was, how the phone sat on the table at the end of the davenport and how she would be coming across the room to lift the receiver and in a moment he would hear her voice.

The phone rang on. And on.

She did not answer.

The operator said, "That number doesn't answer, sir."

"Try this one, then," he said, giving the operator the number of her office.

He waited again and heard the ringing of the signal.

"That number doesn't answer, sir," the operator said.

"Thank you," said Vickers.

"Shall I try again?"

"No," said Vickers. "Cancel the call, please."

He had to think and plan. He had to try to figure out what it was all about. Before this it had been easy to seek refuge in the belief that it was imagination, that he and the world were half insane, that everything would be all right if he'd just ignore whatever might be going on.

That sort of belief was no longer possible.

For now he must believe what he had half believed before, must accept at face value the story that Crawford had told, sitting in this room, with his massive bulk bulging in the chair, with his face unchanging and his voice a flat monotone that pronounced words, but gave them no inflection and no life.

He must believe in human mutation and in a world divided and embattled. He must believe even in the fairyland of childhood, for if he were a mutant then fairyland was a mark of it, a part of the thing by which he might know himself and be known by other men.

He tried to tie together the implications of Crawford's story, tried to understand what it all might mean, but there were too many ramifications, too many random factors, too much he did not know.

There was a world of mutants, men and women who were more than normal men and women, persons who had certain human talents and certain human understandings which the normal men and women of the world had never known, or having known, could not utilize in their entirety, unable to use intelligently all the mighty powers which lay dormant in their brains.

This was the next step up. This was evolution. This was how the human race advanced.

"And God knows," said Vickers to the empty room, "it needs advancement now if it ever did."

A band of mutants, working together, but working undercover since the normal world would turn on them with fang and claw for their very differentness if they revealed themselves.

And what was this differentness? What could they do, what did they hope to do with it?

A few of the things he knew—Forever cars and everlasting razor blades and the light bulbs that did not burn out and synthetic carbohydrates that fed the hungry and helped to hold war at arm's length from the throat of humanity.

But what else? Surely there was more than that.

Intervention, Horton Flanders had said, rocking on the porch. Some sort of intervention that had helped the world advance and then had staved off, somehow or other, the bitter, terrible fruits of progress wrongly used.

Horton Flanders was the man who could tell him, Vickers knew. But where was Horton Flanders now?

"They're hard to catch," Crawford had said. "You ring doorbells and wait. You send in your name and wait. You track them down and wait. And they're never where you think they are, but somewhere else."

First, thought Vickers, plotting out his moves, I've got to get out of here and be hard to catch myself.

Second, find Ann and see that she is hidden out.

Third, find Horton Flanders and, if he doesn't want to talk, choke it out of him.

He picked up the top and went downstairs and turned in his key. The clerk got out his bill.

"I have a message for you," said the clerk, reaching back into the pigeonhole that held the key. "The gentleman who was up to see you just a while ago gave it to me just before he left."

He handed across an envelope and Vickers ripped it open, pulled out a folded sheet.

"A very funny kind of business," said the clerk. "He'd just been talking to you."

"Yes," said Vickers, "It is a very funny business."

The note read:

Don't try to use that car of yours. If anything happens keep your mouth shut.

It *was* a very funny kind of business.

26

He drove toward the dawn. The road was deserted and the car ran like a fleeing thing, with no sound but the whistle of the tires as they hugged the pavement on the curves. Beside him, on the seat, the gaily painted top rolled back and forth to the motion of the car.

There were two things wrong, two immediate things:

He should have stopped at the Preston house.

He should not have used the car.

Both, of course, were foolish things, and he berated himself for thinking of them and pushed the accelerator down so that the whistle of the tires became a high, shrill scream as they took the curves.

He should have stopped at the Preston house and tried out the top. That, he told himself, was what he had planned to do, and he searched in his mind for the reasons that had made him plan it that way, but there were no reasons. For if the top worked, it would work anywhere. If the top worked, it worked and that was all there could be to it; it wouldn't matter where it worked, although deep inside him was a whisper that it did matter where it worked. For there was something special about the Preston house. It was a key point—it must be a key point in this business of mutants.

I couldn't take the time, he told himself. I couldn't mess around. There wasn't time to waste. The first job is to get back to New York and find Ann and get her out of sight.

For Ann, he told himself, must be the other mutant, although once again, as with the Preston house, he could not be entirely sure. There was no reason, no substantial proof, that Ann Carter was a mutant.

Reason, he thought. Reason and proof. And what are they? No more than the orderly logic on which Man had built his world. Could there be inside a man another sense, another yardstick by which one could live, setting aside the matter of reason and of proof as childish things which once had been good enough, but clumsy at the best? Could there be a way of knowing right from wrong, good and bad without the endless reasoning and the dull parade of proof? Intuition? That was female nonsense. Premonition? That was superstition.

And yet, were they really nonsense and superstition? For years researchers had concerned themselves with extrasensory perception, a sixth sense that Man might hold within himself, but had been unable to develop to its full capacity.

And if extrasensory perception were possible, then many other abilities were possible as well—the psycho-kinetic control of objects through the power of mind alone, the ability to look into the future, the recognition of time as something other than the movement of the hands upon a clock, the ability to know and manipulate unsuspected dimensional extensions of the space-time continuum.

Five senses, Vickers thought—the sense of smell, of sight, of hearing, of taste and touch. Those were the five that Man had known since time immemorial, but did it mean that it was all he had? Were there other senses waiting in his mind for development, as the opposable thumb had been developed, as the erect posture had been developed, as logical thinking had been developed throughout the years of Man's existence? Man had developed slowly. He had evolved from a tree-dwelling, fear-shivering thing into a club-carrying animal, into a fire-making animal. He had made, first of all, the simplest of tools, then more complex tools and finally the tools were so complex that they were machines.

All of this had been done as the result of developing intelligence and was it not possible that the development of intelligence, the development of the human senses was not finished yet? And if this were true, why not a sixth sense, or a seventh, or an eighth, or any number of additional senses, which, in their development, would come under the general heading of the natural evolution of the human race?

Was that, Vickers wondered, what had happened to the mutants, the sudden development of these additional and only half-suspected senses? Was not the mutation logical in itself—the thing that one might well expect?

He swirled through little villages still sleeping between the night and dawn and went past farmhouses lying strangely naked in the half light that ran on the eastern sky-line.

Don't try to use the car, Crawford's note had read. And that was foolish, too, for there was no reason why he should not use the car. No reason other than Crawford's saying so. And who was Crawford? An enemy? Perhaps, although at times he didn't act like one. A man afraid of the defeat that he felt sure would come, more fearful perhaps of the commission of defeat than of defeat itself.

Reason once again.

No reason why he should not use the car. But he was faintly uneasy, using it.

No reason why he should have stopped at the Preston house and still, in his heart, he knew he had somehow failed in not stopping there.

No reason to believe Ann Carter was a mutant, and yet he was sure she was.

He drove through the morning, with the fog rising from all the little streams he crossed, with the flush of sun against the eastern sky, with, finally, boys and dogs going after cows, and the first, well spaced traffic on the road.

He suddenly knew that he was hungry and a little sleepy, but he couldn't stop to sleep. He had to keep on going. When it became dangerous to drive, he would have to sleep, but not until then and not for very long.

But he'd have to stop someplace to eat. The next town he came to, if it were big enough, if it had an eating place that was open, he would stop and eat. Perhaps a cup or two of coffee would chase away the sleep.

27

The town was large and there were eating places and people on the street, the six o'clock factory workers on the move to their seven o'clock jobs.

He picked out a place that didn't look too bad, that had less of the cockroach look about it than some of the other places, and slowed to a crawl, looking for a parking place. He found one, a block beyond the restaurant.

He parked and got out, locked the door. Standing on the sidewalk, he sniffed the morning. It still was fresh and cool, with the deceptive coolness of a summer morning.

He'd have breakfast, he told himself. Take his time eating it, give himself a little time in which to relax, let some of the road fatigue drop from his bones.

Maybe he should try to call Ann again. Maybe this morning, he could catch her in. He'd feel safer if she knew, if she were in hiding. Perhaps instead of just meeting him at the place where they sold the houses, she should go there and explain to them what the situation was and maybe they would help her. But to do that, to explain that to Ann, would take too long. He had to tell her fast and sure and she had to go on faith.

He went back down the street and turned in at the restaurant door. There were tables but no one seemed to be using them. All the eaters were bellied up to the counter. There were a few stools still left and Vickers took one.

On one side of him a hulking workman in faded shirt and bulging overalls was noisily slurping up a bowl of oatmeal; head bent close above the bowl, shoveling the cereal into his mouth with a rapidly moving spoon that dipped and lifted, dipped and lifted, almost as if the man were attempting to establish a siphoning flow of the food into his mouth. On the other side sat a man in blue slacks and white shirt with a neat black bow. He wore glasses and he read a paper and he was, from the look of him, a book-keeper or something of the sort, a man handy with a column of figures and very smug about it.

A waitress came and mopped the space in front of Vickers with a dirty cloth.

"What'll you have?" she asked, impersonally, running the words together until they were one word.

"Stack of cakes," said Vickers, "with a side of ham."

"Coffee?"

"Coffee," said Vickers.

The breakfast came and he ate it, hurriedly at first, stuffing his mouth with great forkfuls of syrup-dripping cakes, with generous cuts of ham, then more slowly as the first hunger was appeased.

The overalled man got up and left. A wispy girl with drooping eyelids took his place. Some weary secretary, Vickers thought, with only an hour or two of sleep after a night of dancing.

He was almost through when he heard the shouting in the street outside, then the sound of running feet.

The girl beside him swung around on her stool and looked out the window.

"Everybody's running," she said. "I wonder what's the trouble."

A man stopped outside the door and yelled, "They found one of them Forever cars!"

The eaters leaped from their stools and surged toward the door. Vickers followed slowly.

They'd found a Forever car, the shouting man had said. The only one they could have found was the one he'd parked just up the street.

They had tipped the car over and rolled it out into the middle of the street. They were ringed around it, shouting and shaking their fists at it. Someone threw a brick or stone at it and the sound of the object striking its metal boomed through the early morning street like a cannon shot.

Someone picked up whatever had been thrown and heaved it through the door of a hardware store. Reaching in through the broken glass, someone else unlocked the door. Men streamed in and came out again, carrying mauls and axes.

The crowd drew back to give them elbow room. The mauls and axes flashed in the slanted sunlight. They struck and struck again. The street rang with the sound of metallic hammering. Glass shattered with a crunching sound, then came a metallic clanging.

Vickers stood beside the restaurant door, sick in the pit of his stomach, his brain frozen with what later might be fear, but which now was no more than astonishment and blind befuddlement.

Crawford had written: *Don't try to use that car of yours.*

And this was what he'd meant.

Crawford had known what would happen to any Forever car found on the streets.

Crawford had known and had tried to warn him.

Friend or foe?

Vickers reached out a hand and put it, palm flat, against the rough brick of the building.

The touch of the brick, the roughness of it, told him that this was happening, that it was no dream, that he actually stood here in front of a restaurant in which he had just eaten breakfast, and saw a mob, mad with fury and with hate, smashing up his car.

They know, he thought.

The people finally know. They've been told about the mutants. And they hated the mutants.

Of course, they hated them.

They hated them because the existence of the mutants makes them second-class humans, because they are Neanderthalers suddenly invaded by a bow and arrow people.

He turned and went back into the restaurant, walking softly, ready to leap and run if someone should suddenly shout behind him, if a finger tapped his shoulder.

The bespectacled man with the black bow tie had left the paper beside his plate. Vickers picked it up, walked steadily on, down the length of counter. He pushed open the swinging door that led into the kitchen. There was no one there. He walked through the kitchen rapidly, let himself out the rear door into an alley.

He went down that alley, found another narrow one between two buildings, leading to an opposite street. He took it, crossed the street when he came to it, followed another alleyway between two buildings that led to still another alley.

"They'll fight," Crawford had said, sitting in the hotel room the night before, his big body filling the chair to overflowing, "they'll fight with what they have."

So finally they were fighting, striking back with what they had. They had picked up their club and were fighting back.

He found a park and walking through it, came across a bench shielded from the street by a clump of bushes. He sat down and unfolded the paper he had taken from the restaurant, turned its pages back until he found the front page.

And there the story was.

28

The headline said: WE ARE BEING TAKEN OVER! The drop read: PLOT BY SUPERMEN REVEALED.

And under that: Superhuman Race Among Us; Mystery of Everlasting Razor Blades Solved.

And the story:

WASHINGTON (Special)—The greatest danger the human race has faced in all the years of its existence—a danger which may reduce all of us to slavery—was revealed today in a joint announcement by the Federal Bureau of Investigation, the military Chiefs of Staff and the Washington office of the International Bureau of Economics.

The joint announcement was made at a news conference called by the President.

Simultaneous announcements were made in all the other major capitals of the world, in London, Moscow, Paris, Madrid, Rome, Cairo, Peking and a dozen other cities.

The announcement revealed that a new race of human beings, called mutants, has developed, and is banded together in an attempt to win domination over the entire world.

A mutant, in the sense in which the word is here used, is a human being who has undergone a sudden variation, the child differing from the parent, as opposed to the gradual change by which the human race has evolved to its present form. The variation, in this case, has not been noticeably physical; that is, a mutant is indistinguishable, so far as the eye is concerned, from any other human. The variation has been mental, with the mutant possessing certain skills which the normal human does not have—certain "wild talents," the announcement said.

(See adjoining column for full explanation of mutancy.)

The announcement (full text in Column 4) said that the mutants had embarked upon a campaign to destroy the economic system of the world through the manufacture of certain items, such as the everlasting razor blade, the everlasting light bulb, the Forever car, the new prefabricated houses and other items generally sold in the so called "gadget shops."

The mutant group, it was revealed, has been under investigation by various governmental and independent agencies for several years and the findings, when correlated, showed unmistakably that a definite campaign was under way to take over the entire world. The formal announcement of the situation, it was said, was delayed until there could be no doubt concerning the authenticity of the reports.

The announcement called upon the citizenry of the world to join in the fight to circumvent the plot. At the same time it pleaded for a normal continuation of all activity and advised against hysteria.

"There is no occasion for apprehension," the announcement said. "Certain counter-measures are being taken." There was no hint as to what any of these countermeasures might be. When the reporters attempted to question the spokesman concerning them he was told that this was restricted information.

To aid the world governments in their campaign against the intentions of the mutants, the announcement said that every citizen should take these steps:

1—Keep your head. Do not give way to hysteria.

2—Refrain from using any mutant-manufactured items.

3—Refuse to buy any mutant-manufactured items. Persuade others against their use or purchase.

4—Immediately inform the FBI of any suspicious circumstances which might have a bearing upon the situation.

The announcement said that first suspicions of any attempt
(Continued on Page 11)

Vickers did not turn to Page 11. Instead he studied the rest of the front page.

There was the story which explained mutation and the complete text of the announcement. There was a signed article by some professor of biology, discussing the probable effect of mutancy and its probable causes.

There were a half dozen bulletins. He began to read them:

NEW YORK (AP)—Mobs today swept through the city armed with axes and iron bars. They swarmed into gadget shops, destroying the merchandise, smashing the fixtures. Apparently no one was found in any of the shops. One man was killed, but it was not believed he was connected with a gadget shop.

WASHINGTON (UP)—A mob early today attacked and killed a man driving a Forever car. The car was smashed.

LONDON (INS)—The government today threw heavy guard around several housing development projects containing a number of the prefabricated houses attributed to mutant manufacture.

"The people who purchased these houses," said an explanation accompanying the order, "purchased them in good faith. They are in no way connected or to be connected with the conspiracy. The guards were ordered to protect these innocent people and their neighbors against any misdirected public violence."

The fourth:

ST. MALO, FRANCE (Reuters)—The body of a man was found hanging from a lamp post at dawn today. A placard with the crude lettering of "Mutant" was pinned to his shirt front.

Vickers let the paper fall from his hand. It made a ragged tent upon the ground.

He stared out across the park. Morning traffic was flowing by on the roadway a block away. A boy came along a walk, bouncing a ball as he walked. A few pigeons circled down through the trees and strutted on the grass, cooing gently.

Normal, he thought. A normal human morning, with people going to work and kids out playing and the pigeons strutting on the grass.

But underneath it a current of savagery. Behind it all, behind the facade of civilization, the present was crouching in the cave, lying in ambush against the coming of the future. Lying in wait for himself and Ann and Horton Flanders.

Thank God that no one had thought to connect him with the car. Perhaps, later on, someone would. Perhaps someone would remember seeing him get out of the car. Perhaps someone would fasten suspicion upon the man who, of all of them, had not run out of the restaurant and joined the mob around the car.

But for the moment he was safe. How long he would remain safe was another matter.

Now what?

He considered it.

Steal a car and continue his trip?

He didn't know how to steal a car; he would probably bungle it.

But there was something else—something else that needed doing right now.

He had to get the top.

He had left it in the car and he'd have to get it back.

But why risk his neck to get the top?

It didn't make much sense. Come to think of it, it made no sense at all. Still, he knew that he had to do it.

Crawford's warning about not driving the car hadn't made sense either at the time he read it. He had disregarded it and had felt uneasy about disregarding it, had known, against all logic, that he was wrong in not paying it attention. And in this particular case, at least, logic had been wrong and his feeling—his hunch, his premonition, his intuition, call it what you would—had been right.

He had wondered, he remembered, if there might not be a certain sense which would outweigh logic and reason, if within his brain a man might not have another faculty, a divining faculty, which would outdate the old tools of logic and of reason. Maybe that was what it was. Maybe that was one of the wild talents that the mutants had.

Maybe that was the sense that told him, without reason, without logic, that he must get back the top.

29

The street had been blocked to traffic and the police were standing by, although there was little need of them, it seemed, for the crowd was orderly. The car lay in the middle of the street, battered and dented, with its wheels sticking into the air, like a dead cow in a cornfield. Its glass was shattered and strewed about the pavement, crunching under the feet of the milling crowd. Its tires were knocked off and the wheels were bent and people stood around and stared at it.

Vickers mingled with the crowd, moving nearer to the car. The front door, he saw, had somehow been smashed open and was wedged against the pavement and there was just a chance, he told himself, the top might still be there.

If it was, he would have to figure out some way to get it. Maybe he could get down on his knees and pretend that he was simply curious about the instrument panel or the controls. He'd tell his neighbors about how the control panel differed from that of an ordinary car and maybe he could hook in a hand and sneak out the top and hide it under his coat without any of them knowing.

He shuffled about the wreck, gaping at it in what he hoped was an idly curious fashion and he talked a little with his neighbors, the usual banal comments of the onlooker.

He worked his way around until he was beside the door and squatted down and looked inside the car and he couldn't see the top. He stayed there, squatting and looking, craning his neck, and he told his nearest neighbor about the control panel and wondered about the shift, but all the time he was looking for the top.

But there wasn't any top.

He got up again and milled with the crowd, watching the pavement, because the top might have fallen from the car and rolled away from it. Maybe it had rolled into the gutter and was lying there. He searched the gutters, on both sides of the streets, and covered the pavement and there was no top.

So the top was gone—gone before he could try it out, and now he'd never know if it could take him into fairyland.

Twice he had gone into fairyland—once when he was a child and again when he had walked a certain valley with a girl named Kathleen Preston. He had walked with her in an enchanted valley that could have been nothing else but another fairyland and after that he had gone back to see her and had been told that she had gone away and he had turned away from the door and trudged across the porch.

Now wait, he said to himself. *Had* he actually turned from the door and trudged across the porch?

He tried to remember and, dimly, he saw it all again, the soft-voiced man who had told him that Kathleen was gone and then had said, "But won't you come in, lad. I have something you should see."

He had gone in and stood in the mighty hall, filled with heavy shadow, with its paintings on the wall and the massive stairs winding up the other stories and the man had said—

What had he said?

Or had it ever happened?

Why did an experience like this, an incident that he should have remembered without fail, come back to him after all the years of not knowing, as the lost memory of his boyhood venture into fairyland had come back to him after so long?

And was it true or wasn't it?

There was, he told himself, no way that he could judge.

He turned away and walked down the street, past the policeman who leaned against a building and swung his club, smiling at the crowd.

In a vacant lot a group of boys were playing and he stopped to watch them. Once he had played like that, without thought of time or destiny, with the thought of nothing but happy hours of sunshine and the gurgle of delight that bubbled up with living. Time had been non-existent and purpose was for a moment only, or at the most, an hour. Each day had run on forever and there had been no end to living. . . .

There was one little fellow who sat apart from all the others and he held something in his lap and was turning it around, admiring it, happy in the possession of a wondrous toy.

Suddenly he tossed it in the air and caught it and the sun flashed on its many colors and Vickers, seeing what it was, skipped a breath or two.

It was the missing top!

He left the sidewalk and sauntered across the lot.

The playing boys did not notice him, or rather, they ignored him, after the manner of the playing youngsters for whom the adult does not exist, or is no more than a shadowy personage out of some unreal and unsatisfactory world.

Vickers stood above the boy who held the top.

"Hello, son."

"Hello, yourself."

"What you got?"

"I found it," said the boy.

"It's a pretty thing," said Vickers. "I'd like to buy it from you."

"It ain't for sale."

"I'd pay quite a bit," said Vickers.

The boy looked up with interest.

"Enough for a new bicycle?"

Vickers dug into his pocket and pulled out folded bills.

"Gosh, mister . . ."

Out of the corner of his eye, Vickers saw the policeman standing on the sidewalk, watching him. The policeman took a step, started across the lot.

"Here," said Vickers.

He grabbed the top and tossed the folded bills into the boy's lap. He straightened and ran, heading for the alley.

"Hey, you!" the policeman shouted.

Vickers kept on running.

"Hey, you! Stop, or I'll shoot!"

A gun exploded and Vickers heard the thin, high whine of a bullet going past his head. The policeman could not even have guessed what he was doing or who he was, but the morning paper must have left everyone frightened, on edge.

He reached the first of the buildings in the alley and ducked around it.

He couldn't stay in the alley, he knew, for when the policeman came around the corner of the building, he would be a sitting duck.

He ducked into a passageway between two buildings and realized, even as he did it, that he'd turned in the wrong direction, for the passageway would lead him back onto the street on which lay the wrecked and battered car.

He saw an open basement window and knew, without even thinking of it, that it was his only chance. He gauged his distance and threw himself, feet first, and was through the window. The sill caught him in the back and he felt the fire of pain run along his body, then his head smashed into something and the basement was a place of darkness filled with a million stars. He came down sprawling and the wind was knocked out of him and the top, flying from his hand, bounced along the floor.

He clawed himself to his hands and knees and ran down the top. He found a water pipe and grasped it and pulled himself erect. There was a raw place on his back that burned and his head buzzed with the violence of the blow. But he was safe, for a little while.

He found a stairs and climbed them and saw that he was in the back room of a hardware store. The place was filled with haphazardly piled rolls of chicken wire, rolls of roofing paper, cardboard cartons, bales of binder twine, lengths of stove pipe, crated stoves, coils of Manila rope.

He could hear people moving up in front, but there was no one in sight. He ducked behind a crated stove and from the window above his head a splash of sun came down so that he crouched in a pool of light.

Outside, in the alleyway, he heard running feet go past and from far away he heard men shouting. He hunkered down, pressing his body against the rough board crating of the stove and tried to control his labored breathing, afraid that if someone came into the room they might hear his rasping breath.

He'd have to figure out some way to get away, he knew, for if he stayed where he was they finally would find him. They would start combing the area, police and citizens alike. And, by that time, they would know who it was they hunted. The boy would tell them he had found the top lying near the car and someone then might remember they had seen him park the car and the waitress in the restaurant might remember him. From many little bits of information, they would know their fugitive was the man whose Forever car they'd smashed.

He wondered what would happen to him when they found him. He remembered the bulletin from St. Malo, about the man hanging from the lamp post with a placard on his chest.

But there was no way to escape. He was caught and there wasn't, for the moment, much that he could do. He couldn't sneak out into the alley, for they'd be watching for him. He could go back into the basement, but that wasn't any better than the place he was. He could saunter out into the store and act like a customer, finally walk out into—the street, doing his best to look like an ordinary citizen who had dropped into the place to look at some treasured gun or tool he wished that he could buy. But he doubted that he could carry it off.

So the illogic hadn't paid off, after all. Logic and reason were still the winners, still the factors that ruled the ordering of men's lives.

There was no escape from this sun-lit nest behind the crated stove.

There was no escape, unless—

He had found the top again. He had the top there with him.

There was no escape—unless the top should work, there was no escape.

He put the top's point on the floor and spun it slowly, pumping on the handle. It picked up speed; he pumped the faster. He let go and it spun, whistling. He hunkered in front of it and watched the colored stripes. He saw them come into being and he followed them into infinity and he wondered where they went. He forced his attention on the top, narrowing it down until the top was all he saw.

It didn't work. The top wobbled and he put out a hand and stopped it.

He tried again.

He had to be an eight-year old. He had to go back to childhood once again. He must clear away his mind, sweep out all adult thoughts, all the adult worry, all sophistication. He must become a child.

He thought of playing in the sand, of napping under trees, of the feel of soft dust beneath bare feet. He closed his eyes and concentrated and caught the vision of a childhood and the color and the smell of it.

He opened his eyes and watched the stripes and filled his mind with wonder, with the question of their being and the question of where they went when they disappeared.

It didn't work. The top wobbled and he stopped it.

A frantic thought wedged its way into his consciousness. He didn't have much time. He had to hurry.

He pushed the thought away.

A child had no conception of time. For the child, time went on forever and forever. He was a little boy and he had all the time there was and he owned a brand new top.

He spun the top again.

He knew the comfort of a home and a loved mother and the playthings scattered on the floor and the story books that Grandma would read to him when she came visiting again. And he watched the top, with a simple, childish wonder—watching the stripes come up and disappear, come up and disappear, come up and disappear—

He fell a foot or so and thumped upon the ground and he was sitting atop a hill and the land stretched out before him for miles and miles and miles, an empty land of waving grass and groves of trees and far-off, winding water.

He looked down at his feet and the top was there, slowly spinning to a wobbling halt.

30

The land lay new and empty of any mark of Man, a land of raw earth and sky; even the wildness of the wild that swept across it seemed to say that the land was untamed.

From his hilltop, Vickers saw bands of dark, moving shapes that he felt sure were small herds of buffalo and even as he watched three wolves came loping up the slope, saw him and veered off, angling down the hill. In the blue sweep of sky that arched from horizon to horizon with a single cloud a bird wheeled gracefully, spying out the land. It screeched and the screech came down to Vickers as a high, thin sound filtered through the sky.

The top had brought him through. He was safe in this empty land with wolves and buffalo.

He climbed to the ridgetop and looked across the reaches of the grassland, with its frequent groves and many watercourses, sparkling in the sun. There was no sign of human habitation—no roads, no threads of smoke sifting up the sky.

He looked at the sun and wondered which way was west and thought he knew, and if he was right, it was midmorning. But if he was wrong, it was midafternoon and in a few hours darkness would come upon the land. And when darkness came, he would have to figure out how to spend the night.

He had meant to go into "fairyland" and this, of course, wasn't it. If he had stopped to think about it, he told himself, he would have known that it would not be, for the place he had gone to as a child could not have been fairyland. This was a new and empty world, a lonely and perhaps a terrifying world, but it was better than the back room of a hardware store in some unknown town with his fellow men hunting him to death.

He had come out of the old, familiar world into this new, strange world and if the world were entirely empty of human life, then he was on his own.

He sat down and emptied his pockets and made an inventory of what he had. A half a package of cigarettes; three packs of matches, one almost finished, one full, one with just a match or two gone from it; a pocket knife; a handkerchief; a billfold with a few dollars in it; a few cents in change; the key to the Forever car; a key ring with the key to the house and another to the desk and a couple of other keys he couldn't identify; a mechanical pencil; a few half sheets of paper folded together, pocket size, on which he had intended to make notes if he saw anything worth noting—and that was all. Fire and a tool with a cutting edge and a few hunks of worthless metal— that was the sum of what he had.

If this world were empty, he must face it alone. He must feed himself and defend himself and find shelter for himself and, in time to come, contrive some way in which to clothe himself.

He lit a cigarette and tried to think, but all that he could think about was that he must go easy on the cigarettes, for the half pack was all he had and when those were gone, there would be no more.

An alien land—but not entirely alien, for it was Earth again, the old familiar Earth unscarred by the tools of Man. It had the air of Earth and the grass and sky of Earth, and even the wolves and buffalo were the same as old Earth had borne. Perhaps it was Earth. It looked for all the world like the primal Earth might have looked before it lay beneath Man's hand, before Man had caught and tamed it and bound it to his will, before Man had stripped and gutted it and torn all its treasures from it.

It was no alien land—no alien dimension into which the top had flung him, although, of course, it had not been the top at all. The top hadn't had anything to do with it. The top was simply something on which one focused one's attention, simply a hypnotic device to aid the mind in the job which it must do. The top had helped him come into this land, but it had been his mind and that strange otherness that was his which had enabled him to travel from old familiar Earth to this strange, primal place.

There was something he had heard or read. . . .

He went searching for it, digging back into his brain with frantic mental fingers.

A news story, perhaps. Or something he had heard. Or something he had seen on television.

It came to him finally—the story about the man in Boston— a Dr. Aldridge, he seemed to remember, who had said that there might be more worlds than one, that there might be a world a second ahead of ours and one a second behind ours and another a second behind that and still another and another and another, a long string of worlds whirling one behind the other, like men walking in the snow, one man putting his foot in the same track and so on down the line.

An endless chain of worlds, one behind the other. A ring around the Sun.

He hadn't finished reading the story, he remembered; something had distracted him and he'd laid the paper down. Smoking the cigarette down to its final shred, he wished that he had read it all. For Aldridge might have been right. This might be the next world after the old, familiar Earth, the next link on an endless chain of earths.

He tried to puzzle out the logic of such a ring of worlds but he gave it up, for he had no idea of why it should be so.

Say, then, that this was Earth No. Two, the next earth behind the original Earth which he had left behind. Say, then, that in topographical features the earths would resemble one another, not exactly like one another perhaps, but very close in their topography, with little differences here and there, each magnified in turn until probably a matter of ten earths back the change would become noticeable. But this was only the second earth and perhaps its features were but little changed, and on old Earth he had been somewhere in Illinois and this, he told himself, was the kind of land the ancient Illinois would have been.

As a boy of eight he had gone into a land where there had been a garden and a house in a grove of trees and maybe this was the very earth he had visited then. If that were so, the house might still be there. And in later years he had walked an enchanted valley and it, too, might have been this earth, and if that were true, then there was another Preston house on this very earth, exactly like the one which stood so proudly in the Earth of his childhood.

There was a chance, he told himself. A slim chance, but the only chance he had.

He'd head for the Preston house, toward the northwest, retracing on foot the many miles he had driven since leaving his boyhood home. He knew there was little reason to believe there'd be any Preston house, little reason to think anything other than that he was trapped in an empty, lonely world. But he shut his mind to reason, for this was the only hope he had.

He checked the sun and saw that it had climbed higher in the sky, and that meant that it was morning and not afternoon and by that he knew which way was west, and that was all he needed.

He set off, striding down the hill, heading for the northwest, toward the one hope he had in all the world.

31

Well before dark, he picked a camping site, a grove through which ran a stream.

He took off his shirt and tied it to the stick to form a crude seine, then went down to a small pool in the creek and after some experimenting found how to use the seine to the best advantage. At the end of an hour, he had five good-sized fish.

He cleaned the fish with his pocket knife and lit the fire with a single match and congratulated himself upon his woodsmanship.

He cooked one of the fish and ate it. It was not an easy thing to eat, for he had no salt and the cooking was very far from expert— part of the fish was singed by flame, part of the rest was raw. But he was ravenous and it didn't taste too bad until the edge was off his hunger. After that it was a hard job choking down the rest, but he forced himself to do it, for he knew that he faced hard days ahead and to get through them he must keep his belly filled.

By this time darkness had fallen and he huddled beside the fire. He tried to think, but he was too tired for thinking. He caught himself dozing as he sat.

He slept, awoke to find the fire almost out and the night still dark, built up the fire with cold sweat breaking out on him. The fire was for protection as well as warmth and cooking and on the day's march he had seen not only wolves, but bear as well, and once a tawny shape had run through one of the groves as he passed through, moving too fast for him to make out what it was.

He woke again and dawn was in the sky. He built up the fire and cooked the rest of the fish. He ate one and the part of another, tucked the others, messy as they were, into his pocket. He would need food, he knew, throughout the day, and he did not want to waste the time to stop and make a fire.

He hunted around the grove and found a stout, straight stick, tested it with his weight and knew that it was sound. It would serve him for a walking staff and might be of some use as a club if he were called upon to defend himself. He checked his pockets to see that he was leaving nothing behind. He had his pocket knife and the matches and they were the important things. He wrapped the matches carefully in his handkerchief, then took off his undershirt and added it to the handkerchief. If he were caught in rain or fell in crossing a creek, the wrappings might help to keep the matches dry. And he needed those matches. He doubted very seriously that he could make fire with struck flint or by the Boy Scout bow and arrow method.

He was off before the sun was up, slogging northwestward, but going slower than he had gone the day before, for now he realized that it was not speed, but stamina that counted. To wear himself out in these first few days of hiking would be silly.

He lost some time making a wide detour in the afternoon around a fair-sized herd of buffalo. He camped that night in another grove, having stopped an hour or so earlier beside a stream to catch another supply of fish with his shirt-and-staff seine. In the grove he found a few bushes of dewberries, with some fruit still on them, so he had dessert as well as fish.

The sun came up and he moved on again. The sun descended.

And another day began and he went on. And another and another.

He caught fish. He found berries. He found a deer that had been freshly killed, no doubt by some animal that his appearance had scared off. Hacking away with his pocket knife, he cut as many ragged hunks of venison as he could carry. Even without salt, the meat was a welcome change from fish. He even learned to eat a little of it raw, hacking off a mouthful and chewing it methodically as he walked along. He had to discard the last of the meat when it got so high that he couldn't live with it.

He lost track of time. He had no idea how many miles he had covered, nor how far he might be from the place where he was heading, nor even if he could find it at all.

His shoes broke open and he stuffed them with dried grass and bound them together with strips cut off his trouser legs.

One day he knelt to drink at a pool and in the glass-clear water saw a strange face staring at him. With a shock he realized that it was his own face, that of a bearded man, ragged and dirty and with the lines of fatigue upon him.

The days came and went. He moved ahead, northwestward. He kept putting first one foot out and then the other, moving almost automatically. The sun burned him at first and the burn turned to a tan. He crossed a wide, deep river on a log. It took a long time to get across and once the log almost spun and spilled him, but he made it.

He kept going on. There was nothing else to do.

He walked through an empty land, with no sign of habitation, although it was a land that was well suited for human occupation. The soil was rich and the grass grew tall and thick and the trees, which sprang skyward from groves along the watercourses, were straight and towered high into the sky.

Then one day, just before sunset, he topped a rise and saw the land fall away beneath his feet, sweeping downward toward the far-off ribbon of a river that he thought he recognized.

But it was not the river which held his attention, but the flash of setting sun on metal, on a large area of metal far down the sloping land.

He put up his hand and shielded his eyes against the sunlight and tried to make out what it was, but it was too far far away and it shone too brightly.

Climbing down the slope, not knowing whether to be glad or frightened, Vickers kept a close watch on the gleam of far-off metal. At times he lost sight of it when he dipped into the swales, but it was always there when he topped the rise again, so he knew that it was real.

Finally he was able to make out that what he saw were buildings—metallic buildings glinting in the sun, and now he saw that strange shapes came and went in the air above them and that there was a stir of life around them.

But it was not a city or a town. For one thing, it was too metallic. And for another, there were no roads leading into it.

As he came nearer, he made out more and more of the detail of the place and finally, when he was only a mile or two away, he stopped and looked at it and knew what it was.

It was not a city, but a factory, a giant, sprawling factory and to it came, continually, the strange flying things that probably were planes, but looked more like flying boxcars. The most of them came from the north and west and they came flying low, not too fast, dipping down to land in an area behind a screen of buildings that stood between him and the landing field.

And the creatures that moved about among the buildings were not men—or did not seem to be men, but something else, metallic things that flashed in the last rays of the sun.

All about the buildings, standing on great towers, were cup-shaped discs many feet across and all the faces of the discs were turned toward the sun and the faces of the discs glowed as if there were fires inside of them.

He walked slowly toward the buildings and as he came closer to them he realized for the first time the sheer vastness of them. They covered acre after acre and they towered for many stories high and the things that ran among them on their strange and many errands were not men, nor anything like men, but self-propelled machines.

Some of the machines he could identify, but most of them he couldn't. He saw a carrying machine rush past with a load of lumber clutched within its belly and a great crane lumbered past at thirty miles an hour with its steel jaws swinging. But there were others that looked like mechanistic nightmares and all of them went scurrying about, as if each of them were in a terrific hurry.

He found a street, or if not a street, an open space between two buildings, and went along it, keeping close to the side of one of the buildings, for it would have been what one's life was worth to walk down the center, where the machines might run one down.

He came to an opening in the building, from which a ramp led out to the street, and he cautiously climbed the ramp and looked inside. The interior was lighted, although he could not see where the light came from, and he looked down long avenues of machinery, busily at work. But there was no noise—that, he knew now, was the thing that bothered him. Here was a factory and there was no noise. The place was utterly silent except for the sound of metal on the earth as the self-propelled machines flashed along the street.

He left the ramp and went down the street, hugging the building, and came out on the edge of the airfield where the aerial boxcars were landing and taking off.

He watched the machines land and disgorge their freight, great piles of shining, newly sawed lumber, which was at once snatched up by the carrying machines and hustled off in all directions, great gouts of raw ore, more than likely iron, dumped into the maw of other carrying machines that looked, or so Vickers thought, like so many pelicans.

Once the boxcar had unloaded it took off again—took off without a single sound, as if a wind had seized and wafted it into the upper air.

The flying things came in endless streams, disgorging their endless round of cargo, which was taken care of almost immediately. Nothing was left piled up. By the time the machine had lifted into the air, the cargo it had carried had been rushed off somewhere.

Like men, thought Vickers—those machines act just like men. Their operation was not automatic, for to have been automatic each operation must have been performed at a certain place and at a regular time—and each ship did not land in exactly the same place, nor was the time of their arrival spaced regularly. But each time that a ship landed the appropriate carrying machine would be on hand to take charge of the cargo.

Like intelligent beings, Vickers thought, and even as he thought of it, he knew that that was exactly what they were. Here, he knew, were robots, each one designed to take care of its own particular task. Not the man-like robots of one's imagination, but practical machines with intelligence and purpose.

The sun had set and as he stood at the corner of the building, he looked up at the towers which had faced the sun. The discs atop the towers, he saw, were slowly turning back toward the east, so that when the sun came up next morning they would be facing it.

Solar power, thought Vickers—and where else had he heard of solar power? Why, in the mutant houses! The dapper little salesman had explained to him and Ann how, when you had a solar plant, you could dispense with public utilities.

And here again was solar power. Here, too, were frictionless machines that ran without the faintest noise. Like the Forever car that would not wear out, but would last through many generations.

The machines paid no attention to him. It was as if they did not see him, did not suspect he was there. Not a single one of them faltered as they rushed past him, not a single one had moved out of its way to give him a wider berth. Nor had any made a threatening motion toward him.

With the going of the sun, the area was lighted, but once again he could not determine the source of the light. The fall of night did not halt the work. The flying boxcars, great, angular, box-like contraptions, still came flying in, unloaded and flew off again. The machines kept up their scurrying. The long lines of machines within the buildings kept up their soundless labor.

The flying boxcars, he wondered, were they robots, too? And the answer seemed to be that they probably were.

He wandered about, hugging the building to keep out of the way.

He found a mighty loading platform, where the boxes were piled high, carried there by machines, loaded into the flying boxcars by machines, steadily going out to their destination, wherever it might be. He edged his way onto the platform and looked at some of the boxes closely, trying to determine what it was they held, but the only designations on them were stenciled code letters and numerals. He thought of prying some of them open, but he had no tools to do it, and he was just a bit afraid to do it, for while the machines continued to pay no attention to him, they might pay disastrous attention if he interfered.

Hours later he came out on the other side of the sprawling factory area and walked away from it, then turned back and looked at it and saw it glowing with its strange light and sensed the bustle of it.

He looked at the factory and wondered what was made there and thought he could guess. Probably razor blades and lighters and maybe light bulbs and perhaps the houses and the Forever cars. Maybe all of them.

For this, he felt certain, was the factory, or at least one of the factories, that Crawford and North American Research had been looking for and had failed to find.

No wonder, he thought, that they had failed to find it.

32

He came to the river late in the afternoon, a river filled with tree-covered, grape-vined islands, clogged with sandbars and filled with wicked gurgling and the hiss of shifting sands and it could be, he was sure, no other stream than the Wisconsin River, flowing through its lower reaches to join the Mississippi. And if that were so, he knew where he was going. From here he could reach the place where he was going.

Now he feared he would not find the place he sought, that in this land there was no Preston house. Rather, he had fallen upon a strange land where there were no men, but robots, a complex robotic civilization in which Man played no part. There were no men connected with the factory, he was sure, for the place had been too self-sufficient, too sure of its purpose to need the hand or the brain of Man.

As the last daylight faded, he camped on the river's shore, and sat for a long time before he went to sleep, staring out over the silvered mirror of the moonlit water, feeling the loneliness strike into him, a deeper, more bitter loneliness than he'd ever known before.

When morning came, he'd go on; he'd tread the trail to its dusty end. He'd find the place where the Preston house should stand and when he found that there was no house—what would he do then?

He did not think about that. He did not want to think about it. He finally went to sleep.

In the morning he went down the river and studied the bluff-studded southern shore as he slogged along and was more sure than ever from the character of the bluffs that he knew where he was.

He followed the river down and finally saw the misty blue of the great rock-faced bluff that rose at the junction of the rivers and the thin violet line of the bluffs beyond the greater river, so he climbed one of the nearer bluffs and spied out the valley he had hunted.

He camped that night in the valley and the next morning followed it and found the other, branching valley that would lead to the Preston house.

He was halfway up it before it became familiar, although he had seen here and there certain rock formations and certain clumps of trees that had seemed to him to bear some similarity to ones he had seen before.

The suspicion and the hope grew in him, and at last the certainty, that he tread familiar ground.

Here, once again, was the enchanted valley he had travelled twenty years before!

And now, he thought—and now, if the house is there.

He felt faint and sick at the certainty it would not be there, that he would reach the valley's head and would see the land where it should have stood and it would not be there. For if that happened, he would know that the last of hope was gone, that he was an exile out of his familiar Earth.

He found the path and followed it and he saw the wind blow across the meadow grass so that it seemed as if the grass were water and the whiteness of its wind-blown stems were whitecaps rolling on it. He saw the clumps of crabapple trees and they were not in bloom because the season was too late, but they were the same that he had seen in bloom.

The path turned around the shoulder of a hill and Vickers stopped and looked at the house standing on the hill and felt his knees go wobbly beneath him and he looked away, quickly, and brought his eyes back slowly to make sure it was not imagination, that the house was really there.

It was really there.

He started up the path and he found that he was running and forced himself to slow to a rapid walk. And then he was running again and he didn't try to stop.

He reached the hill that led up to the house and he went more slowly now, trying to regain his breath, and he thought what a sight he was, with weeks of beard upon his face, with his clothing ripped and torn and matted with the dirt and filth of travel, with his shoes falling to shreds, tied upon his feet with strips of cloth ripped from his trouser legs, with his frayed trousers blowing in the wind, showing dirt-streaked, knobby knees.

He reached the white picket fence that ran around the house and stopped beside the gate and leaned upon it, looking at the house. It was exactly as he had remembered it, neat, well-kept, with the lawn well-trimmed and flowers growing brightly in neat beds, with the woodwork newly painted and the brick a mellow color attesting to years of sun upon it and the force of wind and rain.

"Kathleen," he said, and he couldn't say the name too well, for his lips were parched and rough. "I've come back again."

He wondered what she'd look like, after all these years. He must not, he warned himself, expect to see the girl he once had known, the girl of seventeen or eighteen, but a woman near his own age.

She would see him standing at the gate and even with the beard and the tattered clothes and the weeks of travel on him, she would know him and would open the door and come down the walk to greet him.

The door opened and the sun was in his eyes so that he could not see her until she'd stepped out on the porch.

"Kathleen," he said.

But it wasn't Kathleen.

It was someone he'd never seen before—a man who had on almost no clothes at all and who glittered in the sun as he walked down the path and who said to Vickers, "Sir, what can I do for you?"

33

There was something about the glitter of the man in the morning sun, something about the way he walked and the way he talked that didn't quite fit in. He had no hair, for one thing. His head was absolutely bald and there was no hair on his chest. His eyes were funny, too. They glittered like the rest of him and he seemed to have no lips.

"I'm a robot, sir," said the glittering man, seeing Vickers' puzzlement.

"Oh," said Vickers.

"My name is Hezekiah."

"How are you, Hezekiah?" Vickers asked inanely, not knowing what else to say.

"I'm all right," replied Hezekiah. "I am always all right. There is nothing to go wrong with me. Thank you for asking, sir."

"I had hoped to find someone here," said Vickers. "A Miss Kathleen Preston. Does it happen she is home?"

He watched the robot's eyes and there was nothing in them.

The robot asked, "Won't you come in, sir, and wait?"

The robot held the gate open for him and he came through, walking on the walk of mellowed brick and he noticed how the brick of the house was mellowed, as well, by many years of sun and by the lash of wind and rain. The place, he saw, was well kept up. The windows sparkled with the cleanliness of a recent washing and the shutters hung true and straight and the trim was painted and the lawn looked as if it had not been only mowed, but razored. Gay beds of flowers bloomed without a single weed and the picket fence marched its eternal guard around the house straight as wooden soldiers and painted gleaming white.

They went around the house, and the robot turned and went up the steps to the little porch that opened on the side entrance and pushed the door open for Vickers to go through.

"To your right, sir," Hezekiah said. "Take a chair and wait. If there is anything you wish, there is a bell upon the table."

"Thank you, Hezekiah," Vickers said.

The room was large for a waiting room. It was gaily papered and had a small marble fireplace with a mirror over the mantle and there was a hush about the room, a sort of official hush, as if the place might be an antechamber for important happenings.

Vickers took a chair and waited.

What had he expected? Kathleen bursting from the house and running down the steps to meet him, happy after twenty years of never hearing of him? He shook his head. He had indulged in wishful thinking. It didn't work that way. It wasn't logical that it should.

But there were other things that were not logical, either, and they had worked out. It had not been logical that he should find this house in this other world, and still he had found it and now sat beneath its roof and waited. It had not been logical that he should find the top he had not remembered and finding it, know what to use it for. But he had found it and he had used it and was here.

He sat quietly, listening to the house.

There was a murmur of voices in the room that opened to the waiting room and he saw that the door which led into it was open for an inch or two.

There was no other sound. The house lay in morning quiet.

He got up from his chair and paced to the window and from the window back to the marble fireplace.

Who was in that other room? Why was he waiting? Who would he see when he walked through that door and what would they say to him?

He swung around the room, walking softly, almost sneaking. He stopped beside the door, standing with his back against the wall, holding his breath to listen.

The murmur of voices became words.

". . . going to be a shock."

A deep, gruff voice said, "It always is a shock. There's nothing you can do to take the shock away. No matter how you look at it, it always is degrading."

A slow, drawling voice said, "It's unfortunate we have to work it the way we do. It's too bad we can't let them go on in their legal bodies."

Businesslike, clipped, precise, another voice, the first voice said, "Most of the androids take it fairly well. Even knowing what it means, they take it fairly well. We make them understand. And, of course, out of the three, there's always the lucky one, the one that can go on in his actual body."

"I have a feeling," said the gruff voice, "that we started in on Vickers just a bit too soon."

"Flanders said we had to. He thinks Vickers is the only one that can handle Crawford."

And Flanders' voice saying, "I am sure he can. He was a late starter, but he was coming fast. We gave it to him hard. First the bug got careless and he caught it and that set him to thinking. Then, after that, we arranged the lynching threat. Then he found the top we planted and the association clicked. Give him just another jolt or two. . . ."

"How about that girl, Flanders? That—what's her name?"

"Ann Carter," Flanders said. "We've been jolting her a bit, but not as hard as Vickers."

"How will they take it?" asked the drawling voice. "When they find they're android?"

Vickers lurched away from the door, moving softly, groping with his hands, as if he were walking in the dark through a room peopled with obstructing furniture.

He reached the door that led into the hall and grasped the casing and hung on.

Used, he thought.

Not even human.

"Damn you, Flanders," he said.

Not only he, but Ann—not mutants, not superior beings at all, not any sort of humans. Androids!

He had to get away, he told himself. He had to get away and hide. He had to find a place where he could curl up and hide and lick his wounds and let his mind calm down and plan what he meant to do.

For he was going to do something. It wasn't going to stay this way. He'd deal himself a hand and cut in on the game.

He moved along the hall and reached the door and opened it a crack to see if anyone was there. The lawn was empty. There was no one in sight.

He went out the door and closed it gently behind him and when he hit the ground, jumping from the tiny porch, he was running. He leaped the fence and hit the ground, still running.

He didn't look back until he reached the trees. When he did, the house stood serenely, majestically, on its hilltop at the valley's head.

34

So he was an android, an artificial man, a body made of a handful of chemicals, shaped by the cunning of man's mind and the wizardry of man's technology—but the cunning and the wizardry of the mutant mind, for the ordinary, normal man who walked the parent Earth, the original Earth, had no such cunning, and no such wizardry. It was the mutants, and the mutants only, who could make an artificial man so well and cleverly that even he, himself, would never know for sure. And artificial women, too—like Ann Carter.

The mutants could make androids and robots and Forever cars and everlasting razor blades and a host of other gadgets, all designed to wreck the economy of the race from which they sprang. They had synthesized the carbohydrate as food and the protein to make the bodies of their androids, and they knew how to travel from one earth to another—all those earths that trod on one another's heels down the corridors of time. This much he knew they could do and were doing. What other things they might be doing, he had no idea. Nor no idea, either, of the things they dreamed or planned.

"You're a mutant," Crawford had told him, "an undeveloped mutant. You're one of them." For Crawford had an intelligent machine that could pry into the mind and tell its owner what was in the mind, but the machine was stupid in the last analysis, for it couldn't even tell a real man from a fake.

No mutant, but a mutant's errand boy. Not even a man, only an artificial copy.

How many others, he wondered, could there be like him? How many of his kind might roam the Earth, going about their appointed tasks for the mutant master? How many of his kind did Crawford's men trail and watch, not suspecting that they did not trail and watch the mutant, but a thing of mutant manufacture? That, thought Vickers, was the true measure of the difference between the normal man and mutant—that the normal man could mistake the mutant's scarecrow for the mutant.

The mutants made a man and turned him loose and watched him and allowed him to develop and set a spying mechanism that they called a bug to watch him, a little mechanical mouse that could be smashed with a paper weight.

And in the proper time they jolted him—they jolted him for what? They stirred up his fellow townsmen so he fled a lynching party; they planted for him to find a toy out of childhood and waited to see if the toy might not trip a childhood association; they fixed it so he would drive a Forever car when they knew that driving such a car could cause him to be mobbed.

And after they had jolted an android, what happened to him then?

What happened to the androids once they had been used for the purpose of their making?

He had told Crawford that when he knew what was going on, he'd talk to him again. And now he knew something of what was going on and Crawford might be very interested.

And something else as well—some tugging, nagging knowledge that seemed to bubble in his brain, trying to get out. Something that he knew, but could not remember.

He walked on through the woods, with its massive trees and its deep-laid forest mold and thick matting of old leaves, with its mosses and its flowers and its strange silence filled with uncaring and with comfort.

He had to find Ann Carter. He had to tell her what was going on and together, the two of them would somehow stand against it.

He halted beside the great oak tree and stared up at its leaves and tried to clear his mind, to wipe it clean of the chaos of his thinking so he could start fresh again.

There were two things that stood out above all others:

He had to get back to the parent Earth.

He had to find Ann Carter.

35

Vickers did not see the man until he spoke.

"Good morning, stranger," someone said, and Vickers wheeled around. The man was there, standing just a few feet away, a great, tall, strong man dressed much as a farm hand or a factory worker might be dressed, but with a jaunty, peaked cap set upon his head and a brilliant feather stuck into the cap.

Despite the rudeness of his clothing, there was nothing of the peasant about the man, but a cheerful self-sufficiency that reminded Vickers of someone he'd read about and he tried to think who it might be, but the comparison eluded him.

Across the man's shoulder was a strap that held a quiver full of arrows and in his hand he held a bow. Two young rabbits hung lifeless from his belt and their blood had smeared his trouser leg.

"Good morning," said Vickers, shortly.

He didn't like the idea of this man popping up from nowhere.

"You're another one of them," the man said.

"Another one of what?"

The man laughed gaily, "We get one of you every once in a while," he said. "Someone who has blundered through and doesn't know where he is. I've often wondered what happened to them before we were settled here or what happens to them when they pop through a long ways from any settlement."

"I don't know what you're talking about."

"Another thing you don't know," said the man, "is where you are."

"I have a theory," Vickers said. "This is a second earth."

The man chuckled. "You got it pegged pretty close," he said. "You're better than the most of them. They just flounder around and gasp and won't believe it when we tell them that this is Earth Number Two."

"That's neat," said Vickers. "Earth Number Two, is it? And what about Number Three?"

"It's there, waiting when we need it. Worlds without end, waiting when we need them. We can go on pioneering for generation after generation. A new earth for each new generation if need be, but they say we won't be needing them that fast."

"They?" challenged Vickers. "Who are they?"

"The mutants," said the man. "The local ones live in the Big House. You didn't see the Big House?"

Vickers shook his head, warily.

"You must have missed it, coming up the ridge. A big brick place with a white picket fence around it and other buildings that look like barns, but they aren't barns."

"Aren't they?"

"No," said the man. "They are laboratories and experimental buildings and there is one building that is fixed up for listening."

"Why do they have a place for listening? Seems to me you could listen almost anywhere. You and I can listen without having a special place fixed up for us."

"They listen to the stars," the man told him.

"They listen . . ." began Vickers, and then remembered Flanders sitting on the porch in Cliffwood, rocking in the chair and saying that great pools and reservoirs of knowledge existed in the stars, that it was there for the taking and you might not need rockets to go there and get it, but might reach out with your mind and that you'd have to sift and winnow, but you'd find much you could use.

"Telepathy?" asked Vickers.

"That's it," said the man. "They don't listen to the stars really, but to people who live on the stars. Now ain't that the screwiest thing you ever heard of—listening to the stars!"

"Yes, I guess it is," said Vickers.

"They get ideas from these people. They don't talk to them, I guess. They just listen in on them. They catch some of the things they're thinking and some of the things they know and a lot of it they can use and a lot of it don't make no sense at all. But it's the truth, so help me, mister."

"My name is Vickers. Jay Vickers."

"Well, I'm glad to know you, Mr. Vickers. My name is Asa Andrews."

He walked forward and held out his hand and Vickers took it and their grip was hard and sure.

And now he knew where he'd read of this man before. Here before him stood an American pioneer, the man who carried the long rifle from the colonies to the hunting grounds of Kentucky. Here was the stance, the independence, the quick good will and wit, the steady self reliance. Here, once again, in the forests of Earth Number Two, was another pioneer type, sturdy and independent and a good man for a friend.

"These mutants must be the people who are putting out the everlasting, razor and all that other stuff in the gadget shops," said Vickers.

"You catch on quick," said Andrews. "We'll go up to the Big House in a day or two and you can talk to them."

He shifted the bow from one hand to another. "Look, Vickers, did you leave someone back there? A wife and some kids, maybe?"

"No one," said Vickers. "Not a single soul."

"Well, that's all right. If you had, we'd gone up to the Big House right away and told them about it and they would have fixed it up to bring the wife and kids through, too. That's the only thing about this place. Once you get here, there's no going back. Although why anyone would want to go back is more than I can figure out. So far as. I know, there's no one who has wanted to."

He looked Vickers up and down, laughter tugging at his mouth.

"You look all gaunted down," he said. "You ain't been eating good."

"Just fish and some venison I found. And berries."

"The old lady will have the victuals on. We'll get some food into your belly and get those whiskers off and I'll have the kids heat up some water and you can take a bath, and then we can sit and talk. We got a lot to talk about."

He led the way, with Vickers following, down the ridge through the heavy timber.

They came out on the edge of a cleared field green with growing corn.

"That's my place down there," said Andrews. "Down there at the hollow's head. You can see the smoke."

"Nice field of corn you have," said Vickers.

"Knee high by the Fourth. And over there is Jake Smith's place. You can see the house if you look a little close. And just beyond the hogsback you can see John Simmon's fields. There are other neighbors, but you can't see from here."

They climbed the barbed wire fence and went across the field, walking between the corn rows.

"It's different here," said Andrews, "than back on Earth. I was working in a factory there and living in a place that was scarcely fit for hogs. Then the factory shut down and there was no money. I went to the carbohydrates people and they kept the family fed. Then the landlord threw us out and the carbohydrates people had been so friendly that I went to them and told them what had happened. I didn't know what they could do, of course. I guess I didn't really expect them to do anything, because they'd helped already more that there was any call to. But, you see, they were the only ones I knew of I could turn to. So I went to them and after a day or two one of them came around and told us about this place—except, of course, he didn't tell us what it really was. He just said he knew of a place that was looking for settlers. He said it was a brand new territory that was opening up and there was free land for the taking and help to get you on your feet and that I could make a living and have a house instead of a two by four apartment in a stinking tenement and I said that we would go. He warned me that if we went, we couldn't come back again and I asked him who in their right mind would want to. I said that no matter where it was, we would go, and here we are."

"You've never regretted it?" asked Vickers.

"It was the luckiest thing," said Andrews, "that ever happened to us. Fresh air for the kids and all you want to eat and a place to live with no landlord to throw you out. No dues to pay and no taxes to scrape up. Just like in the history books."

"The history books?"

"Sure, you know. Like when America was first discovered and the pioneers piled in. Land for the taking. Land to roll in. More land than anyone can use and rich, so rich you just scratch the ground a little and throw in some seed and you got a crop. Land to plant things in and wood to burn and build with and you can walk out at night and look up at the sky and the sky is full of stars and the air is so clean it seems to hurt your nose when you draw it in."

Andrews turned and looked at Vickers, his eyes blazing.

"It was the best thing that ever happened to me," he said, as if daring Vickers to contradict him.

"But these mutants," asked Vickers. "Don't they get into your hair? Don't they lord it over you?"

"They don't do anything but help us. They send us a robot to help out with the work when we need to have some help and they send a robot that lives with us nine months of the year to teach the kids. One robot teacher for each family. Now ain't that something. Your own private teacher, just like you went out and hired yourself a high-toned private tutor like the rich folks back on Earth."

"And you don't resent these mutants? You don't feel they are better than you are? You don't hate them because they know more than you do?"

"Mister," said Asa Andrews, "you don't want to let anyone around these parts hear you talking like that. They're apt to string you up. When we first came, they explained it all to us. They had indoct—indoctrin—"

"Indoctrination courses."

"That's it. They told us what the score was. They told us what the rules were and there aren't many rules."

"Like not having any firearms," said Vickers.

"That's one of them," Andrews admitted. "How did you know that?"

"You're hunting with a bow."

"Another one is that if you get into a row with anybody and can't settle it peaceable the two of you are to go up to the Big House and let them settle it. And if you get sick you're to let them know right away so they can send you a doctor and whatever else you need. Most of the rules work to your benefit."

"How about work?"

"Work?"

You have to earn some money, haven't you?"

"Not yet," said Andrews. "The mutants give us everything we want or need. All we do is work the land and grow the food. This is what they call . . . let me see now . . . what was that word—oh, yes, this is what they call the pastoral-feudal stage. You ever hear a word like that?"

"But they must have factories," Vickers persisted, ignoring the question. "Places where they make the razor blades and stuff. They'd need men to work in them."

"They use robots. Just lately they started making a car that would last forever. The plant is just a ways from here. But they use robots to do the entire job. You know what a robot is."

Vickers nodded. "There's another thing," he said. "I was wondering about natives."

"Natives?"

"Sure, the people on this earth. If there are people on this earth."

"There aren't any," Andrews said.

"But the rest of it is the same as the other Earth," said Vickers. "The trees, the rivers, the animals . . ."

"There aren't any natives," Andrews said. "No Indians or nothing."

So here, thought Vickers, was the difference from the Earth ahead, the tiny aberration that made a different world. Far back, somehow, there had been a difference that had blocked Man from rising, some minor incident, no doubt; some failing of the spark of intellect. Here there had been no striking of the flint for fire, no grasping of a stone that would become a weapon, no wonder glowing in the brutish brain—a wonder that in later years would become a song or painting or a single paragraph of exquisite writing or a flowing poem . . .

"We're almost home," said Andrews.

They climbed the fence that edged the cornfield and walked across a pasture toward the house.

Someone yelled a joyous greeting and a half dozen kids came running down the hill, followed by a dozen yelping dogs. A woman came to the door of the house, built of peeled logs, and peered toward them, holding her hand to shade her eyes against the sun. She waved to them and Andrews waved back and then the kids and dogs descended on them in a yelping, howling, happy pack.

36

He lay in bed, in the loft above the kitchen, and listened to the wind pattering on bare feet across the shingles just above his head. He turned and burrowed his head into the goose-down pillow and beneath him the corn shuck mattress rustled in the dark.

He was clean, washed clean in the tub behind the house, with water heated in a kettle on an outdoors fire, lathering himself with soap while Andrews sat on a nearby stump and talked and the children played in the yard and the hound dogs lay sleeping in the sun, twitching their hides to chase away the flies.

He had eaten, two full meals of food such as he had forgotten could exist after days of half-cooked fish and half-rotten venison—cornbread and sorghum and young rabbits fried in a smoking skillet, with creamed new potatoes and greens the children had gone out and gathered and a salad of water cress pulled from the spring below the house and for supper fresh eggs just taken from the nest.

He had shaved, with the children ringed around him watching, after Andrews had seated him on a stump and had used the scissors to trim away the beard.

And after that he and Andrews had sat on the steps and talked while the sun went down and Andrews had said that he knew of a place that was crying for a house—a tucked-in place just across the hill, with a spring a step or two away and some level ground on a bench above the creek where a man could lay out his fields. There was wood in plenty for the house, great tall trees and straight, and Andrews said that he would help him cut them. When the logs were ready the neighbors would come in for the raising and Jake would bring along some of the corn that he'd been cooking and Ben would bring his fiddle and they'd have themselves a hoedown when the house was up. If they needed help beyond what the neighbors could supply, all they'd have to do was send word up to the Big House and the mutants would send a gang of robots. But that probably wouldn't be necessary, Andrews had said. The neighbors were a willing lot, he said; and always ready to help; glad, too, to see another family moving in.

Once the house was built, said Andrews, Simmons had some daughters running around his place that Vickers might want to have a look at, although you could do your picking blind if you wanted to, for they were a likely lot. Andrews had dug Vickers in the ribs with his elbow and had laughed uproariously and Jean, Andrews' wife, who had come out to sit with them a while, had smiled shyly at him and then had turned to watch the children playing in the yard.

After supper, Andrews had showed him with some pride the books on the shelf in the living room and had said that he was reading them, something he had never done before—something he had never wanted to do before, nor had the time to do. Vickers, looking at the books, had found Homer and Shakespeare, Montaigne and Austen, Thoreau and Steinbeck.

"You mean you're reading these?" he asked.

Andrews had nodded. "Reading them and liking them, mostly. Once in a while I find it a little hard to wade through them, but I keep reading on. Jean likes Austen best."

It was a good life here, said Andrews, the best life they'd ever known and Jean smiled her agreement and the kids had lost an argument about letting the dogs come in and sleep the night with them.

It *was* a good life, Vickers silently agreed. Here again was the old American frontier, idealized and bookish, with all the frontier's advantages and none of its terror and its hardship. Here was a paternal feudalism, with the Big House on the hill the castle that looked down across the fields where happy people lived and took their living from the soil. Here was a time for resting and for gathering strength. And here was peace. Here there was no talk of war, no taxes to fight a war, or to prevent a war by a proved willingness to fight.

Here was—what had Andrews said?—the pastoral-feudal stage. And after that came what stage? The Pastoral-feudal stage for resting and thinking, for getting thoughts in order, for establishing once again the common touch between Man and soil, the stage in which was prepared the way for the development of a culture that would be better than the one they had left.

This was one earth of many earths. How many others followed close behind: hundreds, millions? Earth following earth, and now all the earths lay open.

He tried to figure it out and he thought he saw the pattern that the mutants planned. It was simple and it was brutal, but it was workable.

There was an Earth that was a failure. Somewhere, on the long path that led up from apedom, they had taken the wrong turning and had travelled since that day a long road of misery. There was brilliance in these people, and goodness, and ability—but they had turned their brilliance and their ability into channels of hate and arrogance and their goodness had been buried in selfishness.

They were good people and were worth the saving, as a drunkard or a criminal is worthy of rehabilitation. But to save them, you must get them out of the neighborhood they live in, out of the slums of human thought and method. There could be no other way of giving them the opportunity to break themselves of old habits, of the ingrown habits of generation after generation of hate and greed and killing.

To do this, you must break the world they live in and you must have a plan to break it and after it is broken, you must have a program that leads to a better world.

But first of all, there must be a plan of action.

First you shattered the economic system on which old Earth was built. You shattered it with Forever cars and everlasting razor blades and with synthetic carbohydrates that would feed the hungry. You destroyed industry by producing, once and for all, things that industry could not duplicate and things that made industry obsolete and when you shattered industry to a certain point, war was impossible and half the job was done. But that left people without jobs, so you fed them with carbohydrates while you tried to funnel them to the following earths that lay waiting for them. If there wasn't room enough on Earth Number Two, you sent some of them to Number Three and maybe Number Four, so that you had no crowding, so there was room enough for all. On the new earths there was a beginning again, a chance to dodge the errors and skirt the dangers that had bathed Old Earth in blood for countless centuries.

On these new earths you could build any sort of culture that you wished. You could even experiment a little, aim at one culture on the Second Earth and a slightly different one on Number Three and yet a different one on Four. And after a thousand years or so you could compare these cultures and see which one was best and consult the bales of data you had kept and pinpoint each mistake in each particular culture. In time you could arrive at a formula for the best in human cultures.

Here on this earth, the pastoral-feudal culture was the first step only. It was a resting place, a place for education and for settling down. Things would change or be changed. The son of the man in whose house he lay would build a better house and probably would have robots to work his fields and make his living, while he himself would live a leisured life and out of a leisured people, with their energies channeled by good leadership, would come paradise on earth—or on many earths.

There had been that article in the paper he had read on that morning—was it only days ago?—which had said that the authorities were alarmed at mass disappearances. Whole families, the article had said, were dropping out of sight for no apparent reason and with no apparent thing in common except abject poverty. And, of course, it would be the ones in abject poverty who would be taken first—the homeless and the jobless and the sick—to be settled on these earths that followed in the track of the dark and bloody Earth inhabited by Man.

Soon there would be little more than a handful of people on the dark and bloody Earth. Soon, in a thousand years or less, it would go tumbling on its way alone, its hide cleansed of the ravening tribe which had eaten at it and gutted it and mangled it and ravished it—and this same tribe would be established on other earths, under better guidance, to create for themselves a life that would be a better life.

Beautiful, he thought. Beautiful—and yet, there was this matter of the androids.

Begin at the beginning, he told himself. Start with first facts, try to see the logic of it, to figure out the course of mutancy.

There always had been mutants. If there had not been, Man would still be a little skittering creature hiding in the jungle, taking to the trees, terrified and skulking.

There had been the mutation of the opposable thumb. There had been mutations within the little brain that made for creature cunning. Some mutation, unrecorded, had captured fire and tamed it. Another mutation had evolved the wheel. Still another had invented the bow and arrow. And so it went, on down the ages. Mutation on mutation, building the ladder that mankind climbed.

Except that the creature who had captured and tamed the flame did not know he was a mutant. And neither had the tribesman who had thought up the wheel, nor the first bowman.

Down through the ages there had been unsuspected and unsuspecting mutants—men who were Successful beyond the success of others, great business figures or great statesmen, great writers, great artists, men who stood so far above the herd of their fellow men that they had seemed giants in comparison.

Perhaps not all of them were mutants, though most of them must have been. But their mutancy would have been a crippled thing in comparison with what it could have been, for they were forced to limit themselves, forced to conform to the social and economic pattern set by a nonmutant society. That they had been able to conform, that they had been able to fit themselves to a smaller measure than their normal stature, that they had been able to get along with men who were less than they and still stand out as men of towering ability was in itself a measure of their mutancy.

Although their success had been large in the terms of normal men, their mutancy had been a failure in that it never reached its full realization and this was because these men had never known what they were. They had been just a little smarter or a little handier or somewhat quicker than the common run of mankind.

But suppose that a man should realize that he was a mutant? Suppose that he knew from a piece of indisputable evidence—what would happen then?

Suppose, for example, a man should find that he could reach out to the stars and that he could catch the thoughts and plans of the thinking creatures who lived on planets circling those far suns—that would be full and sufficient proof that he was a mutant. And if he could obtain from his seeking in the stars some specific information of certain economic value—say, the principle of a frictionless machine—then without question he would know that he had a mutant gift. Once knowing, he would not be able to fit so snugly, nor so smugly, into his contemporary niche as those men who had been mutants but had never known they were. Knowing, he would have the itch of greatness, would know the necessity of following his own path and not the beaten path.

He might be slightly terrified by the things he learned winnowing the stars and he might be terribly lonesome and he might see the necessity of humans other than him alone working on the information that he was dredging from the depths of space.

So he would seek for other mutants and he would do it cleverly and it might take him a long time before he found one of them and he would have to approach the other cautiously and win his confidence and finally tell him what he had in mind. Then there'd be two mutants, banded together, and in the course of years they would seek and find other mutants. Not all of them, of course, would be able to send their minds out to the stars, but they would be able to do other things. Some of them would understand electronics, almost as if by instinct, more completely than any normal man, even with years of intensive training, and another one of them might sense the strange alignment of time and space that allowed for other worlds than one, following on each other's heels in a magnificent, eternal ring.

Some would be women and to the mutants-found would be added mutants-born and in twenty years or so there would be a mutant organization of, say, several hundred persons, pooling their talents.

From the information they gathered from the stars, plus the mutant abilities of certain others of them, they would invent and market certain gadgets that would bring in the necessary money for them to continue with their work. How many of the now common, workaday, almost prosaic gadgets used in the world today, Vickers wondered, were the products of this mutant race?

But the time would come when the mutant organization and the work they did would become too prominent to pass unnoticed and they would seek a place to hide—a safe place where they could continue the work that they were doing. And what safer place could there be than one of the other earths?

Vickers lay on the corn shuck mattress and stared into the darkness and wondered at the glibness of his imagination, with the nagging feeling that it was not imagination—that it was something that he knew. But how could he know it?

Conditioning, perhaps, of his android mind. Or an actual knowledge gained in some period of his life that had been blotted out, as the time he had gone into fairyland at the age of eight had been blotted out—a knowledge that now was coming back again, as the remembrance of the visit to fairyland had come back again.

Or ancestral memory, perhaps, actual specific memory passed to child from parent as instinct was passed—but the catch was that, as an android, he didn't have a parent.

He was parentless and raceless and a mockery of a man, created for a purpose he did not even know.

What purpose could the mutants have for him? What talent did he possess that made him useful to them? What would they use him for?

That was the thing that hurt—that he should be *used* and not know, that Ann should have some purpose she did not even guess.

The work of the mutants was greater than the mere gadgetry they would like it to appear, something greater than Forever cars and everlasting razor blades and synthetic carbohydrates. Their work was the rescue and the re-establishment of the race—the starting over again of a badly muddled race. It was the development of a world or worlds where war would not be merely outlawed, but impossible, where fear would never raise its head, where progress would have a different value than it had in mankind's world today.

And into a program of this sort, where did Jay Vickers fit?

In this house in which he lay there was a new beginning and it was a crude beginning, but a solid one. In another two or three generations the people of this family would be ready for the gadgets and the progress that was due them, and when they were ready the progress would be waiting for them.

The mutants would take from the human race the deadly playthings and keep them in trust until the child of Man was old enough to use them without hurting himself or injuring his neighbor. They would take from the three-year-old the twelve-year-old toy he was using dangerously and when he was twelve years old would give it back again, probably with refinements.

And the culture of the future, under mutant guidance, would be not merely a mechanistic culture, but a social and an economic and an artistic and spiritual culture as well as mechanical. The mutants would take lopsided Man and mold him into balance and the years that were lost in the remolding would pay interest in humanity in the years to come.

But that was speculation, that was day-dreaming, that was getting nothing done. The thing that counted now was what he, Jay Vickers, android, meant to do about it.

Before he could do anything, he'd have to know more of what was happening, would have to get some solid fact. He needed information and he couldn't get it here, lying on a corn shuck mattress in the loft above the kitchen of a neo-pioneer home.

There was only one place where he could get that information.

He slid noiselessly out of bed and fumbled in the dark to find his ragged clothes.

37

The house was dark, sleeping in the moonlight, with the tall shadows of the trees cast against its front. He stood in the shadow just outside the front gate and looked at it, remembering how he had seen it in the moonlight once before, when a road ran past the gate, but now there was no road. He recalled how the moonlight had fallen on the whiteness of the pillars and had turned them to ghostly beauty and of the words the two of them had said as they stood and watched the moonlight shattered on the pillars.

But that was dead and done, that was gone and buried and all that was left was the bitterness of knowing that he was not a man, but the imitation of a man.

He opened the gate and went up the walk and climbed the steps that led to the porch. He crossed the porch and his footsteps rang so loudly in the stillness of the moonlight that he felt certain those in the house would hear him.

He found the bell and put his thumb upon it and pressed, then stood waiting, as he had waited once before. But this time there would be no Kathleen to come to the door to greet him.

He waited and a light sprang into life in the central hall and through the glass he saw a man-like figure fumbling at the door.

The door came open and he stepped inside and the gleaming robot bowed a little stiffly and said, "Good evening, sir."

"Hezekiah, I presume," said Vickers.

"Hezekiah, sir," the robot confirmed. "You met me this morning."

"I went for a walk," said Vickers.

"And now perhaps, I could show you to your room." The robot turned and went up the winding staircase, with Vickers following him.

"It's a nice night, sir," the robot said.

"Very nice."

"You have eaten, sir?"

"Yes, thank you."

"I could bring you up a snack, if you haven't eaten," Hezekiah offered. "I believe there is some chicken left."

"No," said Vickers. "Thank you just the same."

Hezekiah shoved open a door and turned on a light, then stepped aside for Vickers to go in.

"Perhaps," said Hezekiah, "you would like a nightcap."

"That's a good idea, Hezekiah. Scotch, if you have it handy."

"In just a moment, sir. You will find some pajamas in the third drawer from the top. They may be a little large, but probably you can manage."

He found the pajamas and they were fairly new and very loud and they seemed quite a bit too big, but they were better than nothing.

The room was pleasant, with a huge bed covered by a white, stitched counterpane and the white curtains at the windows blew in on the nighttime breeze.

He sat down in a chair to wait for Hezekiah and the drink and for the first time in many days he knew how tired he was. He'd have the drink and climb into bed and when morning came he'd go stomping down the stairs, looking for a showdown.

The door opened.

It wasn't Hezekiah; it was Horton Flanders, in a crimson dressing robe fastened tight about his neck and slippers on his feet that slapped against the floor as he crossed the room.

He crossed the room and sat down in another chair and looked at Vickers, with a half smile on his face.

"So you came back," he said.

"I came back to listen," Vickers told him. "You can start talking right away."

"Why, certainly," said Flanders. "That's why I got up. As soon as Hezekiah told me you had arrived, I knew you'd want to talk."

"I don't want to talk. I want you to talk."

"Oh, yes, Certainly. I am the one to talk."

"And not about the reservoirs of knowledge, of which you talk most beautifully. But certain practical, rather mundane things."

"Like what?"

"Like why I am an android and why Ann Carter is an android. And whether there ever was a person named Kathleen Preston or is that just a story that was conditioned in my mind? And if there ever was a person named Kathleen Preston, where is she now? And, finally, where do I fit in and what do you intend to do?"

Flanders nodded his head. "A very admirable set of questions. You *would* pick the very ones I can't answer to your satisfaction."

Vickers said: "I came to tell you that the mutants are being hunted down and killed on that other world, that the gadget shops are being wrecked and burned, that the normal humans are finally fighting back. I came to warn you because I thought I was a mutant, too . . ."

"You are a mutant, I can assure you, Vickers, a very special kind of mutant."

"A mutant android."

"You are difficult," said Flanders. "You let your bitterness—"

"Of course I'm bitter," Vickers cut in. "Who wouldn't be? For forty years I think I am a man and now I find I'm not."

"You fool," said Horton Flanders, sadly, "you don't know what you are."

Hezekiah rapped on the door and came in with a tray. He set the tray on a table and Vickers saw that there were two glasses and some mix and an ice bucket and a fifth of liquor.

"Now," said Flanders, more happily, "perhaps we can talk some sense. I don't know what it is about the stuff, but put a drink into a man's hand and you tend to civilize him."

He reached into the pocket of his robe, brought out a pack of cigarettes and passed them to Vickers. Vickers took the pack and saw that his hand was shaking a little as he pulled out a smoke. He hadn't realized until then just how tense he was.

Flanders snapped the lighter and held out the flame. Vickers got his light.

"That's good," he said. "I ran out of smokes after the fourth day."

He sat in the chair, smoking, thinking how good the tobacco tasted, feeling the satisfaction run along his nerves. He watched Hezekiah busy with the drinks.

"I eavesdropped this morning," Vickers said. "I came here this morning and Hezekiah let me in. I eavesdropped when you and some others were talking in the room."

"I know you did," said Flanders.

"How much of that was staged?"

"All of it," said Flanders, blithely. "Every blessed word of it."

"You *wanted* me to know I was an android."

"We wanted you to know."

"You set the mouse on me?"

"We had to do something to shake you out of your humdrum life," said Flanders. "And the mouse served a special purpose."

"It tattled on me."

"Oh, exceedingly well. The mouse was a most efficient tattler."

"The thing that really burns me," Vickers said, "is that business about making Cliffwood think I had done you in."

"We had to get you out of there and headed back to your child-hood haunts."

"How did you know I'd go to my childhood haunts?"

Flanders said: "My friend, have you ever thought about the ability of hunch. I don't mean the feeble hunch that is used on the racetrack to pick a winner or the hunch about whether it is going to rain or not, or whether some other minor happening is going to take place . . . but the ability in the fullness of its concept. You might say it is the instinctive ability to assess the result of a given number of factors, to know, without actually thinking the matter out, what is about to happen. It's almost like being able to peek into the future."

"Yes," said Vickers, "I have thought about it. A good deal in the last few days, as a matter of fact."

"You have speculated on it?"

"To some extent. But what has . . ."

"Perhaps," said Flanders, "you have speculated that it might be a human ability that we never developed, that we scarcely knew was there and so never bothered with, or that it might be one of those abilities that it takes a long time to develop, a sort of an ace-in-the-hole ability for mankind's use when he was ready for it or might have need of it."

"I did think that, or at least some of it, but . . ."

"Now's the time we need it." Flanders interrupted again. "And that answers the question that you asked. We hunched you would go back."

"At first I thought Crawford was the one, but he said he wasn't."

Flanders shook his head. "Crawford wouldn't have done it. He needs you too badly. Crawford wouldn't scare you off. Your hunch on that one wasn't working too hot."

"No, I guess it wasn't."

"Your hunches don't work," said Flanders, "because you don't give them a chance. You still have the world of reason to contend with. You put your reliance on the old machine-like reasoning that the human race has relied on since it left the caves. You figure out every angle and you balance it against every other angle and you add up and cancel out as if you were doing a problem in arithmetic. You never give hunch a chance. That's the trouble with you."

And that *was* the trouble, Vickers thought. He'd had a hunch to spin the top on the porch of the Preston house and if he had done that he'd saved himself days of walking through the wilderness of this second world. He'd had a hunch that he should have paid attention to Crawford's note and not driven the Forever car and if he'd done that he'd saved himself a lot of trouble. And there had been the hunch, which he had finally obeyed, that he must get back the top—and that one had paid off.

"How much do you know?" asked Flanders.

Vickers shook his head. "I don't really know anything much," he admitted. "I know there's a mutant organization. One that must have started years ago, one that had something to do with kicking the human race out of the rut you talked about that night back in Cliffwood. And the organization has gone underground, back here on the other worlds, because its operations were getting too widespread and too significant to escape attention. You've got factories working, turning out the mutant gadgets you're using to wreck the industry of the old world. I saw one of those. Run by robots. Tell me, do the robots run it or . . ."

Flanders chuckled. "The robots run it. We just tell them what we want."

"Then there's this business of listening to the stars."

"We've gotten many good ideas that way," said Flanders. "Not all of us can do it. Just some of us, who are natural telepaths. And as I told you that night we talked, not all the ideas are ones that we can use. Sometimes we just get a hint of something and we go on from there."

"And where are you headed? Where do you intend to go?"

"That's one that I can't answer. There are so many new possibilities being added all the time, so many new directions opening out. We're close to many great discoveries. For one thing, immortality. There is one listener . . ."

"You mean," asked Vickers, "everlasting life?"

"Why not?"

Of course, thought Vickers, why not? If you had everlasting razor blades and everlasting light bulbs, why not everlasting life? Why not shoot the works?

"And androids?" he asked. "Where would an android like myself fit in? Surely, an android can't be too important."

"We have a job for you," said Flanders. "Crawford is your job."

"What do I do with Crawford?"

"You stop him."

Vickers laughed. "Me? You know what's back of Crawford?"

"I know what's back of you."

"Tell me," Vickers said.

"Hunch—the highest, most developed hunch ability that ever has been registered in a human being. The highest ever registered and the most unsuspected, the least used of any we have ever known."

"Wait a minute. You're forgetting that I'm not a human being."

"Once you were," said Flanders. "You will be again. Before we took your life."

"Took my life!"

"The life essence," said Flanders, "the mind, the thoughts and impressions and reactions that made up Jay Vickers—the real Jay Vickers—aged eighteen. Like pouring water from one vessel to another. We poured you from your body into an android body and we've kept and guarded your body against the day we can pour it back again."

Vickers came half out of his chair.

Flanders waved a hand at him. "Sit down. You were going to ask me why."

"And you're going to answer me," said Vickers.

"Certainly I will answer you. When you were eighteen you were not aware of the ability you had. There was no way to make you aware of it. It would have done no good to tell you or to attempt to train you, for you had to grow into it. We figured it would take fifteen years and it took more than twenty and you aren't even yet as aware as you should be."

"But I could have . . ."

"Yes," said Flanders, "you could have grown aware of it in your own body, except that there is another factor—inherent memory. Your genes carry the inherent memory factor, another mutation that occurs as infrequently as our telepathic listeners. Before Jay Vickers started fathering children we wanted him to be entirely aware of his hunch ability."

Vickers remembered how he had speculated on the possibility of inherent memory, lying on the corn shuck mattress in the loft of Andrew's house. Inherent memory, memory passed on from father to son. His father had known about inherent memory, so he had guessed it, too. He had known about it, or at least he'd remembered it when the time had come for him to know about it, when he was growing—he groped for the word—aware.

"So that is it," said Vickers. "You want me to put the hunch on Crawford and you want to have my children because they will have hunch, too."

Flanders nodded. "I think we understand one another now."

"Yes," said Vickers. "I am sure we do. First of all, you want me to stop Crawford. That is quite an order. What if I put a price on it?"

"We have a price," said Flanders. "A most attractive price. I think it will interest you."

"Try me."

"You asked about Kathleen Preston. You asked if there were such a person and I can tell that there is. How old were you when you knew her, by the way?"

"Eighteen."

Flanders nodded idly. "A very fine age to be." He looked at Vickers. "Don't you agree?"

"It seemed so then."

"You were in love with her," said Flanders.

"I was in love with her."

"And she in love with you."

"I think so," Vickers said. "I can't be sure—thinking of it now, I can't be sure, of course. But I think she was."

"You may be assured that she was in love with you."

"You will tell me where she is?"

"No," said Flanders. "I won't."

"But, you . . ."

"When your job is done, you'll go back to eighteen again."

"And that's the price," said Vickers. "That's the pay I get. To be given back a body that was mine to start with. To be eighteen again."

"It is attractive to you?"

"Yes, I guess so," Vickers said. "But don't you see, Flanders. The dream of eighteen is gone. It has been killed in a forty-year-old android body. It's not just the physical eighteen—it's something else than that. It's the years ahead and the promise of those years and the wild, impractical dreaming of those years and the love that walks beside you in the spring of life."

"Eighteen," said Flanders. "Eighteen and a good chance at immortality and Kathleen Preston, herself seventeen again."

"Kathleen?"

Flanders nodded.

"Just like it was before," said Vickers. "But it won't be the same, Flanders. There is something wrong. Something that has slipped away."

"Just like it was before," insisted Flanders. "As if all these years had never been."

38

So he was a mutant, after all, in the guise of android, and once he had stopped Crawford, he'd be an eighteen-year-old mutant in love with a seventeen-year-old mutant and there was just a possibility that before they died the listener might pin down immortality. And if that were so, then he and Kathleen would walk enchanted valleys forever and forever and they'd have mutant children who would have terrific hunch and all of them would live a life such as the old pagan gods of Earth would look upon with envy.

He threw back the covers and got out of bed and walked to the window. Standing there, he looked down the moonlit enchanted valley where he'd walked that day of long ago and he saw that the valley was an empty place and would stay empty no matter what he did.

He had carried the dream for more than twenty years and now that the dream was coming true, he saw that it was tarnished with all the time between, that there was no going back to that day in 1966, that a man never can go back to a thing he once has left.

You could not wipe out the years of living, you could not pile them neatly in a corner and walk away and leave them. They could be wiped from out your mind and they would be forgotten, but not forever, and the day would come when they'd break through again.

And once they'd found you out you'd know that you had lived not one lie, but two.

That was the trouble, you couldn't hide away the past.

The door creaked open and Vickers turned around.

Hezekiah stood in the doorway, the dim light from the landing sparkling on his metal-plastics hide.

"You cannot sleep?" asked Hezekiah. "Perhaps there's something I can do. A sleeping powder, perhaps, or . . ."

"There's something you can do," said Vickers. "There's a record that I want to see."

"A record, sir?"

"Yes, a record. My family record. You must have it here somewhere."

"In the files, sir. I can get it right away. If you will only wait."

"And the Preston file as well," added Vickers. "The Preston family record."

"Yes, sir," said Hezekiah. "It will take a moment."

Vickers turned on the light beside the bed and sat down on the edge of the bed and he knew what he had to do.

The enchanted valley was an empty place. The moonlight shattering on the whiteness of the pillar was a memory without life or color. The rose-scent upon the long-gone night of June had blown away with the wind of yesteryear.

Ann, he said to himself. I've been a fool too long about Ann. "What about it, Ann?" he spoke, half-aloud. "We've bantered and quarreled and we've used the bantering and the quarreling to cover the love that both of us have held and if it hadn't been for me and my dreaming of a valley, the dream growing cold and my never knowing it, we would have known long ago the way it was with us."

They took from us, he thought, the two of us, the birthright that was ours of living out our life in the body in which we first knew the world. They've made of us neither man nor woman, but something that passes for a man and woman and we walk through the streets of life like shadows flickering down the wall. And now they would take from us the dignity of death and the knowing that our task was done and they make us live a lie—I an android powered by the life force of a man that is not myself, and you alive with a life that is not your own.

"To hell with them," he said. "To hell with all this double living, with this being a manufactured being."

He'd go back to that other Earth and find Ann Carter and he'd tell her that he loved her, not as one loved a moonlight-and-roses memory, but as a man and woman love when the flush of youth is gone and together they would live out what was left to them of life and he would write his books and she would go on with her work and they'd forget, as best they could, this matter of the mutants.

He listened to the house, the little murmurings of a house at night, unnoticed in the daytime when it is filled with human sound. And he thought, if you listened closely and if you knew the tongue, the house would tell you the tales that you wished to know, could tell you the look upon the face and the way a word was spoken and what a man might do or think when he was alone.

The record would not tell the tale that he wished to know, not all the truth that he hoped to find, but it would tell him who he'd been and something about that tattered farmer and his wife who had been his father and his mother.

The door opened and Hezekiah pattered in, with a folder tucked beneath his arm. He handed the folder to Vickers and stood to one side, waiting.

Vickers opened the folder with trembling fingers and it was there upon the page.

Vickers, Jay, b. Aug. 5, 1947, l.t. June 20, 1966, h.a., t., i.m., lat.

He studied the line and it made no sense.

"Hezekiah."

"Yes, sir."

"What does all this mean?"

"To what do you refer, sir?"

"This line here," said Vickers, pointing. "This l.t. business and the rest of it."

Hezekiah bent and read it:

"Jay Vickers, born August 5, 1947, life transferred June 20, 1966, hunch ability, time sense, inherent memory, latent mutation. Meaning, sir, that you are unaware."

Vickers glanced at the line above and there he found the names, the place on the bracketed lines that indicated marriage, from which the line bearing his own name sprouted.

Charles Vickers, b. Jan. 10, 1917, cont. Aug. 8, 1938, aw., t., el., i.m., s.a. Feb. 6, 1971.

And:

Sarah Graham, b. Apr. 16, 1920, cont. Sept. 12, 1937, aw., ind. comm., t., i.m., s.a. Mar. 9, 1970.

His parents. Two paragraphs of symbols. He tried to make it out.

"Charles Vickers, born January 10, 1917, continued, no, that wouldn't be right . . ."

"Contacted, sir," said Hezekiah.

"Contacted August 8, 1938, aware, t., el., what's that?"

"Time sense and electronics, sir," said Hezekiah.

"Time sense?"

"Time sense, sir. The other worlds. They are a matter of time, you know."

"No, I didn't," Vickers said.

"There is no time," said Hezekiah. "Not as the normal human thinks of time, that is. Not a continuous flow of time, but brackets of time, one second following behind the other. Although there are no seconds, no such things as seconds, no such measurement, of course."

"I know," said Vickers. And he did know. Now it all came back to him, the explanation of those other worlds, the following worlds, each one encapsulated in a moment of time, in some strange and arbitrary division of time, each time bracket with its own world, how far back, how far ahead, no one could know or guess.

Somewhere inside of him the secret trigger had been tripped and the inherent memory was his, as it always had been his, but hidden in his unawareness, as his hunch ability still was largely trapped in his unawareness.

There was no time, Hezekiah had said. No such thing as time in the terms of normal human thought. Time was bracketed and each of its brackets contained a single phase of a universe so vastly beyond human comprehension that it brought a man up short against the impossibility of envisioning it.

And time itself? Time was a never-ending medium that stretched into the future and the past—except there was no future and no past, but an infinite number of brackets, extending either way, each bracket enclosing its single phase of the Universe.

Back on Man's original Earth, there had been speculation on traveling in time, of going back into yesterday or forward into tomorrow. And now he knew that you could not do it, that the same instant of time remained forever within each bracket, that Man's Earth had ridden the same bubble of the single instant from the time of its genesis and that it would die and come to nothing within that self-same instant.

You could travel in time, of course, but there would be no yesterday and no tomorrow. But if you held a certain time sense you could break from one bracket to another, and when you did you would not find yesterday or tomorrow, but another world.

And that was what he had done when he had spun the top, except, of course, that the top had had nothing to do with it—had simply been an aid.

He went on with line.

"*S.a.* What is s.a., Hezekiah?"

"Suspended animation, sir."

"My father and my mother?"

"In suspended animation, sir. Waiting for the day when the mutants finally achieve immortality."

"But they died, Hezekiah. Their bodies . . ."

"Android bodies, sir. We must keep the records straight. Otherwise the normal ones would suspect."

The room was bright and cold and naked with the monstrous nakedness of truth.

Suspended animation. His mother and his father waited, in suspended animation, for the day they could have immortality!

And he, Jay Vickers, the real Jay Vickers, what of him? Not suspended animation, certainly, for the life was gone from the real Jay Vickers and was in this android body that sat in this room holding the family record in two android hands.

"Kathleen Preston?" Vickers asked.

Hezekiah shook his head. "I do not know about Kathleen Preston," he said.

"But you got the Preston family record."

Hezekiah shook his head again. "There is no Preston record! I searched the cross-index, sir. There is no Preston mentioned. No Preston anywhere."

39

He had made a decision and now the decision was no good—made no good by the memory of two faces. He closed his eyes and remembered his mother, remembered every feature, a little idealized, perhaps, but mainly true, and he recalled how she had been horrified by his adventure into fairyland and how Pa talked to him and how the top had disappeared.

Of course the top had disappeared. Of course he had been lectured about too much imagination. After all, they probably had a hard enough time keeping an eye on him and knowing where he was without his wandering into other worlds. An eight-year-old would be hard enough to keep track of on one world, let alone a hundred.

The memory of his mother's face and of his father's hand upon his shoulder, with the fingers of the hand digging into his flesh with a manly tenderness—these were things a man could not turn his back upon.

In utter faith they waited, knowing that when the blackness came upon them it would not be the end, but the beginning of an even greater adventure in living than they had even hoped when they banded themselves with the little group of mutants so many years before.

If they held such faith in the mutant plan, could his be any less?

Could he refuse to do his part toward the establishment of that world for which they had done so much?

They themselves had given what they could; the labor they had expended, the faith they had lavished must now be brought to realization by the ones they had left behind. And he was one of those—and he knew he could not fail them.

What kind of world, he wondered.

Suppose the mutant listeners finally were able to track down the secret of immortality, what kind of world would you have then?

Suppose it really came to pass that Man never need to die, but could live forever and forever?

It would not be the same world then. It would be a different world, with different values and incentives.

What factors would be necessary to make an immortal world keep going? What incentives and conditions to keep it from running down? What opportunity and interest, continually expanding, to save it from the dead-end street of boredom?

What would you need in an immortal world?

Endless economic living room, for one thing; and there would be endless economic living room. For now all the following and preceding worlds lay open. And if that were not enough, there would be the universe, with all its suns and solar systems, for if one earth of a single planet had following and preceding earths, then so must every star and planet in the entire universe be repeated endlessly.

Take the universe and multiply it by an unknown number—take all the worlds there were in all the universe and multiply them by infinity and you would have the answer. There would be room enough, room enough forever.

You would need endless opportunity and endless challenge and in those worlds would lie opportunity and challenge that even eternal Man could not exhaust.

But that would not be the end of it: there would be endless time as well as endless space, and in that time would arise new techniques and new sciences, new philosophies, so that eternal Man need never lack for tasks to do or thoughts to think.

And, once you had immortality, what did you use it for?

You used it to keep up your strength. Even if your tribe were small, even if the birthrate were not large, even if new members of the tribe were discovered but infrequently, you still would be sure of growth, if no one ever died.

You used it to conserve ability and knowledge. If no one ever died, you could count on the ultimate strength and knowledge and ability of each member of the tribe. When a man died, his ability died with him, and to some extent, his knowledge. But it wasn't only that. You lost, not only his present ability and knowledge, but all his future ability and knowledge.

What knowledge, Vickers wondered, did the Earth now lack because a certain man died a dozen years too soon? Some of the knowledge, of course, would be recovered through the later work of other men, but certainly there was much that could never be recovered, ideas that would not be dreamed again, concepts that were blotted out forever by the death of a man within whose brain the first faint stirring of their development had just begun to ferment.

Within an immortal society, such a thing could never happen. An immortal society would be certain of total ability and total knowledge of its manpower.

Take the ability to tap the knowledge of the stars, take the business of inherent memory, take the technical knowledge that made everlasting merchandise—and add immortality.

That was the formula—of what? Of the ultimate in life? Of the pinnacle of intellect? Of godhood itself?

Go back a hundred thousand years. Consider the creature, Man. Give him fire, the wheel, the bow and arrow, domesticated animals and plants, plus tribal organization and the first, faint dawning concept of Man as the lord of Earth. Take that formula and what did you have?

The beginning of civilization, the foundation of a human culture. That was what you had.

And in its way the formula of fire and wheel and domestic animals was as great as the formula of immortality and time sense and inherent memory.

The formula of the mutants, he knew, was simply another step upward as the fire-wheel-dog formula of a hundred thousand years before had been an earlier forward step.

The mutant formula was not the end result of human effort nor of human intellect and knowledge; it was but a step. There was yet another step. In the future there was still another step. Within the human mind still dwelled the possibility of even greater steps, but what the concepts of those steps might be was as inconceivable to him, Jay Vickers, as the time structure of the following worlds would have been to the man who discovered fire or tamed the dog.

We still are savages, he thought. We still crouch within our cave, staring out beyond the smoky fire that guards the entrance of our cave against the illimitable darkness that lies upon the world.

Some day we'll plumb that darkness, but not yet.

Immortality would be a tool that might help us, and that is all it is. A simple, ordinary tool.

What was the darkness out beyond the cave's mouth?

Man's ignorance of what he was or why he was or how he came to be and what his purpose and his end. The old, eternal questions.

Perhaps with the tool of immortality Man could track down these questions, could gain an understanding of the orderly progression and the terrible logic which fashioned and moved the universe of matter and of energy.

The next step might be a spiritual one, the finding and understanding of a divine pattern that was law unto the entire universe. Might Man find at last, in all humility, a universal God—the Deity that men now worshipped with the faintness of human understanding and the strength of human faith? Would Man find at last the concept of divinity that would fill, without question and without quibble, Man's terrible need of faith, so clear and unmistakable that there could be no question and no doubt, as there now was question and doubt; a concept of goodness and of love with which Man could so identify himself that there would then be no need of faith, but faith replaced with knowing and an everlasting sureness?

And if Man outlawed death, he thought, if the doorway of death were closed against the final revelation and the resurrection, then surely Man must find such a concept or wander forever amid the galaxies a lost and crying thing. . . .

With an effort, Vickers brought his thoughts back to the present.

"Hezekiah," he asked, "you are sure?"

"Of what, sir?"

"About the Prestons. You are sure there are no Prestons?"

"I am sure," said Hezekiah.

"There was a Kathleen Preston," Vickers said. "I am *sure* there was . . ."

But how could he be so sure?

He remembered her.

Flanders said there was such a person.

But his memory could be conditioned and so could Flanders' memory.

Kathleen Preston could be no more than an emotional factor introduced into his brain to keep him tied to this house, a keyed-in response that would not let him forget, no matter where he went or what he might become, this house and the ties it held for him.

"Hezekiah," Vickers asked, "Who is Horton Flanders?"

"Horton Flanders," said the robot, "is an android, just the same as you."

40

So he was supposed to stop Crawford.

He was supposed to hunch him.

But first he had to figure out the angles. He had to take the factors and balance one against another and see where the weak spots were and the strong points, too. There was the might of industry, not one industry alone, but the might of all the industry in the entire world. There was the fact that Crawford and industry had declared open war upon the mutants. And there was the matter of the secret weapon.

"Desperation and a secret weapon," Crawford had said, sitting in the hotel room. But the secret weapon, he had added, wasn't good enough.

First of all, Vickers had to know what the weapon was. Until he knew that, there would be no point in making any plans.

He lay in bed and stared at the ceiling and sorted out the facts and laid them in orderly rows and had a look at them. Then he juggled them a bit, changing their position in regard to one another and he balanced the strength of normal human against the strength of mutant and there were many places where they canceled one another and there were other instances where one stood forth, unassailable and uncancelable.

He got exactly nowhere.

"And of course I won't," he said. "This is the old awkward normal human way of doing. This is reasoning."

Hunch was the thing.

And how to do the hunching?

He swept the factors clean away, swept them from his mind, and lay upon the bed, staring at the darkness where the ceiling was and did not try to think.

He could feel the factors bumping in his brain, bouncing together, then fleeing from each other, but he kept himself from recognizing them.

The idea came: War.

He thought about it and it grew and gripped him.

War, but a different kind of war than the world had ever known. What was that phrase from the old history of World War II? A phony war. And yet, not a phony war.

It was a disturbing thing to think about something that you couldn't place—to have a hunch—that was it, a hunch gnawing at you and not know what it was.

He tried to think about it and it retreated from him. He stopped thinking and it came back again.

Another idea came: Poverty.

And poverty was somehow tied up with war and he sensed the two of them, the two ideas, circling like coyotes around the campfire that was himself, snarling and growling at one another in the darkness beyond the flame of his understanding.

He tried to banish them utterly into the darkness and they would not go.

After a time he grew accustomed to them and it seemed that the campfire flickered lower and the coyote-ideas did not run so fast nor snap so viciously.

There was another factor, too, said his sleepy mind. The mutants were short on manpower. That's why they had the robots and the androids.

There would be ways you could get around a manpower shortage. You could take one life and split it into many lives. You could take one mutant life and you could spread it thin, stretch it out and make it last longer and go further. In the economy of manpower, you could do many things if you just knew how.

The coyotes were circling more slowly now and the fire was growing dimmer and I'll stop you, Crawford, I'll get the answer and I'll stop you cold and I love you, Ann, and—

Then, not knowing, he had slept, he woke and sat bolt upright in the bed.

He knew!

He shivered in the slight chill of summer dawn and swung his legs from beneath the covers and felt the bite of the cold floor against his bare feet.

Vickers ran to the door and jerked it open and came out on the landing, with the stairway winding down into the hall below him.

"Flanders!" he shouted. "Flanders."

Hezekiah appeared from somewhere and began to climb the stairs, calling: "What is the matter, sir? Is there something that you want?"

"I want Horton Flanders!"

Another door opened and Horton Flanders stood there, bony ankles showing beneath the hem of a nightshirt, sparse hair standing almost erect.

"What's going on?" he mumbled, tongue still thick with sleep. "What's all the racket?"

Vickers strode across the hall and grabbed him by the shoulders and demanded: "How many of us are there? How many ways was Jay Vickers' life divided?"

"If you'll stop shaking me—"

"I will when you tell me the truth."

"Oh, gladly," Flanders said. "There are three of us. There's you and I and . . ."

"*You?*"

"Certainly. Does it surprise you?"

"But you're so much older than I."

"We can do a great deal with synthetic flesh," said Flanders. "I don't see why you should be surprised at all."

And he wasn't, Vickers suddenly realized. It was as if he had always been aware of it.

"But the third one?" Vickers asked. "You said there are three. Who's the other one?"

"I can't tell you yet," Flanders said. "I won't tell you who it is. I've told you too much already."

Vickers reached out and grasped the front of Flanders' nightshirt and twisted the fabric until it tightened on his throat.

"There's no use in violence," Flanders said. "No possible use in violence. It was only because we reached a crisis sooner than expected that I've told you what I have. You weren't ready for even that much. You weren't fit to know. We were taking quite a chance of pushing you too fast. I couldn't possibly tell you more."

"Not fit to know!" Vickers repeated savagely.

"Not ready. You should have had more time. And to tell you what you ask, to tell you now, just isn't possible. It would—create complications for you. Impair your efficiency and your value."

"But I know *that* answer already," Vickers told him angrily. "Ready or not, I know the answer to Crawford and his friends, and that's more than the rest of you have done, with all the time you've spent on it. I have the answer now, everything you'd hoped for; I know the secret weapon and I know how to counteract it. You said I should stop Crawford and I can."

"You're sure of that?"

"Completely sure," Vickers said. "But this other person, this third person. . . ."

There was a suspicion creeping into his mind, a frightful suspicion.

"I have to know," he said.

"I just can't tell you; I can't possibly tell you," Flanders repeated.

Vickers' grip on the nightshirt had loosened; now he let his hand drop. The nagging thing tearing at his mind was a torture, a terrible, rising torture. Slowly he turned away.

"Yes, I'm sure," Vickers said again. "I'm sure I know *all* the answers. I know, but what the hell's the use."

He went into his room and shut the door.

41

There had been a moment when he had seen his course straight and clear before him—the realization that Kathleen Preston might have been no more than a conditioned personage, that for years the implanted memory of the walk in the enchanted valley had blinded him to the love he bore Ann Carter and the love that he now was sure she felt for him, glossed over with their silly quibbling and their bitter quarreling.

Then had come the realization, too, that his parents slept away the years in suspended animation, waiting for the coming of that world of peace and understanding to which they had given so much.

And he had not been able to turn his back upon them.

Perhaps, he told himself, it was as well, for now there was this other factor—making more than one life out of a single life.

It was a sensible way to do things, and perhaps a valid method, for the mutants needed manpower and when you needed manpower you did the best you could with what you had at hand. You placed in the hands of robots the work that could be left to robots and you took the life of living men and women and out of each of those lives you made several lives, housing the divisional lives in the bodies of your androids.

He was not a person in his own right, but a part of another person, a third of that original Jay Vickers whose body lay waiting for the day when his life would be given back to him again.

And Ann Carter was not a person in her own right, either, but the part of another person. Perhaps a part—and for the first time he forced himself to allow his suspicion to become a clear and terrible thought—perhaps a part of Jay Vickers, sharing with him and with Flanders the life that had been held originally by one.

Three androids now shared the single life: he and Flanders and someone else. And the question beat at him, whispering in his brain: who could that other be?

The three of them were bound by a common cord that almost made them one, and in time the three of them must let their lives flow back into the body of the original Jay Vickers. And when that happened, he wondered, which of them would continue as Jay Vickers? Or would none of them—would it be an equivalent of death for all three and a continuation of the consciousness that Jay Vickers himself had known? Or would the three of them be mingled, so that the resurrected Jay Vickers would be a strange three-way personality combining what was now himself and Flanders and the unknown other?

And the love he bore Ann Carter? In the face of the possibility that Ann might be that unknown other, what about the tenderness he suddenly had felt for her after the moonlight-and-roses years—what of that love now?

There could be no such love, he knew. If Ann were the third, there could be no love between them. You could not love yourself as you would another person. You could not love a facet of yourself or let a facet of yourself love you. You could not love a person who was closer than a sister or a mother. . . .

Twice he had known love of a woman and twice it had been taken from him and now he was trapped with no other choice but to do the job that had been assigned him.

He had told Crawford that when he knew what was going on, he'd come back and talk to him and between the two of them they'd see if there was a compromise.

But there was no compromise now, he knew.

Not if his hunch was right.

And Flanders had said that hunch was a better way of reasoning, a more mature, more adult way of arriving at the answer to a problem that was up to you to solve. A method, Flanders had told him, that did away with the winding path of reason that the human race had used through all its formative years.

For the secret weapon was the old, old weapon of deliberate war, waged with mathematical cynicism and calculated precision.

And how many wars, he wondered, could the human race survive? And the answer seemed to be: *Just one more real war.*

The mutants were the survival factor in the race of Man; and now there was nothing left to him, neither Kathleen nor Ann, nor even, perhaps, the hope of personal humanity—he must work as best he could to carry forward the best hope of the human race.

Someone tapped at the door.

"Yes," said Vickers. "Come on in."

"Breakfast will be ready, sir," said Hezekiah, "by the time that you get dressed."

42

Flanders was waiting in the dining room when Vickers came down the stairs.

"The others left," said Flanders. "They had work to do. And you and I have plotting."

Vickers did not answer. He pulled out a chair and sat down across from Flanders. The sunlight from the windows came down across Flanders' shoulders and his head stood out against the window glass in bold relief, with the whiteness of his hair like a fuzzy halo. His clothes, Vickers saw, still were slightly shabby and his necktie had seen better days, but he still was neat and his face shone with the scrubbing he had given it.

"I see that Hezekiah found some clothes for you," said Flanders. "I don't know what we'd do without Hezekiah. He takes care of us."

"Money, too," said Vickers. "A pack of it was lying on the dresser with the shirt and tie. I didn't take the time to count it, but there'd seem to be several thousand dollars."

"Of course. Hezekiah thinks of everything."

"But I don't want several thousand dollars."

"Go ahead," said Flanders. "We've got bales of it."

"Bales of it!"

"Certainly. We keep making it."

"You mean you counterfeit it?"

"Oh, bless me, no," said Flanders. "Although it's something we have often thought of. Another string to our bow, you might say."

"You mean flood the normal world with counterfeit money?"

"It wouldn't be counterfeit. We could duplicate the money exactly. Turn loose a hundred billion dollars of new money in the world and there'd be hell to pay."

"I can see the point," said Vickers. "I'm amazed you didn't do it."

Flanders looked sharply at him. "I have a feeling that you disapprove of us."

"In some ways I do," said Vickers.

Hezekiah brought in a tray with tall glasses of cold orange juice, plates of scrambled eggs and bacon, buttered toast, a jar of jam and a pot of coffee.

"Good morning, sir," he said to Vickers.

"Good morning, Hezekiah."

"Have you noticed," asked the robot, "how fine the morning is?"

"I have noticed that," said Vickers.

"The weather here is most unusually fine," said Hezekiah. "Much finer, I am told, than on the Earth ahead."

He served the food and left, out through the swinging door into the kitchen, where they could hear him moving about at his morning chores.

"We have been humane," said Flanders, "as humane as possible. But we had a job to do and once in a while someone got his toes stepped on. It may be that we will have to get a little rougher now, for we are being pushed. If Crawford and his gang had just taken it a little easier, it would have worked out all right and we wouldn't have had to hurt them or anyone. Ten years more and it would have been easier. Twenty years more and it would have been a cinch. But now it's neither sure nor easy. Now it has to amount almost to revolution. Had we been given twenty years, it would have been evolution.

"Given time and we would have taken over not only world industry and world finance, but world government as well, but they didn't give us the time. The crisis came too soon."

"What we need now," said Vickers, "is a countercrisis."

Flanders seemed not to have heard him. "We set up dummy companies," he continued. "We should have set up more, but we lacked the manpower to operate even the ones we did set up. Given the manpower, we would have gone more extensively into the manufacture of certain basic gadgets. But we needed the little manpower we had at so many other places—at certain crisis points or to hunt down other mutants to enlist into our group."

"There must be many mutants," Vickers said.

"There are a number of them," agreed Flanders, "but a large percentage of them are so entangled in the world and the affairs of the normal world that you can't dislodge them. Take a mutant man married to a normal woman. You simply can't, in the name of humanity, break up a happy marriage. Say some of their children are mutants—what can you do about them? You can't do a thing about it. You simply watch and wait. When they grow up and go out on their own, you can approach them, but not before that time.

"Take a banker or an industrialist upon whose shoulders rest an economic empire. Tell him he's a mutant and he'll laugh at you. He's made his place in life; he's satisfied; whatever idealism or liberalism he may have had at one time has disappeared beneath the exterior of rugged individualism. His loyalties are set to the pattern of the life he's made and there's nothing we can offer that will interest him."

"You might try immortality," suggested Vickers.

"We haven't got immortality."

"You should have attacked on the governmental level."

Flanders shook his head. "We couldn't. We did a little of it, but not much. With a thousand major posts in the governments of the world, we would have turned the trick quickly and easily. But we didn't have the thousand mutants to train for government and diplomatic jobs.

"By various methods, we did head off crisis after crisis. The carbohydrates relieved a situation which would have led to war. Helping the West get the hydrogen bomb years ahead of time held off the East just when they were set to strike. But we weren't strong enough and we didn't have the time to carry out any well defined, long-range program, so we had to improvise. We introduced gadgets as the only quick way we knew to weaken the socio-economic system of the Earth and, of course, that meant that sooner or later we would force Earth's industry to band against us."

"What else would you expect?" asked Vickers. "You interfere . . ."

"I suppose we do," said Flanders. "Let's say, Vickers, that you were a surgeon and you had a patient suffering from cancer. To try to make the patient well, you would not hesitate to operate. You would be most zealous in your interference with the patient's body."

"I presume I would," said Vickers.

"The human race," said Flanders, "is our patient. It has a malignant growth. We are the surgeons. It will be painful for the patient and there will be a period of convalescence, but at least the patient will live and I have the gravest doubts that the human race could survive another war."

"But the high-handed methods that you use!"

"Now wait a moment," Flanders objected. "You think there must be other methods and I will agree, but all of them would be equally objectionable to humanity and the old human methods themselves have been discredited long ago. Men have shouted peace and preached the brotherhood of man and there has been no peace and only lip service to brotherhood. You would have us hold conferences? I ask you, my friend, what is the history of the conference?

"Or maybe we should go before the people, before the heads of government, and say to them we are the new mutations of the race and that our knowledge and our ability are greater than theirs and that they should turn all things over to us so we could bring the world to peace. What would happen then? I can tell you what would happen. They'd hate us and drive us out. So there is no choice for us. We must work underground. We must attack the key points. No other way will work."

"What you say," said Vickers, "may be true so far as 'the people' are concerned, but how about the *person,* the individual? How about the little fellow who gets socked in the teeth?"

"Asa Andrews was here this morning," Flanders told him. "He said you'd been at his place and had disappeared and he was worried about what might have happened to you. But that is beside the point. What I want to ask you is, would you say that Asa Andrews was a happy man?"

"I've never seen anybody happier."

"And yet," said Flanders, "we interfered with him. We took away his job—the job he had to have to feed his family and clothe them and keep a roof above their heads. He searched for jobs and could find none. When he finally came for help, we knew that we were the ones who cost him his job, who forced him finally to be evicted, to stand in the street and not know where his family would lay their heads that night. We did all this and yet, in the end, he is a happy man. There are thousands of others throughout this earth who have thus been interfered with and now are happy people. Happy, I must contend, because of our interference."

"You can't claim," Vickers contended, "that there is no price for this happiness. I don't mean the loss of job, the bread of charity— but what comes afterwards. You are settling them here on this earth in what you are pleased to call a pastoral-feudal stage, but the fancy name you call it can't take away the fact that in being settled here they have lost many of the material advantages of human civilization."

"We have taken from them," Flanders said, "little more than the knife with which they'll cut their own or their neighbor's throat. Whatever else we've taken from them will in time be given back, in full measure and with fantastic interest. For it is our hope, Mr. Vickers, that in time to come they all will be like us, that in time the entire race may have everything we have.

"We are not freaks, you understand, but human beings, the next step in evolution. We're just a day or two ahead, a step or two ahead of all the rest of them. To survive, Man had to change, had to mutate, had to become something more than what he was. We are only the first forerunners of that mutation of survival. And because we are the first, we must fight a delaying action. We must fight for the time that it will take for the rest of them to catch up with us. In us you see not one little group of privileged persons, but all of humanity."

"Humanity," said Vickers, sourly, "seems to be taking a dim view of your delaying fight to save them. Up on that world of ours they're smashing gadget shops and hunting down the mutants and hanging them from lamp posts."

"That's where you come in," Flanders pointed out.

Vickers nodded. "You want me to stop Crawford."

"You told me you could."

"I had a hunch," said Vickers.

"Your hunches, my friend, are more likely to be right than seasoned reasoning."

"I will need some help," said Vickers.

"Anything you say."

"I want some of your pioneers—men like Asa Andrews, sent back to do some missionary work."

"But we can't do that," protested Flanders.

"They're in this fight, too," said Vickers. "They can't expect to sit and not lift a finger."

"Missionary work? You want them to go back to tell about these other worlds?"

"That is exactly what I want."

"But no one would believe them. With the feeling running as it is on earth they would be mobbed and lynched."

Vickers shook his head. "There is one group that would believe them—the Pretentionists. Don't you see, the Pretentionists are fleeing from reality. They pretend to go back and live in the London of Pepys' day, and to many other eras of the past, but even there they find certain restraining influences, certain encroachments upon their own free will and their security. But here there is complete freedom and security. Here they could go back to the simplicity, the uncomplicated living that they are yearning for. No matter how fantastic it might sound, the Pretentionists would embrace it."

"You're sure of this?" asked Flanders.

"Positive."

"But that's not all. There is something else?"

"There is one thing more," said Vickers. "If there were a sudden demand on the carbohydrates, could you meet it?"

"I think we could. We could reconvert our factories. The gadget business is shot now and so is the carbohydrates business. To dispense carbohydrates we'd have to set up a sort of black market system. If we went out in the open, Crawford and his crew would break it up."

"At first, perhaps," agreed Vickers. "But not for very long. Not when tens of thousands of people would be ready to fight him to get their carbohydrates."

"When the carbohydrates are needed," Flanders said, "they'll be there."

"The Pretentionists will believe," said Vickers. "They are ripe for belief, for any kind of fantastic belief. To them it will be an imaginative crusade. Against a normal population, we might have no chance, but we have a great segment of escapists who have been driven to escape by the sickness of the world. All they need is a spark, a word—some sort of promise that there is a chance of real escape as against the mental escape they have been driven to. There will be many who will want to come to this second world. How fast can you bring them through?"

"As fast as they come," said Flanders.

"I can count on that?"

"You can count on that." Flanders shook his head. "I don't know what you're planning. I hope your hunch is right."

"You said it was," Vickers declared.

"You know what you're going up against? You know what Craw-ford's planning?"

"I think he's planning war. He said it was a secret weapon, but I'm convinced it's war."

"But war . . ."

"Let's look at war," said Vickers, "just a little differently than it ever has been looked at, just a little differently than the historians see it. Let's see it as a business. Because war, in certain aspects, is just that. When a country goes to war, it means that labor and indus-try and resources are mobilized and controlled by governments. The businessman plays as important a part as does the military man. The banker and the industrialist is as much in the saddle as the general.

"Now let's go one step further and imagine a war fought on strictly business lines—for the strictly business purpose of obtaining and retaining control in those very area where we are threatening. War would mean that the system of supply and demand would be suspended and that certain civilian items would cease to be manu-factured and that the governments could crack down on anyone who would attempt to sell them . . ."

"Like cars, perhaps," said Flanders, "and lighters and even razor blades."

"Exactly," Vickers told him. "That way they could gain the time, for they need time as badly as we do. On military pretext, they'd seize complete control of the world economy."

"What you're saying," Flanders said, "is that they plan to start war by agreement."

"I'm convinced that's it," said Vickers. "They'd hold it to a mini-mum. Perhaps one bomb on New York in return for a bomb on Moscow and another on Chicago for one on Leningrad. You get the idea—a restricted war, a gentleman's agreement. Just enough fight-ing to convince everyone that it was real.

"But phony as it might be, a lot of people would die and there'd always be the danger that someone would get sore and instead of one bomb on Moscow it might be two, or the other way around, or an admiral might get just a bit too enthusiastic and a bit too accurate and sink a ship that wasn't in the deal or a general might—"

"It's fantastic," Flanders said.

"You forget that they are very desperate men. You forget that they are fighting, every one of them, Russian and American, French and Pole and Czech, for the kind of life that Man has built upon the Earth. To them we must appear to be the most vicious enemy mankind's ever faced. To them we are the ogre and the goblin out of the nursery tale. They are frightened stiff."

"And you?" asked Flanders.

"I'd go back to the old Earth, except I lost the top. I don't know where I lost it, but . . ."

"You don't need the top. That was just for novices. All you have to do is will yourself into the other world. Once you've done it, it's a cinch."

"If I need to get in touch with you?"

"Eb's your man," said Flanders. "Just get hold of Eb."

"You'll send Asa and the others back?"

"We will."

Vickers rose and held out his hand.

"But," said Flanders, "you don't need to leave just yet. Sit down and have another cup of coffee."

Vickers shook his head. "I'm anxious to get going."

"The robots could get you lined up with New York in no time at all," suggested Flanders. "You could return to the old Earth from there."

Vickers said, "I want time to think. I have to do some planning—hunching, you'd call it. But I think I'll want to start from right here, before going to New York."

"Buy a car," advised Flanders. "Hezekiah left you enough cash to buy one and have some left over. Eb will have more if you need it. It wouldn't be safe to travel any other way. They'll have traps set out for mutants. They'll be watching all the time."

"I'll be careful," Vickers promised.

43

The room was dusty and festooned with spider webs and its emptiness made it seem much larger than it was. The paper was peeling from the walls and the plaster cracks ran like jagged chains of lightning from the ceiling molding to the baseboard at the floor.

But one could see that at one time the peeling paper had been colorful, with festoons of little flowers and the larger figure of a Dresden shepherdess guarding woolly sheep and beneath the film of dust one knew the woodwork lay with some of the old wax still on it, ready to shine again when rescued from neglect.

Vickers turned slowly in the center of the room and he saw that the doors were where they had been and the windows, too, in that other room where he'd just risen from the chair after eating breakfast. But here the door to the kitchen stood open and the windows were dark with the shutters closed against them.

He took a step or two and he saw that he left footprints in the dust and the footprints started at the center of the room. There were no footprints leading from anywhere to the center of the room. The tracks just started there.

He stood and looked at the room and tried to reconstruct it, not as he had known it less than sixty seconds before, but as he first had seen it twenty years before.

Or was it fantasy—conditioned fantasy? Had he ever, actually, stood in this room before? Had there ever been a Kathleen Preston?

He knew that a Vickers family, a poor farm family, had lived not more than a mile from where he stood. He thought of them—the woman, courageous in her ragged dress and drab sweater; the man with the pitiful little shelf of books beside his bed and how he used to sit in faded overalls and too-big shirt, reading the books in the dim yellowness of the kerosene lamp; the boy, a helter-skelter sort of kid who had too much imagination and once went to fairyland.

Masquerade, he thought—a bitter masquerade, a listening post set out to spy out the talk of enemies. But it had been their job and they had done it well and they had watched their son grow into a youth and knew by the manner of his growing that he was no throw-back, but truly one of them.

And now they waited, those two who had posed as lonely farmer folk for all the anxious years, fitting themselves into an ordinary niche which was never meant for such as they, against the day when they could take their rightful place in the society which they had given up to stand outpost duty for the big brick house standing proudly on its hill.

He could not turn his back on them and now there was no need to turn his back on them—for there was nothing else.

He walked across the dining room and along the hall that led to the closed front door and he left behind him a trail of footprints in the dust.

Outside the door, he knew, was nothing—not Ann, nor Kathleen, nor any place for him—nothing but the cold knife-edge of duty to a life he had not chosen.

He had his moments of doubt while he drove across the country, savoring the goodness of the things he saw and heard and smelled—the little villages sleeping in the depth of summer with their bicycles and canted coaster wagons, with their shade trees along neat avenues of homes; the first reddening of the early summer apples on the orchard trees; the friendly bumbling of the great transport trucks as they howled along the highways; the way the girl behind the counter smiled at you when you stopped at a roadside eating place for a cup of coffee.

There was nothing wrong, he told himself, nothing wrong with the little villages or the trucks or the girl who smiled. Man's world was a pleasant and a fruitful place, a good place in which to live.

It was then that the mutants and their plans seemed like a nightmare snatched from some lurid Sunday supplement and he wondered, as he drove along, why he didn't simply pull off the road and let the car sit there while he walked off into this good life he saw on every hand. Surely there was within it some place for a man like him; somewhere in the flat corn lands, where the little villages clung to every crossroad, that a man could find peace and security.

But he saw, reluctantly, that he did not seek these things for themselves alone. He sought a place to hide from the thing one could sense in the very air. In wanting to leave his car beside the road and walk away, he knew, he was responding to the same bone-deep fear as the Pretentionists when they escaped emotionally to some other time and place. It was the urge to flee that made him want to leave the car and find a hiding place in the calmness of these corn lands.

But even here, in the agricultural heart of the continent, there was no real peace and security. There was creature comfort and, at times, some measure of unthinking security—if you never read a paper nor listened to a broadcast and did not talk with people. For, he realized, the signposts of insecurity could be found everywhere under the sunlit exteriors: on every doorstep and in every home and at every drugstore corner.

He read the papers and the news was bad. He listened to the radio and the commentators were talking about a new and deeper crisis than the world had ever faced. He listened to the people talking in the lobbies of the hotels where he stopped to spend the nights or in the eating places where he stopped along the road. They would talk and shake their heads and one could see that they were worried.

They said: "What I can't understand is how things could change so quick. Here, just a week or two ago, it looked like the East and West would band together against this mutant business. At last they had something they could fight together instead of fighting one another, but now they're back at it again and it's worse than ever."

They said: "If you ask me, it's them Commies that stirred up this mutant business. You mark my word, they're at the bottom of it."

They said: "It just don't seem possible. Here we sit to-night a million miles from war with everything calm and peaceful. And tomorrow . . ."

And tomorrow and tomorrow and tomorrow.

They said: "If it was up to me, I'd get in touch with them mutants. They got stuff up their sleeve that would blow these Commies plumb to hell."

They said: "Like I said forty years ago, we never should have demobilized at the end of World War II. We should have hit them then. We could've knocked them off in a month or two."

They said: "The hell of it is that you never know. No one ever tells you anything and when they do, it's wrong."

They said: "I wouldn't horse around with them a single God damn minute. I'd load me up some bombs and I'd let them have it."

He listened to them talk and there was no talk of compromise nor of understanding. There was no hope in all the talk that war could be averted. "If not this time," they said, "it'll come in five years, or ten, so let's get it over with. You got to hit them first. In a war like this there ain't no second chance. It's either them or us . . ."

And it was then that he fully understood that even here, in the heartland of the nation, in the farms and little villages, in the roadside eating places there was a boiling hate. That, he told himself, was the measure of the culture that had been built upon the earth—a culture founded on a hatred and a terrible pride and a suspicion of everyone who did not talk the same language or eat the same food or dress the same as you did.

It was a lop-sided mechanical culture of clanking machines, a technological world that could provide creature comfort, but not human justice nor security. It was a culture that had worked in metals, that had delved into the atom, that had mastered chemicals and had built a complicated and dangerous gadgetry. It had concentrated upon the technological and had ignored the sociological so that a man might punch a button and destroy a distant city without knowing, or even caring, about the lives and habits, the thoughts and hopes and beliefs of the people that he killed.

Underneath the sleek surface one could hear the warning rumble of machines; and the gears and sprockets, the driving chain, the generator, without the leavening of human understanding, were the guideposts to disaster.

He drove and ate and drove again. He ate and slept and drove. He watched the cornfields and the reddening apples in the orchard and heard the song of mowers and smelled the scent of clover and he looked into the sky and felt the terrible fear that hung high in the sky and he knew that Flanders had been right, that to survive Man must mutate and that the survival mutation must win before the storm of hate could break.

But it was not only news of approaching war which filled the columns of the daily press and the frenzied quarter-hours of the news commentators.

There was still the mutant menace and the hatred of the mutants and the continuing exhortations to the people to keep a watch for mutants. There were riots and lynchings and gadget shops burned.

And something else:

A creeping whisper that spread across the land, that was talked over at the drugstore corners and at the dusty crossroads and in the shadowed night spots of the bigger cities—the whisper that there was another world, a brand new world where one could start his life again, where one would escape from the thousands of years of accumulated mistakes of the present world.

The press at first was wary of the story, then printed cautious stories with very restrained headlines and the news commentators seemed at first to be just as wary, but finally took the plunge. In a very few days the news of the other world and of the strange, starry-eyed people who had talked to someone else (always someone else) who claimed they had come from there ranked with the news of approaching war and with hatred of the mutants.

You could feel the world on edge, as tense as the sudden, strident ringing of a telephone in the dead of night.

44

Cliffwood after dark had the smell and feel of home and he drove along its streets and felt the lump of loss come into his throat, for it had been here that he had thought to settle down and spend his years in writing, in setting down on paper the thoughts that welled inside of him.

His house was here and the furniture and the manuscript and the crudely carpentered shelf that held his freight of books, but it was his home no longer, and now, he knew, could never never be again. And that wasn't all, he thought. The Earth, the original human earth—the earth with the capital E—was his home no longer and never again could be.

He'd go and see Eb first and after he had seen Eb, he'd go to his own house, and get the manuscript. He could give the manuscript to Ann, he thought; she would keep it for him.

On second thought, he'd have to find some other place, for he didn't want to see Ann—although that was not precisely the truth. He did want to see her, but knew he shouldn't, for now there lay between them the almost-certain knowledge that he and she were part of a single life.

He pulled the car to a stop in front of Eb's house an sat there for a moment looking at it, wondering at the neatness of the house and yard, for Eb lived alone without wife or child, and it was not usual that a man alone would keep a place so tidy.

He'd spend just a minute with Eb, would tell him what had happened, what was going on, would make arrangements to keep in touch with him, would learn from him whatever news might be worth knowing.

He closed the car door and went across the walk, fumbling at the latch of the gate that opened to the yard. Moonlight came down through the trees and splotched the walk with light and he followed it to the porch, and now, for the first time, he noticed that there were no lights burning in the house.

He rapped on the door, knowing from poker sessions and other infrequent visits that Eb had no doorbell.

There was no answer. He waited and finally rapped again and then turned from the door and went down the walk. Maybe Eb was still down at the garage, putting in some overtime on an urgent repair job, or he might be down at the tavern, having a quick one with the boys.

He'd sit out in the car and wait for Eb. It probably wouldn't be safe to go down into the village business section where he'd be recognized.

A voice asked: "You looking for Eb?"

Vickers spun around toward the voice. It was the next door neighbor, he saw, standing at the fence.

"Yes," said Vickers. "I was looking for him."

He was trying to remember who lived next to Eb, who this person across the fence might be. Someone that he knew, someone who might recognize him?

"I'm an old friend of his," said Vickers. "Just passing through. Thought I'd stop and say hello."

The man had stepped through a break in the fence and was coming across the lawn.

The man asked: "How well did you know Eb?"

"Not too well," said Vickers. "Haven't seen him in ten or fifteen years. Used to be kids together."

"Eb is dead," the neighbor said.

"Dead!"

The neighbor spat. "He was one of them damned mutants."

"No," protested Vickers. "No, he couldn't be!"

"He was. We had another one, but he got away. We always had a suspicion Eb might have tipped him off."

The bitterness and hatred of the neighbor's words filled Vickers with a feeling of sheer terror.

The mob had killed Eb and they would kill *him* if they knew he had returned to town. And in just a little while they'd know, for any minute now the neighbor would recognize him—now he knew who the neighbor was, the beefy individual who ran the meat market in the town's one chain store. His name was—but it didn't really matter.

"Seems to me," the neighbor said, "I've seen you somewhere."

"You must be mistaken. I've never been East before."

"Your voice . . ."

Vickers struck with all the power he had, starting the fist down low and bringing it up in a vicious arc, twisting his body to line it up behind the blow, to put the weight of his body behind the balled-up fist.

He hit the man in the face and the impact of flesh on flesh, of bone on bone, made a whiplike sound and the man went down.

Vickers did not wait. He spun away and went racing for the gate. He almost tore the car door from its hinges getting in. He thumbed the starter savagely and trod down on the gas and the car leaped down the street, spraying the bushes with gravel thrown by its frightened wheels.

His arm was numb from the force of the blow he'd struck and when he held his hand down in front of the lighted dash panel, he saw that his knuckles were lacerated and slowly dripping blood.

He had a few minutes' start; the neighbor might take that long to shake himself into a realization of what had happened. But once he was on his feet, once he could reach a phone, they'd start hunting him, screaming through the night on whining tires, with shotgun and rope and rifle.

And he had to get away. Now he was on his own.

Eb was dead, attacked without warning, surely, without a chance to escape to the other earth. Eb had been shot down or strung up or kicked to death. And Eb had been his only contact.

Now there was no one but himself and Ann.

And Ann, God willing, didn't even know that she was a mutant.

He struck the main highway and swung down the valley, pouring on the gas.

There was an old abandoned road some ten miles down the highway, he remembered. A man could duck a car in there and wait until it was safe to double back again. Although doubling back probably wouldn't be too safe.

Maybe it would be better to take to the hills and hide out until the hunt blew over.

No, he told himself, there was nothing safe.

And he had no time to waste.

He had to get to Crawford, had to head Crawford off the best way that he could. And he had to do it alone.

The abandoned road was there, halfway up a long, steep hill. He wheeled the car into it and bumped along it for a hundred feet or so, then got out and walked back to the road.

Hidden behind a clump of trees, he watched cars go screaming past, but there was no way to know if any of them might be hunting him.

Then a rickety old truck came slowly up the hill, howling with the climb.

He watched it, an idea growing in his mind.

When it came abreast, he saw that it was closed in the back only with a high end gate.

He ran out into the traffic lane and raced after it, caught up with it and leaped. His fingers caught the top of the end gate and he heaved himself clear of the road, scrambled over the gate and clambered over the piled up boxes stacked inside the truck.

He huddled there, staring out at the road behind him.

A hunted animal, he thought; hunted by men who once had been his friends.

Ten miles or so down the road someone stopped the truck.

A voice asked: "You see anyone up the road a ways? Walking, maybe?"

"Hell, no," the truck driver said. "I ain't seen a soul."

"We're looking for a mutant. Figure he must have ditched his car."

"I thought we had all of them cleaned out," the driver said.

"Not all. Maybe he took to the hills. If he did, we've got him."

"You'll be stopped again," another voice said. "We phoned ahead both ways. They got road blocks set up."

"I'll keep my eyes peeled," the driver said.

"You got a gun?"

"No."

"Well, keep watching anyway."

When the truck rolled on, Vickers saw the two men standing in the road. The moonlight glinted on the rifles that they carried.

He set to work cautiously, moving some of the boxes, making himself a hideout.

He needn't have bothered.

The truck was stopped at three other road blocks. At none of them did anyone do more than flash a light inside the truck. They seemed half-hearted in their search, convinced that they wouldn't find a mutant that easily, perhaps thinking that this one had already vanished, as so many other forewarned mutants had done.

But Vickers could not allow himself to take that avenue of escape. He had a job to do on this Earth.

45

He knew what he would find at the store, but he went there just the same; for it was the only place he could think of where he might establish contact. But the huge show window was broken and the house that had stood there was smashed as utterly as if it had stood in a cyclone's path.

The mob had done its work.

He stood in front of the gaping, broken window and stared at the wreckage of the house and remembered the day that he and Ann had stopped on their way to the bus station. The house, he recalled, had had a flying duck weather vane and a sun dial had stood in the yard and there had been a car standing in the driveway, but the car had disappeared completely. Dragged out into the street, probably, he thought, and smashed as his own car had been smashed in that little Illinois town.

He turned away from the window and walked slowly down the street. It had been foolish to go to the showroom, he told himself, but there had been a chance— although the chance had been a slim one, as he knew all his chances were.

He turned a corner and there, in a dusty square across the street, a good-sized crowd had gathered and was listening to someone who had climbed a park bench and was talking to them.

Idly, Vickers walked across the street, stopped opposite the crowd.

The man on the park bench had taken off his coat and rolled up his sleeves and loosened his tie. He talked almost conversationally, although his words carried clear across the park to where Vickers stood.

"When the bombs come," asked the man, "what will happen then? They say don't be afraid. They say, stay on your jobs and don't be afraid. They have told you to stay and not be afraid, but what will they do when the bombs arrive? Will they help you then?"

He paused and the crowd was tense, tense in a terrible silence. You could feel the knotted muscles that clamped the jaws tight shut and the hand that squeezed the heart until the body turned all cold. And you could sense the fear—

"They will not help," the speaker told them, speaking slowly and deliberately. "They will not help you, for you will be past all help. You will be dead, my friends. Dead by the tens of thousands. Dead in the sun that flamed upon the city. Dead and turned to nothing. Dead and restless atoms.

"You will die. . . ."

From far away came the sound of sirens and at the sound the crowd stirred restlessly, almost angrily.

"You will die," the speaker said, "and there is no need to die, for there is another world that waits you.

"Poverty is the key to that other world. Poverty is the ticket that will take you there. All you need to do is to quit your job and give away everything you have—and *throw* away everything you have. You cannot go except with empty hands . . ."

The sirens were closer and the crowd was murmuring, stirring, like some great animal arousing itself from sleep. The sound of its voice swept across the square like the sudden rustle of leaves in the wind that moved before a storm.

The speaker raised his hand again and there was instant silence.

"My friends," he said, "why don't you heed? The other world awaits. The poor go first. The poor and desperate, the ones for which this world you stand on has no further use. The only way you can go is in utter poverty, with empty hands, with no possessions.

"In that other world there are no bombs. There is a beginning over, a starting over again. An entire new world, almost exactly like this world, with trees and grass and fertile land and game upon the hills and fish teeming in the rivers. The kind of place you dream of. And there is peace."

There were more sirens now and they were getting closer.

Vickers stepped off the sidewalk and dashed across the street.

A squad car screeched around a corner, skidding and whipping to get straightened out, it's tires screaming on the pavement, its siren awail as if in agony.

"I beg your pardon?"

Almost at the curb, Vickers stumbled and went sprawling. Instinctively, he pulled himself to hands and knees and flicked a sidewise glance to see the squad car bearing down upon him and he knew he could not make it, that before he could get his feet beneath him the car would be upon him.

A hand came down out of nowhere and fastened on his arm and jerked and he felt himself catapulting off the street and across the sidewalk.

Another squad car came around the corner, skidding and with flattened tires protesting, almost as if the first had returned to make a second entrance.

The scattered crowd was running desperately.

The hand tugged at his arm and hauled him erect and Vickers saw the man for the first time, a man in a ragged sweater, with an old knife-mark jagged across his cheek.

"Quick," said the man, the knife-mark writhing with the words he spoke, teeth flashing in the whisker-shadowed face.

He shoved Vickers into a narrow alleyway between two buildings and Vickers sprinted, shoulders hunched, between the walls of brick that rose on either side.

He heard the man panting along behind him.

"To your right," said the man. "A door."

Vickers grasped the knob and the door swung open into a darkened hall.

The man stepped in beside him and closed the door and they stood together in the darkness, gasping with their running, the sound of them beating like an erratic heart in the confining darkness.

"That was close," the man said. "Those cops are getting on the ball. You no more than start a meeting and . . ."

He did not finish the sentence. Instead he reached out and touched Vickers on the arm.

"Follow me," he said. "Be careful. Stairs."

Vickers followed, feeling his way down the creaky stairs, with the musty smell of cellar growing stronger with each step.

At the bottom of the stairway, the man pushed aside a hanging blanket and they stepped into a dimly lighted room. There was an old, broken down piano in one corner and a pile of boxes in another and a table in the center, around which four men and two women sat.

One of the men said, "We heard the sirens."

Scar-face nodded. "Charley was just going good. The crowd was getting down to shouting."

"Who's your friend, George?" asked another one.

"He was running," said George, "Police car almost got him."

They looked at Vickers with interest.

"What's your name, friend?" asked George.

Vickers told them.

"Is he all right?" asked someone.

"He was there," said George. "He was running."

"But is it safe . . ."

"He's all right," said George, but Vickers noted that he said it too vehemently, too stubbornly, as if he now realized that he might have made a mistake in bringing a total stranger here.

"Have a drink," said one of the men. He shoved a bottle across the table toward Vickers.

Vickers sat down in a chair and took the bottle.

One of the women, the better-looking of the two, said to him, "My name is Sally."

Vickers said, "I'm glad to know you, Sally."

He looked around the table. None of the rest of them seemed ready to introduce themselves.

He lifted the bottle and drank. It was cheap stuff. He choked a little on it.

Sally said, "You an activist?"

"I beg your pardon?"

"An activist or purist?"

"He's an activist," said George. "He was right in there with the rest of them."

Vickers could see that George was sweating a little, afraid that he had made a mistake.

"He sure as hell doesn't look like one," said one of the men.

"I'm an activist," said Vickers, because he could see that was what they wanted him to be.

"He's like me," said Sally. "He's an activist by principle, but a purist by preference. Isn't that right?" she asked Vickers.

"Yes," said Vickers. "Yes, I guess that's it."

He took another drink.

"What's your period?" Sally asked.

"My period," said Vickers. "Oh, yes, my period."

And he remembered the white, intense face of Mrs. Leslie asking him what historic period he thought would be the most exciting.

"Charles the Second," he said.

"You were a little slow on that one," said one of the men, suspiciously.

"I fooled around some," said Vickers. "Dabbled, you know. Took me quite a while to find the one I liked."

"But you settled on Charles the Second," Sally said.

"That's right."

"Mine," Sally told him, "is Aztec."

"But, Aztec . . ."

"I know," she said. "It really isn't fair, is it? There's so little known about the Aztecs, really. But that way I can make it up as I go along. It's so much more fun that way."

George said, "It's all damn foolishness. Maybe it was all right to piddle around with diaries and pretending you were someone else when there was nothing else to do. But now we got something else to do."

"George is right," nodded the other woman.

"You activists' are the ones who're" wrong," Sally argued. "The basic thing in pretentionism is the ability to lift yourself out of your present time and space, to project yourself into another era."

"Now, listen here," said George. "I . . ."

"Oh, I agree," said Sally, "that we must work for this other world. It's the kind of opportunity we wanted all along. But that doesn't mean we have to give up . . ."

"Cut it out," said one of the men, the big fellow at the table's end. "Cut out all this gabbling. This ain't no place for it."

Sally said to Vickers, "We're having a meeting tonight. Would you like to come?"

He hesitated. In the dim light he could see that all of them were looking at him.

"Sure," he said. "Sure. It would be a pleasure."

He reached for the bottle and took another drink, then passed it on to George.

"There ain't nobody stirring for a while," said George. "Not until them cops have a chance to get cooled off a bit."

He took a drink and passed the bottle on.

46

The meeting was just getting under way when Sally and Vickers arrived.

"Will George be here?" asked Vickers.

Sally laughed a little. "George here?" she asked.

Vickers shook his head. "I guess he's not the type."

"George is a roughneck," said Sally. "A red-hot. A born organizer. How he escaped communism is more than I'll ever know."

"And you? The ones like you?"

"We are the propagandists," she said. "We go to the meetings. We talk to people. We get them interested. We do the missionary work and get the converts who'll go out and preach. When we get them we turn them over to the people like George."

The dowager sitting at the table rapped with the letter opener she was using as a gavel.

"Please," she said. Her voice was aggrieved. "Please. This meeting will come to order."

Vickers held a chair for Sally, then sat down himself. The others in the room were quieting down.

The room, Vickers saw, was really two rooms—the living room and the dining room, with the French doors between them thrown open so that in effect they became one room.

Upper middle class, he thought. Just swank enough not to be vulgar, but failing the grandeur and the taste of the really rich. Real paintings on the wall and a Provencal fireplace and furniture that probably was of some period or other, although he couldn't name it.

He glanced at the faces around him and tried to place them. An executive type over there—a manufacturer's representative, he'd guess. And that one who needed a haircut might be a painter or a writer, although not a successful one. And the woman with the iron-grey hair and the outdoor tan was more than likely a member of some riding set.

But it did not matter, he knew. Here it was upper middle class in an apartment house with its doorman uniformed, while across the city there would be another meeting in a tenement that had never known a doorman. And in the little villages and the smaller cities they would meet in houses, perhaps at the banker's house or at the barber's house. And in each instance someone would rap on the table and say would the meeting come to order, please. At most of the meetings, too, there would be a man or a woman like Sally, waiting to talk to the members, hoping to make converts.

The dowager was saying, "Miss Stanhope is the first member on our list to read tonight."

Then she sat back, contented, now that she had them finally quieted down and the meeting under way.

Miss Stanhope stood up and she was, Vickers saw, the personification of frustrated female flesh and spirit. She was forty, he would guess, and manless, and she would hold down a job that in another fifteen years would leave her financially independent—and yet she was running from a spectre, seeking sanctuary behind the cloak of another personality, one from the past.

Her voice was clear and strong, but with a tendency to simper, and she read with her chin held high, in the manner of an elocution student, which made her neck appear more scrawny than it was.

"My period, you may remember," she said, "is the American Civil War, with its locale in the South."

She read:

> *Oct. 13, 1862—Mrs. Hampton sent her carriage for me today, with old Ned, one of her few remaining servants, driving, since most of the others have run off, leaving her quite destitute of help, a situation in which many of the others of us also find ourselves . . .*

Running away, thought Vickers, running away to the age of crinoline and chivalry, to a war from which time had swept away the filth and blood and agony and made of its pitiful participants, both men and women, figures of pure romantic nostalgia.

She read: . . . *Isabella was there and I was glad to see her, for it had been years since we had met, that time in Alabama . . .*

Fleeing, of course. And yet a fleeing now turned into a ready-made instrument to preach the gospel of that other world, the peaceful second world behind the tired and bloody Earth.

Three weeks, he thought. No more than three weeks and they're already organized, with the Georges who do the shouting and the running and occasionally the dying, and the Sallys who do the undercover work.

And yet, even with the other world before them, even with the promise of the kind of life they seek, they still cling to the old nostalgic ritual of the magnolia-scented past. It was the mark of doubt and despair upon them, making them refuse to give up the dream through fear that the actuality, if they reached for it, would dissolve beneath their fingertips, vanish at their touch.

Miss Stanhope read on: *I sat for an hour beside old Mrs. Hampton's bed, reading "Vanity Fair," a book of which she is fond, having read it herself, and having had it read to her since the occurrence of her infirmity, more times than she can remember.*

But even if some of them still clung to the scented dream, there were others, the Georges among them, the "activists" who would fight for the promise that they sensed in the second world, and each day there would be more and more of them who would recognize the promise and go out and work for it.

They would spread the word and they would flee the police when the sirens sounded and they would hide in dark cellars and come out again when the police were gone.

The word is safe, thought Vickers. It has been placed in hands that will guard and cherish it, that can do no other than guard and cherish it.

Miss Stanhope read on and the old dowager sat behind the table, nodding her head just a little drowsily, but with a firm grip still upon the letter opener, and all the others were listening, some of them politely, but most with consuming interest. When the reading was done, they would ask questions on points of research and pose other points to be clarified and would make suggestions for the revision of the diary and would compliment Miss Stanhope on the brilliance of her work. Then someone else would stand up and read about their life in some other time and place and once again all of them would sit and listen and repeat the performance.

Vickers felt the futility of it, the dead, pitiful hopelessness. It was as if the room were filled with the magnolia scent, the rose scent, the spice scent of many dusty years.

When Miss Stanhope had finished and the room was stirring with the questions asked and the questions to be asked, he rose quietly from his chair and went out into the street.

He saw that the stars were shining. And that reminded him of something.

Tomorrow he would go to see Ann Carter.

And that was wrong, he knew. He shouldn't see Ann Carter.

47

He rang the bell and waited. When he heard her footsteps coming across the floor he knew that he should turn from the door and run. He had no right to come here and he knew he shouldn't have—he should have done first things first and there was no reason why he should see her at all, for the dream of her was dead as the dream of Kathleen.

But he had had to come, literally *had* to. He had paused twice before the door of the apartment building and then had turned around and gone away again. This time he had not turned back, could not turn back, but had gone in and now here he was, before her door, listening to the sound of footsteps coming towards him.

And what, he wondered wildly, would he say to her when the door was opened? What would he do then? Go in as if nothing at all had happened, as if he were the same person and she the same person as they had been the last time they had met?

Should he tell her she was a mutant and, more than that, an android, a manufactured woman?

The door came open and she was a woman, as lovely as he remembered her, and she reached out a hand and drew him in and closed the door behind them and stood with her back against it.

"Jay," she said. "Jay Vickers."

He tried to speak, but he couldn't. He only stood there looking at her and thinking: It can't be true. It's a lie. It simply isn't true.

"What happened, Jay? You said that you would call me."

He held out his arms, fighting not to, and she made a quick, almost desperate motion and was in them. He held her close against him and it was as if the two of them stood in the final consolation of a misery which each had believed the other did not know.

"I thought at first you were just a little crazy," she told him. "Remembering some of the things you said over the phone from that Wisconsin town, I was almost sure there was something wrong with you—that you'd gone a little off the beam. Then I got to remembering things, strange little things you had done or said or written and . . ."

"Take it easy, Ann," he said. "You don't need to tell me."

"Jay, have you ever wondered if you were quite human? If there might not be something in you that wasn't quite the usual pattern—something unhuman?"

"Yes," he said. "I've often wondered that."

"I'm sure you aren't. Not quite human, I mean. And that's all right. Because I'm not human, either."

He held her closer then. Feeling her arms around him, he knew finally that here were the two of them, clinging to one another, two wan souls lost and friendless in a sea of humanity. Neither of them had anyone but the other. Even if there were no love between them they still must be as one and stand against the world.

The telephone buzzed at them from its place upon the end table and they scarcely heard it.

"I love you, Ann," he said, and a part of his brain that was not a part of him, but a cold, detached observer that stood off to one side, reminded him that he had known he could not love her, that it was impossible and immoral and preposterous to love someone who might be closer than a sister, whose life surely had once been a part of his life and once again would blend with his life into another personality that might be unaware of them.

"I remembered," Ann told him in a vague and distant voice. "And I haven't got it straight. Maybe you can help me get it straight."

He asked, lips stiff with apprehension: "What did you remember, Ann?"

"A walk I had with someone. I've tried, but I can't recall his name, although I'd know his face, after all these years. We walked down a valley, from a big brick house that stood up on a hill at the valley's head. We walked down the valley and it was springtime because the wild crab apple blossoms were in bloom and there were singing birds and the funny thing about that walk is that I know I never took it, but I remember it. How can you remember something, Jay, when you know it never happened?"

"I don't know," said Vickers. "Imagination, maybe. Something that you read somewhere."

But this was it, he knew. This was the proof of what he had suspected.

There were three of them, Flanders had said, three androids made out of one human life. The three of them had to be himself and Flanders and Ann Carter. For Ann remembered the enchanted valley as he remembered it—but because he was a man he had walked with a woman by the name of Kathleen Preston, and since Ann was a woman, she had walked with a man whose name she could not recall. And when and if she did recall it, of course it would be wrong. For if he had walked with anyone, it had not been with a girl named Kathleen Preston, but a girl with some other name.

"And that's not all," said Ann. "I know what other people think. I . . ."

"Please, Ann," he said.

"I try not to know what they think, now that I realize that I can do it. Although I know now that I've been doing it, more or less unconsciously, all the time for years. Anticipating what people were about to say. Getting the jump on them. Knowing their objections before they even spoke them. Knowing what would appeal to them.

I've been a good business woman, Jay, and that may be why I am. I can get into other people's minds. I did just the other day. When I first suspected that I could do it, I tried deliberately, just to see if I could or was imagining it. It wasn't easy, and I'm not very good at it yet. But I could do it! Jay, I could . . ."

He held her close and thought: Ann's one of the telepaths, one of those who can go out to the stars.

"What are we, Jay?" she asked. "Tell me what we are."

The telephone shrieked at them.

"Later," he said. "It's not so terribly bad. In some ways it's wonderful. I came back because I loved you, Ann. I tried to stay away, but I couldn't stay. Because it isn't right . . ."

"It's right," she said. "Oh, Jay, it's the rightest thing there ever was. I prayed that you would come back to me again. When I knew there was something wrong, I was afraid you wouldn't—that you might not be able to, that something awful might have happened to you. I prayed and the prayer was wrong because prayer was strange to me and I felt hypocritical and awful . . ."

The ringing was a persistent snarl.

"The phone," she said.

He let her go and she walked to the davenport and sat down and took the receiver out of its cradle, while he stood and looked at the room and tried to bring it and Ann into the focus with his memory of them.

"It's for you," she said.

"For me?"

"Yes, the phone. Did anyone know that you were coming here?"

He shook his head, but walked forward and took the receiver and stood with it in his hand, balancing it, trying to guess who might be calling him and why they might be calling.

Suddenly, he knew that he was frightened, felt the sweat break out beneath his armpits because he knew that it could only be one person at the other end of the phone.

A voice said: "This is the Neanderthaler, Vickers."

"Club and all?" asked Vickers.

"Club and all," said Crawford. "We have a bone to chew."

"At your office?"

"There's a cab outside. It is waiting for you."

Vickers laughed and it was a more vicious sound than he intended it to be. "How long have you been tracking me?"

Crawford chuckled. "Ever since Chicago. We have the country plastered with our analyzers."

"Picking up much stuff?"

"A few strays here and there."

"Still confident about that secret weapon?"

"Sure, I'm confident, but . . ."

"Go ahead," said Vickers. "You're talking to a friend."

"I have to hand it to you, Vickers. I really got to hand it to you. But get over here fast."

He hung up. Vickers took the receiver down from his ear and stared at it a moment, then placed it in the cradle.

"That was Crawford," he said to Ann. "He wants to talk to me."

"Is everything all right, Jay?"

"Everything's all right."

"You'll come back?"

"I'll come back," said Vickers.

"You know what you are doing?"

"Now I do," said Vickers. "I know what I'm doing now."

48

Crawford motioned to the chair beside the desk. Vickers saw with a start that it was the same chair he'd sat in when he'd come to the office, only weeks ago, with Ann.

"It's nice seeing you again," said Crawford. "I'm glad we can get together."

"Your plans must be going well," said Vickers. "You are more affable than when I saw you last."

"I'm always affable. Worried and scared sometimes, but always affable."

"You haven't picked up Ann Carter."

Crawford shook his head. "There's no reason to. Not yet."

"But you're watching her."

"We're watching all of you. The few that are left."

"Any time we want to, we can come unwatched."

"I don't doubt it," Crawford admitted, "but why do you stick around? If I were a mutant, I wouldn't."

"Because we have you licked, and you're the one who knows it," said Vickers. He wished he were half as confident as he hoped he sounded.

"We can start a war," said Crawford. "All we have to do is lift a finger and the shooting begins."

"You won't start it."

"You played your hand too hard. You've pushed us just a bit too much. Now we have to do it—as a last defense."

"You mean the other world idea."

"Exactly," Crawford said.

He sat and stared at Vickers with the pale blue bullet eyes peering out from the rolls of flesh.

"What do you think we'll do?" he asked. "Stand still and let you steamroller us? You tried the gadgets and we stopped them with, I admit, rather violent methods. But now there's this other thing. The gadgets didn't work, so you tried an idea, a religion, a piece of park bench fanaticism—tell me, Vickers, what do you call this business?"

"The blunt truth," said Vickers.

"No matter what it is, it's good. Too good. It'll take a war to stop it."

"You'd call it subversive, I suppose."

"It is subversive," Crawford said. "Already, just a few days since it started, it has shown results. People quitting their jobs, walking away from their homes, throwing away their money. Poverty, they said, that was the key to the other world. What kind of a gag have you cooked up, Vickers?"

"What happens to these people? The ones who quit their jobs and threw away their money. Have you kept a check on what happens to them?"

Crawford leaned forward in his chair. "That's the thing that scares us. Those people disappeared; before we could round them up, they disappeared."

"They went to the other world," said Vickers.

"I don't know where they went, but I know what will happen if we let it continue. Our workers will leave us, a few at first and then more and more of them and finally . . ."

"If you want to turn on that war, start reaching for the button."

"We won't let you do this to us," Crawford said. "We will stop you somehow."

Vickers came to his feet and leaned across the desk. "You're done, Crawford. We're the ones who won't let you and your world go on. We're the ones . . ."

"Sit down," Crawford said.

For a moment Vickers stared at him, then slowly eased his way back into the chair.

"There is one other thing," said Crawford. "Just one other thing. I told you about the analyzers in this room. Well, they're not only in this room. They are everywhere. In railroad terminals, bus depots, hotel lobbies, eating joints . . ."

"I thought as much. That's how you picked me up."

"I warned you once before. Don't despise us because we're merely human. With an organization of world industry you can do a lot of things and do them awfully fast."

"You outsmart yourself," said Vickers. "You've found out a lot of things from those analyzers that you didn't want to know."

"Like what?"

"Like a lot of your industrialists and bankers and the others who are in your organization are really the mutants you are fighting."

"I said I had to hand it to you. Would you mind telling me how you planted them?"

"We didn't plant them, Crawford."

"You didn't . . ."

"Let's take it from the start," said Vickers. "Let me ask you what a mutant is."

"Why, I suppose he's an ordinary man who has some extra talents, a better understanding, an understanding of certain things that the rest of us can't grasp."

"And suppose a man were a mutant and didn't know he was, but regarded himself as an ordinary man, what then? Where would he wind up? Doctor, lawyer, beggarman, thief? He'd wind up at the top of the heap somewhere. He'd be an eminent doctor or a smart attorney or an artist or a highly successful editor or writer. He might even be an industrialist or banker."

The blue bullets of the eyes stared out from Crawford's face.

"You," said Vickers, "have been heading up one of the finest group of mutants in the world today. Men we couldn't touch because they were tied too closely to the normal world. And what are you going to do about it, Crawford?"

"Not a single thing. I'm not going to tell them."

"Then, I will."

"No, you won't," said Crawford. "Because you, personally, are washed up. How do you think you've lived this long in spite of all the analyzers we have? I've let you, that's how."

"You thought you could make a deal."

"Perhaps I did. But not any more. You were an asset once. You're a danger now."

"You're throwing me to the wolves?"

"That's just what I'm doing. Good day, Mr. Vickers. It was nice knowing you."

Vickers rose from the chair. "I'll see you again."

"That," said Crawford, "is something I doubt."

49

Going down in the elevator, Vickers thought furiously.

It would take Crawford half an hour or so to spread the word that he was unprotected, that he was fair game, that anyone could pot him like a sitting duck.

If it had only been himself, it would have been an easy matter, but there was Ann.

Ann, without a doubt, would become fair game, too, for now the die was cast, now the chips were down, and Crawford wasn't the kind of man who would play according to any rules now.

He had to reach Ann. Reach and tell her fast, keep her from asking questions and make her understand.

At the ground floor he stepped out with the other passengers. As he walked away he saw the operator leave the elevator open and dash for a phone booth.

Reporting me, he thought. There was an analyzer on the elevator and it made some sort of a signal that would go undetected to anyone but the operator. And there were other analyzers everywhere, Crawford had said, in railroad terminals and bus stations and eating places—anywhere that a man might go.

Once one of the analyzers spotted a mutant, the word would be called in somewhere—to an exterminator squad, perhaps—and they would hunt the mutant down. Maybe they spotted him with portable analyzers, or maybe there were other ways to spot him, and once they spotted him it would be all over.

All over because the mutant would not know, because he would have no warning of the death that tracked him. Given a moment's warning, given a moment to concentrate, and he could disappear, as the mutants had disappeared at will when Crawford's men had tried to track them down for interview and parley.

What was it Crawford had said? "You ring the bell and wait. You sit in a room and wait."

But now no one rang a doorbell.

They shot you down from ambush. They struck you in the dark. They knew who you were and they marked you for the death. And you had no chance because you had no warning.

That was the way Eb had died and all the others of them who had died, struck down without a chance because Crawford's men could not afford to give a moment's chance to one who was marked to die.

Except that always before, when Jay Vickers had been spotted, he'd been known as one of the few who were not to be molested—he and Ann and maybe one or two others.

But now it would be different. Now he was just another mutant, a hunted rat, just like all the others.

He reached the sidewalk outside the building and stood for a moment, looking up and down the street.

A cab, he thought, but there would be an analyzer in a cab. Although, as far as that was concerned, there would be analyzers everywhere. There must be one at Ann's apartment building, otherwise how could Crawford have known so quickly that he had arrived there?

There was no way in which he could duck the analyzers, no way to hide or prevent them from knowing where he might be going.

He stepped to the sidewalk's edge and hailed a cruising cab. The cab drew up and he stepped inside and gave the driver the address.

The man threw a startled backward look at him.

"Take it easy," said Vickers. "You won't be in any trouble as long as you don't try anything."

The driver did not answer.

Vickers sat hunched on the edge of the seat.

"It's all right, chum," the driver finally told him. "I won't try a thing."

"That's just fine," said Vickers. "Now let's go."

He watched the blocks slide by, keeping an eye on the driver, watching for any motions that might signal that a mutant was in the taxi. He saw none.

A thought struck him. What if they were waiting at Ann's apartment? What if they had gone there immediately and had found her there and were waiting for him now?

It was a risk, he decided, he'd have to take.

The cab stopped in front of the building. Vickers opened the door and leaped out. The driver gunned the car, not waiting for his fare.

Vickers ran toward the door, ignored the elevator, and went pounding up the stairs.

He reached Ann's door and seized the knob and turned it, but the smooth metal slid beneath his fingers. It was locked. He rang the bell and nothing happened. He rang it again and again. Then he backed to the opposite wall and hurled his body forward across the corridor, smashing at the door. He felt it give, slightly. He backed up again. The third try and the lock ripped open and sent him sprawling.

"Ann," he shouted, leaping up.

There was no answer.

He went running through the rooms and found no one there.

He stood for a moment, sweat breaking out on him.

Ann was gone! There was little time left to them and Ann was gone!

He plunged out the door and went tearing down the stairs.

When he reached the sidewalk, the cars were pulling up, three of them, one behind the other, and there were two more across the street. Men were piling out of them, men who carried guns.

He tried to swing around to get back into the door again and as he swung he bumped into someone and he saw that it was Ann, arms filled with shopping bags and from one of the bags, he saw, protruded the leafy top of a bunch of celery.

"Jay," she said. "Jay, what's going on? Who are all these men?"

"Quick," he said, "get into my mind. Like you did the others. The way you know how people think."

"But . . ."

"Quick!"

He felt her come into his mind, groping for his thoughts, fastening onto them.

Something hit the stone wall of the building just above their heads and went tumbling skyward with a howl of tortured metal.

"Hang on," he said. "We're getting out of here."

He closed his eyes and willed himself into the other earth, with all the urgency and will he could muster. He felt the tremor of Ann's mind and then he slipped and fell. He hit his head on something hard and stars wheeled inside his skull and something tore at his hand and something else fell on top of him.

He heard the sound of wind blowing in the trees. He opened his eyes and there were no buildings.

He lay flat on his back, at the foot of a gray granite boulder. A bag of groceries, with the top of a bunch of celery sticking out of it, lay on his stomach.

He sat up.

"Ann," he called.

"Here I am," she said.

"You all right?"

"Physically, yes, but not mentally. What happened?"

"We fell off that boulder," Vickers told her.

He stood up and reached down a hand to help her to her feet.

"But the *boulder*, Jay. Where are we?"

"We're in the second world," said Vickers.

They stood together and looked across the land—wild, desolate, wooded, with scattered boulders and with granite ledges sticking from the hillslopes.

"The second world," repeated Ann. "That crazy stuff that's been in the papers?"

Vickers nodded gravely. "There's nothing crazy about it, Ann. It exists."

"Well, no matter where we are," said Ann, "we brought our dinner with us. Help me pick up these groceries."

Vickers got down on hands and knees to chase down the potatoes that had escaped from the sack. It had split wide open in the tumble from the boulder.

50

It was Manhattan as it must have appeared before the white man came, finally to build upon it the man-made half-wonder, half-monstrosity. It was a primeval Manhattan, a world unspoiled.

"And yet," said Vickers, "there must be something here. The mutants would have to have some sort of supply depot here to store the stuff they'd want to funnel to New York."

"And if they haven't?" Ann asked him.

He looked at her and grinned wryly.

"How are you at travel?"

"All the way to Chicago?"

"Farther than Chicago," he told her. "On foot. Although we might rig up a raft when we hit a westward-flowing river."

"There'd be other mutant centers."

"I suppose there would be, but we might not be lucky enough to stumble on one of them."

She shook her head at him. "This is all so strange."

"Not strange," he said. "Just sudden. If we'd had the time I'd told you, but we didn't have the time."

"Jay, they were shooting at us!"

Vickers nodded grimly. "They're gents who play for keeps."

"But they're human beings, Jay. Just like us."

"Not like us," said Vickers. "Only human. That's the trouble with them. Being human in this day isn't quite enough."

He tossed two or three pieces of wood on the campfire. Then he turned to Ann. "Come on," he said. "Let's go."

"But, Jay, it's getting dark."

"I know. If there's anything on the island, we'll spot it by the lights. Just up on that hill. If we don't see anything we'll come back. When morning comes we can look again."

"Jay," she said, "in lots of ways, it's just like a picnic."

"I'm no good at riddles. Tell me why it's like a picnic."

"Why, the fire and eating in the open and . . ."

"Forget it, lady," Vickers told her. "We're not on any picnic."

He moved ahead and she followed close behind him, threading their way between the thickets and the boulders. Nighthawks skimmed the air above them in graceful, insect-catching swoops. From somewhere far off came the wickering of a coon. A few lightning bugs flashed on and off, dancing in the bushes.

They climbed the hill, not very high, but fairly steep, and when they reached the top they saw the lights, far down toward the island's tip.

"There it is," said Vickers. "I figured they would have to be here."

"It's a long way off. Will we have to walk it?"

"Maybe not."

"But how . . ."

"And you a telepath," said Vickers.

She shook her head.

"Go on and try," said Vickers. "Just want to talk to someone down there."

And he remembered Flanders, rocking on the porch and saying that distance should be no bar to telepathy, that a mile or light year should not make the slightest difference.

"You think I can?"

"I don't know," said Vickers. "You don't want to walk, do you?"

"Not that far."

They stood silently, looking toward the small area of light in the gathering darkness. He tried to pick out the different locations. There was where Rockefeller Center was located on the old Earth, and up there Central Park and down there, where the East River curved in, the old abandoned United Nations structure. But it was all grass and trees here, not steel and concrete.

"Jay!" Her whisper was tense with excitement.

"Yes, Ann."

"I think I have someone."

"Man or woman?"

"No, I think it's a robot. Yes, he says he's a robot. He says he'll send someone—no, not someone—something—for us."

"Ann . . ."

"He says for us to wait right here. They'll be right along."

"Ann, ask him if they can make movies."

"Movies?"

"Sure. Motion pictures. Films. Have they got cameras and stuff like that?"

"But what do you . . ."

"Just go ahead and ask him."

"But motion pictures?"

"I have an idea—we can lick Crawford yet."

"Jay, you aren't going back!"

"Most certainly," said Vickers.

"Jay Vickers, I won't let you."

"You can't stop me," Vickers said. "Here, let's sit down and wait to be picked up."

They sat down, close together.

"I have a story," Vickers said. "It's about a boy. His name was Jay Vickers and he was very young . . ." He stopped abruptly.

"Go on," she said. "Go on with your story."

"Some other time. Later on I'll tell you."

"Why not now? I want to hear it now."

"Not when a moon is coming up," said Vickers. "That's no time for stories."

First he tried hard to close his mind, to erect a barrier against her still-inexpert telepathic powers. Only then did he feel free to wonder: Can I tell her that we are closer than she thinks, that we came from the one life and will go back to the same body and that we cannot love one another?

She leaned against him and put her head against his shoulder and looked up at the sky.

"It's coming clearer," she said. "It's not so strange now. And it seems right. Queer as it may be, it seems right. This other world and the things we have, those strange abilities and all and the strange remembering."

He put his arm around her and she turned her head and kissed him, a quick, impulsive kiss.

"We'll be happy," she said. "The two of us in this new world."

"We'll be happy," Vickers said.

And now, he knew, he could never tell her. She might know soon enough, but he could never be the one to tell her.

51

A girl's voice answered the telephone and Vickers asked for Crawford.

"Mr. Crawford is in conference," said the girl.

"Tell him this is Vickers."

"Mr. Crawford cannot be. . . . Did you say Vickers? Jay Vickers?"

"That's right. I have news for him."

"Just a minute, Mr. Vickers."

He waited, wondering how long he might have, for the analyzer in the phone booth must have sounded the alarm. Even now members of the exterminator squad must be on their way.

Crawford's voice said: "Hello, Vickers."

"Call off your dogs," said Vickers. "They're wasting their time and yours."

He heard the rage in Crawford's voice. "I thought I told you—"

"Take it easy," Vickers said. "You haven't got a chance of potting me. Your men couldn't do it when they had me cornered. So if you can't kill me, you better dicker with me."

"Dicker?"

"That's what I said."

"Listen; Vickers, I'm not—"

"Of course you will," said Vickers. "That other world business is really rolling now. The Pretentionists are pushing it and it's gathering steam and you're getting hurt. It's time you talked sense."

"I'm tied up with my directors," Crawford said.

"That's fine. They're the ones I really want to talk to."

"Vickers, go away," said Crawford. "You'll never get away with it. No matter what you're planning, you'll never get away with it. You'll never leave here alive. No matter what I do, I can't save you if you keep up this foolishness."

"I'm coming up."

"I like you, Vickers. I don't know why. I have no reason to . . ."

"I'm coming up."

"All right," said Crawford, wearily. "The blood is on your head."

Vickers picked up the film case and stepped out of the booth. An elevator car was waiting and he walked swiftly toward it, shoulders hunched a little, as if against the anticipated bullet in the back.

"Third floor," he said.

The elevator operator didn't bat an eye. The analyzer by now must have given its signal, but more than likely the operator had his instructions concerning third floor passengers.

Vickers opened the door to North American Research and Crawford was waiting for him in the reception room.

"Come on," said Crawford.

He turned and marched ahead and Vickers followed him down the long hall. He looked at his watch and did fast mental arithmetic. It was going better than he thought. He still had a margin of two or three minutes. It hadn't taken as long to convince Crawford as he had thought it might.

Ann would be calling in ten minutes. What happened in the next ten minutes would decide success or failure.

Crawford stopped in front of the door at the end of the hall.

"You know what you are doing, Vickers?"

Vickers nodded.

"Because," said Crawford, "one slip and. . . ." He made a hissing sound between his teeth and sliced a finger across his throat.

"I understand," said Vickers.

"Those men in there are the desperate ones There still is time to leave. I won't tell them you were here."

"Cut out the stalling, Crawford."

"What have you got there?"

"Some documentary film. It will help explain what I have to say. You've got a projector in there?"

Crawford nodded. "But no operator."

"I'll run the machine myself," said Vickers.

"A deal?"

"A solution."

"All right, then. Come in."

The shades were drawn and the room was twilit and the long table at which the men sat seemed to be no more than a row of white faces turned toward them.

Vickers followed Crawford across the room, feet sinking into the heavy carpeting. He looked at the men around the table and saw that many of them were public figures.

There, at Crawford's right hand, was a banker and beyond him a man who time and again had been called to the White House to be entrusted with semi-diplomatic missions. And there were others also that he recognized, although there were many that he didn't, and there were a few of them who wore the strange dress of other lands.

Here, then, was the directorate of North American Research, those men who guided the destiny of the embattled normals against the mutant menace—Crawford's desperate men.

"A strange thing has happened, gentlemen," said Crawford. "A most unusual thing. We have a mutant with us."

In the silence the white faces flicked around at Vickers, then turned back again, and Crawford went on talking.

"Mr. Vickers," Crawford went on, "is an acquaintance of some standing. You will recall that we have talked of him before. At one time we hoped he might be able to help us reconcile the differences between the two branches of the race.

"He comes to us willingly and of his own accord and indicated to me he may have a possible solution. He has not told me what that solution might be. I brought him directly here. It's up to you, of course, whether you want to hear what he has to say."

"Why, certainly," said one of them. "Let the man talk."

And another said: "Most happy to."

The others nodded their agreement.

Crawford said to Vickers: "The floor is yours."

Vickers walked to the table's head and he was thinking: So far, so good. Now if only the rest works out. If I don't make a slip. If I can carry it off. Because it was win or lose, there was no middle ground, no backing out.

He set the film case on the table, smiled, and said: "No infernal weapon, gentlemen. It's a film that, with your permission, I'll show you in just a little while."

They did not laugh. They simply sat and looked at him and there was nothing that you could read in their faces, but he felt the coldness of their hatred.

"You're about to start a war," he said. "You're meeting here to decide if you should reach out and turn on the tap. . . ."

The white faces seemed to be leaning forward, all of them straining toward him.

One of them said: "You're either a brave man, Vickers, or an utter fool."

"I've come here," said Vickers, "to end the war before it starts."

He reached into his pocket and his hand came out in a flicking motion and tossed the thing it held onto the table.

"That's a top," he said. "A thing that kids play with—or used to play with, at any rate. I want to talk to you for a minute about a top."

"A top?" said someone. "What is this foolishness?"

But the banker at his right hand said reminiscently: "I had a top like that when I was a boy. They don't make them any more. I haven't seen one of them in years."

He reached out a hand and picked up the top and spun it on the table. The others craned their necks to look at it.

Vickers glanced at his watch. Still on schedule. Now if nothing spoiled it.

"You remember the top, Crawford?" asked Vickers. "The one that was in my room that night?"

"I remember it," said Crawford.

"You spun it and it vanished," said Vickers.

"And it came back again."

"Crawford, why did you spin that top?"

Crawford licked his lips nervously. "Why, I don't really know. It might have been an attempt to rescue boyhood, an urge to be a boy again."

"You asked me what the top was for."

"You told me it was for going into fairyland and I told you that a week before I would have said that we were crazy—you for saying a thing like that and I for listening to you."

"But before I came in, you spun the top. Tell me, Crawford, why did you do it?"

"Go ahead," the banker urged. "Tell him."

"Why, I did," said Crawford. "I just told you the reason."

Behind Vickers a door opened. He turned his head and saw a secretary beckoning to Crawford.

On time, he thought. Working like a charm. Ann was on the phone and Crawford was being called from the room to talk to her. And that was the way he'd planned it, for with Crawford in the room, the plan would be hopeless.

"Mr. Vickers," the banker said, "I'm curious about this business of the top. What connection is there between a top and the problem that we face?"

"A sort of analogy," Vickers replied. "There are certain basic differences between the normals and the mutants and I can explain them best by the use of a top. But before I do, I'd like you to see my film. After that I can go ahead and tell you and you will understand me. If you gentlemen will excuse me."

He lifted the film case from the table.

"Why, certainly," the banker said. "Go right ahead."

Vickers went back to the stairs which led to the projection booth and opened the door and went inside.

He'd have to work fast and surely, for Ann could not hold Crawford on the phone very long and she had to keep Crawford out of the room for at least five minutes.

He slid the film into the holder and threaded it through the lenses with shaking fingers and clipped it on the lower spool and then swiftly checked what he had done.

Everything seemed all right.

He found the switches and turned them on and the cone of light sprang out to spear above the conference table and on the screen before the table was a brilliantly colored top, spinning, with the stripes moving up and disappearing, moving up and disappearing—

The film's sound track said: *Here you see a top, a simple toy, but it presents one of the most baffling illusions . . .*

The words were right, Vickers knew. Robotic experts had picked out the right words, weaving them together with just the right relationship, just the right inflation, to give them maximum semantic value. The words would hold his audience, fix their interest on the top, and keep it there after the first few seconds.

He came silently down the stairs and moved over to the door. If Crawford should come back, he could hold him off until the job was done.

The sound track said: *Now if you will watch closely, you will see that the lines of color seem to move up the body of the top and disappear. A child, watching the lines of color, might wonder where they went, and so might anyone . . .*

He tried to count the seconds. They seemed to drag, endlessly.

The sound track said: *Watch closely now—watch closely—they come up and disappear—they come up and disappear—come up and disappear—*

There were not nearly so many men at the table now, only two or three now and they were watching so closely that they had not even noticed the others disappear. Maybe those two or three would remain. Of them all, those two or three might be the only ones who weren't unsuspecting mutants.

Vickers opened the door softly and slid out and closed the door behind, him.

The door shut out the soft voice of the sound track: *come up and disappear—watch closely—come up and . . .*

Crawford was coming down the hall, lumbering along.

He saw Vickers and stopped.

"What do you want?" he asked. "What are you out here for?"

"A question," Vickers said, "One you didn't answer in there. Why did you spin that top?"

Crawford shook his head. "I can't understand it, Vickers. It doesn't make any sense, but I went into that fairyland once myself. Just like you, when I was a kid. I remembered it after I talked to you. Maybe because I talked to you. I remembered once I had sat on the floor and watched the top go round and wondered where the stripes were going—you know how they come up and disappear and then another one comes up and disappears. I wondered where they went and I got so interested that I must have followed them, for all at once I was in fairyland and there were a lot of flowers and I picked a flower and when I got back again I still had the flower and that's the way I knew I'd really been in fairyland. You see, it was winter and there were no flowers and when I showed the flower to mother . . ."

"That's enough," Vickers interrupted. There was sudden elation in his voice. "That is all I need."

Crawford stared at him. "You don't believe me?"

"I do."

"What's the matter with you, Vickers?"

"There is nothing wrong with me," said Vickers.

It hadn't been Ann Carter, after all!

Flanders and he and *Crawford*—they were the three who had been given life from the body of Jay Vickers!

And Ann?

Ann had within her the life of that girl who had walked the valley with him—the girl he remembered as Kathleen Preston, but who had some other name. For Ann remembered the valley and that she had walked the valley in the springtime with someone by her side.

There might be more than Ann. There might be three of Ann just as there were three of him, but that didn't matter, either. Maybe Ann's name really was Ann Carter as his really was Jay Vickers. Maybe that meant that, when the lives drained back into the rightful bodies, it would be his consciousness and Ann's consciousness that would survive.

And it was all right now to love Ann. For she was a separate person and not a part of him.

Ann—*his* Ann—had come back to this Earth to place a telephone call and to get Crawford from the room, so that he would not recognize the danger of the top spinning on screen, and now she'd gone back to the other world again and the threat was gone.

"Everything's all right," said Vickers. "Everything's just fine."

Soon he'd be going back himself and Ann would be waiting for him. And they'd be happy, the way she'd said they'd be, sitting there on a Manhattan hilltop waiting for the robots.

"Well, then," said Crawford. "Let's go back in again."

Vickers put out his arm to stop him. "There's no use of going in."

"No use?"

"Your directors aren't there," said Vickers. "They're in the second world. The one, you remember, that the Pretentionists preached about on street corners all over town."

Crawford stared at him. "The top!"

"That's right."

"We'll start again," said Crawford. "Another board, another . . ."

"You haven't got the time," said Vickers. "This Earth is done. The people are fleeing from it. Even those who stay won't listen to you, won't fight for you."

"I'll kill you," Crawford said. "I'll kill you, Vickers."

"No, you won't."

They stood face to face silently, tensely.

"No," said Crawford. "No, I guess I won't. I should, but I can't. Why can't I kill you, Vickers?"

Vickers touched the big man's arm.

"Come on, friend," he said softly. "Or should I call you brother?"

ABOUT THE AUTHOR

During his fifty-five-year career, Clifford D. Simak produced some of the most iconic science fiction stories ever written. Born in 1904 on a farm in southwestern Wisconsin, Simak got a job at a small-town newspaper in 1929 and eventually became news editor of the *Minneapolis Star-Tribune,* writing fiction in his spare time.

Simak was best known for the book *City,* a reaction to the horrors of World War II, and for his novel *Way Station.* In 1953 *City* was awarded the International Fantasy Award, and in following years, Simak won three Hugo Awards and a Nebula Award. In 1977 he became the third Grand Master of the Science Fiction and Fantasy Writers of America, and before his death in 1988, he was named one of three inaugural winners of the Horror Writers Association's Bram Stoker Award for Lifetime Achievement.

CLIFFORD D. SIMAK

FROM OPEN ROAD MEDIA

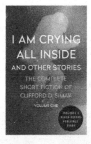
I AM CRYING ALL INSIDE AND OTHER STORIES

THE BIG FRONT YARD AND OTHER STORIES

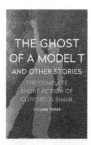
THE GHOST OF A MODEL T AND OTHER STORIES

ALL FLESH IS GRASS

CITY

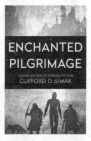
ENCHANTED PILGRIMAGE

A HERITAGE OF STARS

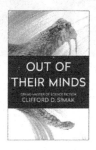
OUT OF THEIR MINDS

TIME IS THE SIMPLEST THING

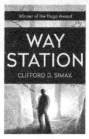
WAY STATION

OPEN ROAD
INTEGRATED MEDIA

OPEN ROAD

INTEGRATED MEDIA

Find a full list of our authors and
titles at www.openroadmedia.com

FOLLOW US
@OpenRoadMedia

EARLY BIRD BOOKS
FRESH DEALS, DELIVERED DAILY

Love to read?
Love great sales?

Get fantastic deals on bestselling ebooks delivered to your inbox every day!

Sign up today at
earlybirdbooks.com/book